Life-Size

Jenefer Shute
Life-Size

SECKER & WARBURG
LONDON

First published in Great Britain in 1992
by Martin Secker & Warburg Limited
Michelin House, 81 Fulham Road, London SW3 6RB

Copyright © Jenefer Shute 1992
Reprinted 1992, 1993

A CIP catalogue record for this book
is available from the British Library

ISBN 0 436 47278 3

The author gratefully acknowledges permission to quote
from *Consuming Passions: The Anthropology of Eating*
by Peter Farb and George Armelagos. Copyright
© 1990 by the Estate of Peter Farb. Reprinted
by permission of Houghton Mifflin Company.
All rights reserved.

The description of an anorexic woman eating an apple
and a cube of cheese originally appeared in
'Food as Enemy', by Caroline Knapp, the Boston
Phoenix, February 1989.

Phototypeset in 12/15 Perpetua
by Wilmaset Ltd, Birkenhead, Wirral
Printed and bound in Great Britain by
Mackays of Chatham PLC, Chatham, Kent

To
JBF
with
thanks

Stars with masses above the Chandrasekhar limit, on the other hand, have a big problem when they come to the end of their fuel. In some cases they may explode or manage to throw off enough matter to reduce their mass and so avoid catastrophic gravitational collapse, but it was difficult to believe this always happened, no matter how big the star. How would it know that it had to lose weight? And even if every star managed to lose enough mass to avoid collapse, what would happen if you added more mass to a white dwarf or neutron star to take it over the limit? Would it collapse to infinite density?

— Stephen Hawking,
A Brief History of Time

1

I'M LYING HERE, just occupying space, drifting in and out of a dream, when I hear something clattering and rumbling down the hall. I know what it is; my jaw and stomach muscles tense, but otherwise I remain exactly as I am. Why should I move? The trolley stops outside the door with a faint tinkle of crockery; after a brief knock (giving me no time to respond), she comes in, smiling and pert, brisk and trim in her white tunic and pants. (Trim, but don't think I don't notice the almost-sagging buttocks, the incipient droop of the upper arm).

As she walks towards me, her blockish, cushiony shoes squeak against the floor, jarring my ears, scraping my brain.

"Hello! Still lying there? It's lunchtime."

I make no response as she puts the tray down next to me and removes some kind of cover from the plate, releasing a sickening, mealy odor.

"Sit up now and enjoy your lunch," she says brightly, pushing it closer to the bed. "I'll be back in half an hour to see how you're doing." I say nothing and she leaves (shoes conversing in shrill, rubbery shrieks across the floor).

I'm not planning even to look at this tray, but the smell is so strong that I turn my head and encounter, at eye level, a brown, oily, pimply thing (chicken! as if I would ever eat that) oozing onto a mound of mashed potato and some big green branches of broccoli. I try, and fail, to imagine eating it, like munching on a tree. Everything is heaped, crowded on the plate, everything touching. There's also a glass of milk, beaded with sweat; a puffy roll plus two pats of butter; a dish of flabby yellow stuff growing a skin (custard? are they kidding?); an apple; a little envelope of salt, one of pepper, one of ketchup. The smell is so overpowering that I know I'm going to have to do something.

Reluctantly, I roll over on to my side and tip myself so that my feet hang over the edge of the bed. Then, very slowly, I push upwards until I'm sitting, curled, with my head on my lap. I rest like this awhile, trying to breathe, and then, tightening my abdominals, raise myself carefully to my feet.

This prevents fainting.

I have to get this tray out of my sight. The smell is entering me as a hollow nausea, and seeing all that . . . food sends a chilly tingle across my skin. Got to get this thing away! I dump it on the other bed and am about to climb back on mine when I reconsider, go back, and pick off a small piece of the roll, which I put in the drawer of my nightstand: just in case.

Then I roll on the bed, flop my arms wide, wait for everything to stop spinning, and, fixing my eye on the ceiling light bulb, return its stern, milky stare.

So this is what my world has shrunk to: a ward with two gray metal beds, barred at head and foot, with thin spreads, waffled, which might once have been white. The walls, an institutional cream, are scuffed and scarred; lying here, I trace and retrace each blister, each blemish, each bruise. The cold floor is tiled in beige and khaki, which might once have been lemon and olive, or even vanilla and lime. Through the high, locked windows — is this perhaps the psycho ward, after all? — limp shades diffuse a sooty light. A metal nightstand with a screeching drawer, a locker in which my clothes are locked from me, and a plastic chair — for visitors I assume (though who would come here, I cannot think) — complete the decor.

Since being admitted two days ago, I've spent most of my time lying on this bed, arms apart, hands splayed, eyes fixed on the blind bulb above me. They want me to get up, put on my robe, perhaps wander down to the dayroom to meet the other inmates. But I won't, of course. I'm just going to lie here, drifting through time, dreams washing over me, retinal dots composing themselves pointillist-style into a private flow of images.

But then I notice that I'm holding my breath, almost choking: a chemical whiff in the air has stopped my throat. At first I think this is a new symptom — already I'm afraid of running water, of restaurants, of licking a postage stamp — but then it makes sense. The last time I was in a hospital was when I was nine, for a tonsillectomy: in my throat I feel again the dry, violent pain, like swallowing ground glass. Dark clotted stuff in the mouth, salting the ice cream, tingeing the vanilla with tinny strawberry.

Vanilla and strawberry and cream. Think about something else. Think about the tonsils, ripped out like tubers.

A brisk knock, and then the door opens immediately (why do they never wait for me to answer?). In comes Squeaky, interrupting my dream — the surgeon is caressing my hair, the anesthetic taking its ecstatic hold — but I don't even move my head. Out of the corner of my eye, I can see her taking in the situation: the full tray dumped on the other bed, me flat on my back, arms outspread, my pelvic bones protruding pointedly under the gray-green hospital gown. She shakes her head and says in what she probably takes for a calm, reasonable tone:

"Josie, you haven't eaten anything, have you? That's very disappointing: you know the rules. You remember what the doctor said."

"I'm not hungry," I say.

"It was too much," I say.

"Anyway, I did eat something," I say. "I ate some of that roll."

"Josie," she says, "you know the rules, you agreed to them yourself. Do you just want to lie here forever? What's the point of that?"

Her measured yet whiny tone is getting to me and I just want her out. Out! Out of my room! Still staring at the ceiling, I say, "I don't like chicken." They say I'm sick, but what about them, all of them, who think nothing of chewing on a carcass, sinking their teeth into muscle and gristle and blood? They say I'm sick, but what about them, who feast on corpses?

"Well, you wouldn't fill out a menu card, so the dietician picked out something for you."

A corpse and a tree; a fluid secreted by bovine mammary glands; gobs of congealed grease.

"Later, if you fill out the card, you can get something you like. A nice fruit salad perhaps, with ice cream? Or a tuna sandwich, with a banana, perhaps, and some cookies . . . ?"

Banana and tuna and cream: the very words, as if secret, obscene, are making me ill, my heart starting to hammer, the same hollow sickness poking at the base of my throat. To get her to stop, I say, "Leave the card here and I'll think about it."

"OK. And we have a busy afternoon planned for you. The endocrinologist is going to stop by to ask you some questions, and then we'll need to take you for some blood samples."

Blood again. They're after my blood.

Sure enough, a chirpy little woman (thin, birdlike, but with a turkey's tired wattle) shows up, armed with a rubber mallet. She

4

asks me a few questions about my periods; that's all anyone seems to care about around here.

"I forget. Maybe when I was about seventeen."

"So you've had no periods for eight years now?"

"No, they come and go. Sometimes I won't have any for a year or two, then they'll come back for a while, then go away again."

"And how long have they been gone this time?"

"I forget. Maybe a year or so."

Why do they think I should care, anyway? Who, given the choice, would really opt to menstruate, invite the monthly hemorrhage — a reminder that the body is nothing but a bag of blood, liable to seep or spatter at any moment?

Then I discover what the mallet is for. She asks me to sit on the edge of the bed and starts tapping away at my knees, a sharp, clean crack on the bone. Nothing happens, so I give a little kick to help things along. Then she tickles the soles of my feet and tells me my reflexes are impaired because the electrolytes are out of balance and the neurons aren't firing properly, or some such jargon.

Fine with me. I don't want any involuntary responses; soon, in this body, everything will be willed.

So I just look at her blankly and flop back on the bed, because all this sitting up and being hammered is making me light-headed. The minute she leaves, I roll over onto my side and begin my leg lifts, hoping I can complete the full hundred on each side without being interrupted.

I am halfway through the second set when the nurse comes back again, pushing a wheelchair, into which she invites me to climb for some blood tests. (More blood.) I tell her I won't get in the chair, I can walk, thank you — I'm desperate to move: my muscles are turning mushy from lying here. But she insists —

says it's "policy" — and wraps a blanket around me when I complain of the cold. So off we go, her shoes squeaking across the tiles.

The assistant who's supposed to take the blood looks startled when she sees me and shakes her head at my arms — my white, well-defined arms, ropy with blue and softly furred (I hate this hair, this down, which keeps growing all over me, even on my stomach: I have tried bleaching it, but more just keeps growing in, dark, like a pelt). She comes at me with the needle, jabbing and wiggling; she tries both arms a few times, getting flustered. "Your veins keep collapsing," she says. "I'm sorry, dear, but I have to keep trying."

It hurts, and though I don't look, distancing myself from this piece of meat that's being probed, I start feeling sick, my head suddenly receding from my feet, which in turn have disconnected from my knees. Squeaky, ever vigilant, pushes my head gently down onto my lap, and, after a few minutes in this pose, I feel ready to continue.

"Come on, let's get it over with," I say.

More prodding, but eventually she finds a vein, and, while I fix my attention on the far wall, she takes eight tubes of blood: to test potassium, calcium, hemoglobin levels. Sugar, too: as if they would find sugar in my blood. Even though I don't watch the blood being sucked out — once I made the mistake of observing the thick, grape-coloured stuff rising in the tube, stood up, and passed out — I still feel light-headed, and the shaken bloodsucker makes me lie down and drink some apple juice (120 calories; I take only a sip) before we leave.

My keeper wheels me back and explains, in her professionally patient, reasonable tone (I'd love to hear how she bitches with other nurses on her coffee break) that, though psychotherapy is part of the treatment plan, "they" have decided that I cannot begin yet because, she says, I am a starving organism and my brain is starving and therefore not working the way it should. I say nothing, but it's hard not to sneer: my brain's not working the way it should! On the contrary, it's never been purer and less cluttered, concentrated on essentials instead of distracted by a body clamoring for attention, demanding that its endless appetites be appeased. Stripped down, the brain is closer to the surface, taking in colors, sounds, with a fine, vibrating intensity.

One day I will be pure consciousness, traveling unmuffled through the world; one day I will refine myself to the bare wiring, the irreducible circuitry that keeps mind alive.

She also explains to me, again in what she thinks is a neutral, measured tone, that they're sure I'm going to co-operate, but if not, as a last resort, they might have to consider hyperalimentation. Hyperalimentation: interesting euphemism for force-feeding, for attaching a helpless human body to a tangle of tubes and pumping — what, I wonder? — into its unwilling ducts. Hyperalimentation: isn't that the word, rather, for the way most people eat?

I never feel hungry and despise those who do, whose lives are governed by the peristatltic pulse. Never have they learned to ignore that gaping maw: its slightest twinge sends them running to the trough. From the day's first mouthful to the last at night, their lives are one long foraging. In the morning, hunched over their desks, they munch on soft dough; at noon, they herd out en masse, meat-hungry, to feed; midafternoon, in a circadian slump, they crave sugar; arriving home, they root in the refrigerator's roaring heart and eat upright before an open door. And all this before the serious eating begins, the ever-to-be-repeated hours of shopping and chopping and mixing and cooking and serving, only to wolf down the result in seconds and greet it the next morning transformed into shit.

But I've freed myself from this compulsion. When I wake, I'm empty, light, light-headed; I like to stay this way, free and pure, light on my feet, traveling light. For me, food's only interest lies in how little I need, how strong I am, how well I can resist — each time achieving another small victory of the will: one carrot instead of two, half a cracker, no more peas. Each gain makes me stronger, purer, larger in my exercise of power, until eventually I see no reason to eat at all. Like a plant, surely, the body can be trained to subsist on nothing, to take its nourishment from the air.

Miss Pert — I think her name is Suzanne — finally leaves me, with a cheery reminder to fill out the menu card for dinner. The minute she's gone, I take it out and study it carefully, reading and rereading it, savoring not the names of the foods so much as the knowledge I will never eat them. Some disgust me, the very words filling my mouth with a viscid sickness: pork chops, hamburger, cheese omelet, clam chowder. But others I linger over, imagining their colors and textures, feeding on images, secure in the knowledge that images alone can fill me.

I prepare myself an imaginary feast, taking about forty minutes to decide on the menu — banana with peanut butter, fried rice, pecan pie — and to imagine consuming it lasciviously with a spoon. When it's over, I look at the menu card again, knowing that Squeaky-Pert will harass me if I don't mark something. Some of the dishes frighten me, their names alone quickening my pulse: spaghetti and meatballs! Imagine eating that, a whole, giant plate of it, everything heaped together, oozing oil. My heart is racing now, so I put a check mark next to "mixed salad" on the card and push it away from me, to the far side of the nightstand.

I lie back again, trying to relax, wondering how big the salad will be and whether they'll try to make me eat the whole thing.

Then panic seizes me: I sit up violently, grab the menu card again, and write in emphatic block letters next to my check mark, "NO DRESSING!!" I underline this three times and then lie back, trying to calm my hammering heart.

To collect myself, I start doing leg lifts again, picking up where I was interrupted earlier and deciding I will do an extra fifty on each side in case the nurse, my jailer, makes me eat the whole salad. The bed isn't really firm enough for calisthenics, but I'm afraid to get down on the floor in case someone comes in. I'm going to have to get down there eventually, to do my push-ups: maybe I can say I'm looking for something on the floor. (A contact lens? A cockroach?) They think they can wear me down by this constant intrusion — I'm supposed to be on an hourly watch — but I know I can outlast them all.

One day I will be thin enough. Just the bones, no disfiguring flesh, just the pure, clear shape of me. Bones. That is what we are, after all, what we're made of, and everything else is storage, deposit, waste. Strip it away, use it up, no deposit, no return.

Every morning the same ritual, the same inventory, the same naming of parts before rising, for fear of what I may have become overnight. Jolting out of sleep — what was that dream, that voice offering me strawberries and cream? — the first thing I do is feel my hipbones, piercingly concave, two naked arcs of bone around an emptiness. Next I feel the wrists, encircling each with the opposite hand, checking that they're still frail and pitiful, like the legs of little birds. There's a deep hollow on the inside of each wrist, suspending delicately striated hands, stringy with tendon and bone. On the outside of the wrist, I follow the bone all the way up to the elbow, where it joins another, winglike, in a sharp point.

Moving down to the thighs, first I feel the hollow behind the knee to check that the tendon is still clean and tight, a naked cord. Then I follow the outside of each thigh up towards the hips: no hint of a bulge, no softening anywhere. Next I grab the inner thigh and pinch hard, feeling almost all the way around the muscle there; finally, turning on one side and then the other, I press each buttock, checking that the bones are still sticking through.

Sitting up in bed, a little more anxiously now, I grasp the collarbone, so prominent that it protrudes beyond the edges of the shoulders, like a wire coat hanger suspending this body, these bones. Beneath it, the rows of ribs, deeply corrugated (and the breasts, which I don't inspect). Then I press the back of my neck and as far down my spine as I can, to make sure the vertebrae are all still there, a row of perfect little buttons: as if they held this body together, as if I could unbutton it and step out any time I wanted to.

Dinner is as bad as I was afraid it would be. At precisely six o'clock, Squeaky squeaks in with a big tray, which she puts down next to the bed, where I am floating again, on my back, imagining myself somewhere else altogether, cool and perfectly hard in a silk-lined gown. Firmly, she says, "Josie, I hope you're going to eat your salad tonight, otherwise the medical team will have to make a decision tomorrow about hyperalimentation."

I look in horror at the huge bowl of salad on the tray. *It's possible to slow yourself down by eating too much salad.* "This *is* hyperalimentation," I say: a mound of lettuce with chunks of pale tomato, shards of green pepper, hunks of purplish raw onion and — they must be nuts if they think I'm going to eat any of this — gobs of cheese and hard-boiled egg, with a bruise-colored line where the white pulls away from the yolk. Even though I didn't ask for it, there's a big, stale-looking roll and butter, an apple, a dish of vanilla ice cream, a glass of milk, and a plastic container of some urine-colored oil labeled "Italian".

"I can't eat if you're watching me," I say, which is true.

"OK," she says, "I'll be back in half an hour to see how you're doing."

As soon as she leaves, I draw the curtain around my bed: no one must ever see me eat, no one must ever catch me in the act — especially now that my appearance excites so much attention, with people always staring at me, willing me to weaken. *The Trobrianders eat alone, retiring to their own hearths with their portions, turning their backs on one another and eating rapidly for fear of being observed.* With the curtains drawn, my heart slows down a little and I concentrate on controlling this food: if I don't deal with it soon, it will exert a magnetic pull on me, commanding me to eat it, filling my consciousness until the only way I could escape would be to run shrieking into the street.

There is a big paper napkin on the tray, so I scrape exactly half the salad out of the bowl and into the napkin, along with half the roll. I bundle this mess up and start looking for a place to hide it: not easy in this cell. My clothes locker is locked and I don't have the key — of course not: this is going to be one of my little "rewards". (Even my shoes have been locked away, my socks.) Under my pillow would be too risky, because the napkin could leak or break, making a big lettucey mess that would be hard to explain. So the only place I can think of is the drawer of the nightstand next to the other bed, the unoccupied one, the one as flat and empty as I would like mine to be.

Once that little bundle is out of the way, I can relax a bit and start working on what's left. I separate the mound of food into piles: lettuce on one side, tomato on the other, pepper pieces neatly stacked and segregated from the rank, juicy onion. The egg and cheese I pick right off and banish to the bread plate: evil.

Cheese is the hardest food to digest and it contaminates everything you eat it with. Then I cut the lettuce, tomato, and pepper into tiny pieces, deciding I won't even pretend to eat the onion because lots of people don't like raw onion: it's legitimate, it's "normal". I cut the half roll into four sections and decide I will eat only one. Of the ice cream, I will eat exactly two spoonfuls, and the apple I will save for another time. So I put it away in my nightstand drawer along with the piece of roll I picked off the lunch tray: just in case.

Now that these decisions have been made, now that the bad stuff has been removed, now that the food is separated, with white space showing on the plate, now I can start eating: one piece at a time, and at least three minutes (timed on a second hand) between mouthfuls, with the fork laid down precisely in the center of the plate after each bite.

Of course the nurse comes back before I'm done and, without even asking, swishes back the bed curtains, revealing me shamefully hunched over the tray, chewing. I freeze, unable to meet her eyes. She says, gently, "There's really no need to close the curtains, dear, when you're alone."

Sullenly I push the tray away and lie back on the pillow, staring up at the mangy acoustic tile.

"Don't stop," she says. "I'll come back in fifteen minutes or so." She leaves, but it's no good: I can't eat any more; I feel sick and upset, with the undigested salad sitting scratchily, bulkily, inside me. My stomach is beginning to swell. I feel it anxiously, palming the dip between my hipbones, sensing a new curvature, a new tightness there. Panicky, before I know what I have done, I have wolfed down three teaspoons of the now almost entirely melted ice cream.

I put the tray on the other bed and draw the bed curtains around it so I don't have to be reminded of my gluttony; climbing back on to my own bed, I draw those curtains too, wanting to be alone, to hide where no one can find me, tempt me, torment my will. I want to find a cave or burrow somewhere where the idea of food becomes an abstraction, and this body, ever clearer and purer, evaporates finally into the dark, leaving only consciousness behind.

When the nurse comes back, I ask her to take me to the bathroom (another of these laws under which I now live: I can't leave the ward unaccompanied). This is partly a diversionary tactic but partly also because I'm desperate to wash my hands and face: my skin feels oily and slimy, as if the fat in the food is oozing through my pores. She helps me tie on the hospital-issue robe, with a faded blue design that makes my skin look even more cyanotic than it is. I'm cold but she won't let me put on any more clothes. So we walk slowly to the bathroom and she stands near the door while I go into a cubicle, where I'm not allowed to close the door in case I make myself vomit (which I've never been able to do — though not for want of trying). I can't pee under these conditions, so I give up and comb my hair instead (it's still coming out, in dry hanks), tying it back tightly with an elastic band. Then I scrub my face and hands once, and again, then again, until the nurse says sharply, "That's enough now," and we trudge back to the cell.

She bustles about, making a big deal of flinging back the curtain on both beds, plumping up pillows, straightening the limp covers. Then, tilting her head to one side, she contemplates the tray and says, "Well, Josie, you did a good job on your dinner."

Relieved, I climb back on the bed and pick up a *Vogue* that's been lying around — I got away with it! again — when she says, "I'm going to have to take a look around, if you don't mind. It's one of the rules."

If I don't mind! What choice do I have, powerless as a child, forced to lie and scheme simply to exercise the elementary — alimentary — right to determine what does and doesn't go into my body?

She looks quickly under both beds and behind the curtains, checks the lock on the clothes locker, runs her hand between the end of the mattress and the metal railing at the foot of the beds, and then, of course, opens the nightstand drawer on the far side.

"What's this?" she says, though she knows.

"I was saving it for later," I say. "I couldn't eat it all now, so I was going to have some more later, before bed."

She says nothing but just stands there, shaking her head, holding the imperfectly closed bundle of salad and bread, already soggy in spots. Then she dumps it on the tray and says, "Anything you don't eat, just leave on the tray." She seems about to pick up the tray and go, but then, as an afterthought, comes over to the side of my bed, opens the screeching drawer — is there no place that's mine? — and finds the apple and the piece of roll I took from lunch. "This is hoarding," she says. "You can have anything you want to eat at any time — just ask, but don't hoard."

Angry and humiliated and bereft, I don't answer. I put the *Vogue* over my face so I won't have to see her, wondering how I must look, lying here flat in a faded robe, my fragile limbs sticking out like a grasshopper's, my skin a dry grayish white, netted with veins, my fingertips and nails blueberry-hued, the crook of each arm a purplish mess dotted with bloody pinpricks, and on top of this all, superimposed over my face, the vivid face of the *Vogue* cover, each eyelash alert, each tooth a dazzling, chunky Chiclet, the skin a sealed and poreless stretch of pink, and the ripe, shiny lips curved into a radiant smirk.

2

It's FIVE A.M. and I should be stretching for my run, but how am I going to run here, when they won't even let me walk farther than the bathroom? I could run in place for forty-five minutes, which is how long it usually takes me to do four miles, but would that burn the same number of calories? Maybe I should run in place a little longer, just in case. By my calculation, I have an hour and a half before Nursey bursts in: she didn't come until six-thirty yesterday.

Sure enough, at precisely six-thirty, there's a knock on the door, which opens immediately, giving me just enough time to leap back on the bed. I try to look as if I'm just lying there contemplating the ceiling, but I feel flushed and a little out of breath from the running. At least I never sweat anymore.

"Good morning," she chirps, eyeing me suspiciously. "How did you sleep?"

"Fine," I lie.

"Have you been awake for long?" she asks. "If you wake up early, or you can't sleep, you can always ring for the night nurse. She can bring you a cup of tea or something, or just stop by to talk."

"No, I'm fine, thanks."

"Well, here's your breakfast," she says, as if I haven't already figured out what the huge tray is. "We're going to weigh you afterwards and decide what needs to be done, so see how much of it you can eat, OK?"

What needs to be done is for everybody just to leave me alone, to let me eat my own food in my own way.

Although I told them exactly what I have to have for breakfast — two cups of tea, no milk, no sugar, exactly a quarter cup of Special K cereal with half a teaspoon of sugar substitute and skim milk, diluted — they refuse to give it to me. Special K has no nutritional value and sugar substitutes are bad for you and you must learn to eat "normal" food, blah blah blah.

"What's 'normal'?" I ask the doctor. "Should we all strive for an IQ of precisely one hundred?" Of course he has no answer. (How would he, the fat, balding frog?)

Every mealtime is going to be the same struggle, I can see, looking over the enormous load.

The more they give me, though, the less I'll eat.

Here I'm confronted with a huge mound of dry flakes — corn or cardboard, who can tell? — heaping over the rim of the bowl; a pitcher of what looks suspiciously like whole milk; half a cantaloupe (cantaloupe: 40 calories per quarter); two pieces of whole wheat toast (180 calories), dry, I'm glad to see, after the tantrum I threw yesterday, though there are four pats of butter (110 calories) in case I change my mind; a vial of glutinous red stuff; a gigantic glass of orange juice (100 calories), a pot of tea, and a boiled egg (79 calories)! How many times do I have to tell them! The very sight of it, freckled and pert in its white china cup, makes me want to take a spoon and smash its shell and smash again and watch it crack and then stab it with the point of the spoon until its membrane that holds it together ruptures

16

once and for all. Except I would be afraid of the terrible smell this would release, the metallic stench, the viscous yellow blood.

I take the egg off the tray, in its cup, and carry it to the windowsill, where it sits like Humpty Dumpty before the fall. Then I get back on the bed and draw the curtains around me. I decide I will drink two cups of tea and eat half the cantaloupe and one piece of toast. *Eat the plain, crispy toast in small bites, savoring the crunchiness and nutty flavour.* That ought to keep them happy. For a moment I think of throwing the cereal away, to make it look as if I've eaten that too, but after the salad fiasco, I can't think of a place to hide it.

Slowly, delicately, precisely, I cut the piece of toast into halves, then quarters, then eighths, then sixteenths, and daintily convey each piece to my mouth, allowing three minutes between bites. Then, in the same way, I eat exactly half the slice of cantaloupe, panicking for a moment: how can anything so heartrendingly sweet and juicy, so intensely orange and alive, have so few calories? What if they've sprinkled sugar all over it, so I can't see it? What if this is some special high-calorie cantaloupe, grown expressly for hospitals? Something is definitely wrong, because this vivid sweetness is titillating my taste buds, tempting me to yield and eat more.

But I don't. When I've finished the cantaloupe, my heart is hammering: I put the tray on the other bed, as far away from me as possible, and slowly drink the weak, bitter tea. The tray still looks loaded, despite everything I've consumed. I hide the other piece of toast under the napkin; if I had a bedpan, I could pour some of the orange juice into it. That would give the lab something to think about.

I wonder if they have me on some kind of drug, because I seem able to spend so much time just lying here, suspended, with time

17

becoming increasingly unreal — a question only of the day nurse versus the night nurse, a different tint behind barred glass. Usually, I can't sit still: it hurts my bones, and a voracious fear funnels up from my gut, driving me out of the house, to the gym, to the jogging track, to the park to pace endlessly, to a store five miles away for a pack of gum.

But here, a prisoner, I pace, yes, but I also lie back and float, the images coming in such a flow that they frighten me, I who have been perfecting emptiness for so long. I thought I had lost the past, starved it away, until nothing remained but a vague dream populated by phantoms: a lifetime of words reaching me through thick languor; other people never really seen but remembered only in terms of how I must have looked to them. (Sullen, lumpish, weighed down with ugliness? Small, delicate, waifish, perfect? A monster of gluttony and sloth, this body gravid with its own greed?) Days, weeks, months, completely lost, lying on the bed too faint and dizzy to consider standing up, counting the hours (eighteen, always, exactly) until the next and only meal: a half cup of cottage cheese.

Time for the big weigh-in and I'm afraid: afraid that I will have gained weight under this regime of force-feeding; afraid that I won't have, and will have to stay here forever, having huge trays of food pushed at me, even perhaps having tubes rammed in. The nurse is chattering away mindlessly as she wheels me to the examining room: it's a beautiful day outside, she says, too bad I'm not "level three" yet, so I could go out: I'm scheduled to see Dr. Frog later in the day, she says; how about a nice long, hot bath after the weigh-in; take off your slippers — no, take them *off* — and step in.

The beam doesn't move at first, and then she slides the weight along and it lifts, quivering gently. With a shock of alarm I see the metal tooth has snagged just above sixty-nine. Sixty-nine and a half pounds! I've gained a pound and a half in three days (not counting the five glasses of water I drank before being wheeled here: half a pound, perhaps?) My belly feels tight to bursting and suddenly looks obscenely round; reflexively, I press it with my palm, resolving not to eat again today.

I have a rule when I weigh myself: if I've gained weight, I starve for the rest of the day. But if I've lost weight, I starve too.

As panic surges in me, I try to remind myself why I'm here. I'm here to become "healthy" again. (But I am healthy: a perfectly functioning, energy-sufficient machine, driven by pure will.) I'm here, basically, because my room-mate couldn't take it anymore and called in the cops: come and get your daughter, I can't cope with her, I'm afraid she's going to die. Nothing too good for the daughter, no expense spared (now), leave her in the institute and get the hell out of town again, as fast as possible.

Hospital, graduate school, prison: it's becoming increasingly difficult to tell the difference. And here at least the rent is paid.

I'm here but — ha! — I'm still nowhere near the seventy-five pounds they've set as a minimum for me to start the rest of the "treatment plan." Intensive inpatient care for "nutritional rehabilitation." Long-term outpatient psychotherapy and "support." Starving organism, blah blah. Neurological deficit, blah blah blah.

Hyperalimentation.

"It's not something we like to do, Josie, and it's certainly not something we like to bandy about as a threat. But sometimes it's the only way we can get people out of danger, or up to a certain level of cognitive functioning."

From a long way away — the parents are on a plane, hushed and bowed, unable to look each other in the eye; my father holds a big key (ornate, theatrical, something a chatelaine would wear on her belt), pops open the plane's porthole, hesitates a moment, and releases it, sending it downward in a dream-slow spiral — I come back, feel the scale's cold metal on my feet, look down at my purple toenails, tune in to the nurse. Why doesn't she ever talk like a normal person? Why doesn't she just say, "Eat, you little shit, or I'll shove tubes into every orifice and blow you up like a blimp"? Then I could say "Fuck you, I'll never eat; you'll have to watch me vanish."

"I'm trying," I say. "I really am."

I keep standing there, staring at the numbers on the scale as if the reading might change if I will it hard enough. It's terribly cold in the thin robe, but I can't think what else to do. There's nowhere to go, nothing to do; time opens up vertiginously beneath my feet.

Usually, around this hour, I would be getting out of my Macro lecture and riding home on my bike to prepare my first meal of the day: diluted skim milk and instant coffee and sugar substitute and ice cubes whirred in the blender for ninety seconds. And drunk with a straw from a special tall glass, at the kitchen table in the sun, reading over my notes — half an hour minimum, no slurping. And then it would be time to start changing for noon aerobics. But here?

I'm shivering; she suggests a shower. But I don't want to undress, to confront my bloated, blotchy body, to feel the shock of hot water on my bones. I want to go back to my room again, close the door, lie down, drift through this thick expanse of time.

I'm eating ground glass from a silver spoon: it's as delicate as spun sugar or shaved ice. As I swallow, the ecstatic friction begins, warmth welling up at the back of my throat and announcing its arrival, savory, on the tongue. I smile slightly: my lips turn vivid red from the inside out, my skin chalk-pale (with my dark hair,

I'm Snow White, I'm an image floating up from a Pre-Raphaelite lake). My smile widens and a gush of hot blood runs out.

"How beautiful she is, doctor."

"Yes. And she'll never eat again."

Dr. Frog is not happy. He wants to see a lot more "meat on my bones," and soon. (Meat. Am I to resemble a pork chop? A leg of lamb? A bloody, dripping steak tartare?)

"We're going to hold off on the hyperalimentation," he explains, hunched forward in his chair, his small, chubby hands working, "because we really hate to do that — it's a last resort. But if we don't see some significant improvement in nutrition — and a weight gain of at least five pounds — we're going to have to do something. The choice is yours, Josie."

I say nothing, focusing on his hooded, baggy eyelids, the slight croak in his voice.

"Tell me something, Josephine," he asks, in a confidential tone, leaning even farther forward in fake bonhomie. "What were mealtimes like in your house, when you were younger?"

Mealtimes. Perfectly normal, doc.

I would always arrive a little late, a few minutes after the bell had sounded. My mother, my father, and my brother would already be at the table, unrolling their napkins, filling their water goblets, with the maid discreetly setting down the last few dishes. As the others helped themselves, I would take my place, filling my glass to exactly three-quarters and taking dainty sips as they heaped their plates. I wouldn't look at them; they resolutely avoided looking at me. As the lids came off the serving dishes, sickening steam escaped, the various smells of matter: mealy (baked potatoes), grassy (green peas, congregating plumply like alien life-forms), bloody (chunks of mutilated muscle and fat, seared in a watery seepage).

Shaking my head primly at each dish, I would continue sipping until my mother — always — could stand it no more. "Josie!" she would burst out. "Aren't you going to eat anything?"

Coldly, triumphantly: "No thanks, I'm not hungry."

"But you *must* eat something," she would continue, two deep vertical lines scoring her oily brow, as if we had never had this conversation before. "I made all these veggies specially for you."

"But I'm not hungry." Another deliberate sip.

A deep sigh, and she would begin shoveling food into her mouth, stuffing in more before the previous mouthful was properly chewed. Avoiding her eye, my father concentrated on his plate, his long, delicate hands slicing the lamb. My brother, absently making tracks with his fork in his food, buttering his bread so thickly that each bite left toothmarks, was always somewhere else, his gray-green-blue eyes vacant and dreamy.

When I felt the beam of their attention wane a little — Dad might ask Anthony something about soccer or school — I would go into the kitchen and fetch myself a whole tomato, returning to place it exactly in the center of the blue and white dinner plate. The tension would increase again, though nobody would look at me directly. Excising its woody navel first, I would cut the tomato into four equal pieces and line them up, side by side, on the plate. Then I would take precisely half a teaspoon of mayonnaise from the silver dish; using knife and fork surgically, I would cut a tiny mouthful of tomato — it had to be pale and underripe, no oozing — dip it lightly in the mayonnaise, and transfer it to my mouth. By the time the others had wolfed down their second helpings, I would still be working on my tomato. Finishing, finally, I would close my knife and fork, bisecting the plate. Then and only then would my mother ring for the maid; as she cleared away the plates, I would ask to be excused.

"Won't you at least have some fruit, Jo? I bought some beautiful ripe peaches."

"No thanks, I'm not hungry."

After folding and rolling my napkin in its engraved silver ring, I would head to the kitchen to make my coffee, unable to trust anyone else with the correct proportion of coffee powder to saccharin. Sometimes, in the bright, cluttered disorder, I would surprise the maid scraping out a serving dish and cramming the crispy residue into her mouth. Sometimes, I would surprise in myself an urge to do the same.

"Just normal?" he asks. "No problems, no tension?"

"No, no tension," I respond. "You know, just sit around, discuss the day's events, what was happening in the world, family jokes, stuff like that."

"No fights?"

"No, not really."

"Not even when you wouldn't eat?"

"Yeah, well, sure, they were worried, but there wasn't much they could do. So they just kind of, you know, accepted it."

He says nothing but looks skeptical (interesting effect on a frog).

She's dragging me by the hair, my hair is coming out in handfuls, the carpet is burning my skin off my elbows, she's trying to gouge my eyes with her other hand, with my teeth and nails I flail at her ankles, missing and screaming, screaming and screaming, the fire engine is at the door, false alarm, yes but what *is* that smell? *In a sample of sixty cannibal societies, about thirty-five percent roasted the meat, regardless of whether it came from kin or from strangers.* It's the roast, officer (my daughter, skinned and burning); sorry to have bothered you. *Out of twenty-six cannibal societies who ate only their relatives, only two actually boiled them. The cannibals not only unpredictably roasted or boiled relatives and strangers alike; they also baked them, smoked them, or ate them raw.* Next time, gag her as well. I will, officer, I will.

As I'm wheeled back from the doctor — Squeaky is chattering away about something; did she really say "Art Therapy"? — I realize I have to make a decision. They seem serious about hyperalimentation — can they do it, against my will? Perhaps I could sue them, drag them through the courts, buy myself some time. They say I am dying, but I know I've never been more intensely alive (right now, for instance, how that honeyed square of sunlight on an olive tile pierces my retina, furs the edge of my tongue).

Yet here I am, "voluntarily." I agreed to come; that is, I didn't actively resist being put in the car. Sick leave. Leave of absence? You can even study at the hospital — rather, rest home — and come back to take your exams.

A seductive image: myself pale and languid, interestingly blue around the eyes, in a narrow metal bed, pinned down by weighty texts, subsisting on cups of bouillon brought by hushed, tender nurses.

Instead of which, this brisk, freckled woman, this Dr. Frog, these huge plates of food. This threat of force-feeding. I have no idea how it's done, but my imagination irresistibly summons two fat tubes, one pushed all the way into my mouth, cramming in a thick, lumpy pap, another rammed into my dry cunt, forcing an even denser mix up into the belly, which swells and swells but always takes more, never bursting. The arms, I see, are handcuffed to the bed rails (tiny handcuffs, hospital issue, for

24

wrists like birds' legs), with a needle in each blue crook and a thinner tube through which drops a heavy red flow: meat. Put some meat on those bones.

At this point, hyperventilating, feeling already the pressure in the mouth, the belly, the veins, I make a decision: I will allow myself to gain the five pounds (five pounds!). I will gain them as quickly as possible — for a week this body will be somebody else's, I won't look, I won't touch — check out of the hospital, and eat nothing until I'm back to sixty-eight pounds. Maybe sixty-five this time, for insurance.

I can't lie still anymore so I pace around the cell a few times, counting the tiles (every other one, the café au lait ones), trying to factor the total into primes, but I can't concentrate, so I look around for a mirror, wanting to see what I look like when I'm this agitated. But of course there's no mirror in here — why not? afraid, when it shatters, that I might open a vein? — so I lie on the cold floor next to the bed and start doing sit-ups.

When she bustles in with the lunch tray, I don't have time to move so I just stay where I am, flat and limp on the floor. She doesn't see me at first, looks alarmed, catches sight of me on the floor, draws in her breath, puts down the tray, heads over towards me, and then sees I'm all right. The blood floods abruptly back into her cheeks, but, ever the professional, she tries to keep the annoyance out of her voice.

"Josie, what are you doing down there on the floor? You gave me quite a fright."

"Nothing. Just lying. Change of scene."

"Aren't you cold? At least put on your robe, dear."

I won't stand up while she's there, so I stay where I am, staring at the ceiling, speckled like an eggshell, in other places — near the water pipes, I suppose — encrusted like Camembert. My spine and the two sharp bones at its base feel crushed by their

25

encounter with the floor, but I don't move. She stands looking at me, hands on hips; if she were wearing a dress, I would be able to see right up it. Instead from this angle I'm struck by her enormous, looming breasts and a fleshy fold under her chin.

"Josephine, please get up now."

"I can lie wherever I want."

"You're in no physical condition to be lying there on a cold floor."

I just did two hundred sit-ups and she tells me I'm in no condition! I'm certainly not going to move now. She looks at me; I look at the ceiling; she gives in.

"Well, I don't have time to stand here and argue with you. You're not the only patient on this floor, you know." Momentarily confused, I look around, half expecting to see a fellow inmate, hitherto unnoticed, also flat on her back. "I'll be back in forty-five minutes to see how you're doing on your lunch."

Lunch. Am I really going to eat all of it, as I had planned? I have to gain those pounds, my exit visa. Maybe if I eat everything on the lunch tray, I will gain it all at once. Well, not everything: if there's dessert, I definitely won't eat that. No, everything: I must eat everything (not butter, though: I could never eat that), otherwise it's the tubes, the pap, the meat. I must eat everything and waddle out of this jail to recover myself, to recapture my own clear shape.

Though I have decided this, though Miss Squirt is long gone, I can't quite make myself get off the floor. A heavy, dreamlike languor has seized me — though my skin is puckered and purple with cold, though my bones ache. The idea of actually standing up, of resuming the vertical seems increasingly improbable. How does one become upright again, from flat on one's back? How does anyone ever figure it out? Where would movement begin — at the head, so heavy and sodden, or at the feet, so lightly elongated? Perhaps the hands, but they seem numb and boneless, with a distant tingle deep inside, as if they were filled with laughing gas. I think I'll just lie here for a while, feeling the earth roll below me through dense, lonely space.

I'm still lying there — floating and rolling, my long, dark hair adrift in the lunar wind — when she comes back, takes one look at me, squats down beside me, takes my hands (without asking) in her own damp paws, and says "Come on, now, we're going to roll up slowly. Take a deep breath and keep your head down as I pull you up." I unravel upwards, the lunar wind is very loud, laughing gas, zero G, but then she somehow has me sitting on the side of the bed with my head in my lap. She has the nerve to leave her hand on my nape.

"Leave me alone, I'm fine," I say crossly, rolling over on my side and curling up tightly into a ball. Closed for repairs. "Don't bug me about the lunch, either," I add. "I'm going to eat it."

But I can't. Even when she has gone and fetched me a fresh bowl of vegetable soup (240 calories) to replace the congealed slime that had grown cold during my space travel, even when she has left me alone again, curtains drawn tightly around the bed, to face this food, I can't. I'm shaking: there is so much of it — a peanut butter sandwich (350 calories), a bowl of soup, a fruit salad, a glass of milk (140 calories) — and it squats there, daring me to eat it. Forcing me to eat it, forcing me to keep going until I have eaten the waffled bedspread and cream pillowcases as well, the dried flowers on the windowsill, the *Vogue* magazine, cramming it all insatiably into my mouth.

I must eat. I have to get out of here.

I can't eat. I'll die.

I must eat something. The tubes. (Thick stuff, like shit, forced into me.)

Still shaking, I start working on the fruit salad. *The life force in*

27

fruit is unsurpassed by any other food. The rest, I've decided, is out of the question, five pounds or no five pounds. I separate it into piles: browning chunks of apple over here; hard, unripe pieces of melon there; hairy little orange segments; a few white-filmed blueberries, wrinkled like rabbit shit. I decide I will eat only the apple chunks, because nothing else seems possible (hard, hairy, wrinkled), but by the time I've cut each chunk into quarters and placed the first one on the spoon, I begin trembling violently, spasmodically, all over, and my gullet closes, opening only when I set the spoon down, in a loud gasp that I recognize, belatedly, as a sob. More come, and more, forced up from somewhere deep inside me, as involuntary as an attack of retching, as strenuous, as inexhaustible.

DIAGNOSTIC PROFILE

Thank You for Your Voluntary Cooperation

DEMOGRAPHIC INFORMATION

Age: Late industrial capitalism
Sex: Rarely
Race: Opted out
Religious affiliation: None
Marital status: None
Current living situation: Barely
Highest level of education: *The Pritikin Program for Diet and Exercise*
Highest occupational level: 122 pounds
Current occupation: Wasting away

3

WAKING UP, I feel huge, my distended limbs spreading in all directions. I have to get out of bed and start running. But first, the inventory, the naming of parts: wrists, knee hollows, quadriceps, outer thighs, inner thighs, iliac crests. The hipbones still arch upward, pure and sharp, but between them — what's this? a definite swelling, a tautness.

This is what happens, once you start.

I made myself eat a whole tomato and a whole orange last night (the memory sickens me now, so much watery blood). I told them that's what I wanted, that's all I would eat, so eventually the night nurse brought it, whisking away the loaded plate in an exaggerated show of pique — the doctor says just this once, to get some calories in, but after that it's normal food, Josephine, we're warning you — and now look at me, beached whalelike on this bed.

I can't continue with the inspection, knowing only too well what I will feel: the heavy, sagging breasts scored with stretch marks; the swollen gut; lumpy gluteals yielding to gravity; wrists coarse; fingers stubby; face like a stupid moon. Dense and polluted, this immense mass of flesh swells like dough as I lie here; raising my hand to the light, I see only my mother's fat paw.

She brings in the breakfast tray — the same as yesterday's — and seems surprised to see me still in bed, sullen and greasy, unable to drag my bloated carcass to its feet, let alone stretch (how would I bend over?), pace, run.

"Sleep well, dear?"

"Would you for god's sake please stop calling me *dear*? And I need you to walk me to the bathroom."

I scrub and scrub but cannot remove the film from my face; even my hair, normally so brittle, seems lank, scummy, this morning.

"Can I take a shower right now?" I ask, panicky.

"No," she says, "after breakfast, at the usual time."

"But I have to," I insist.

"I'm sorry, de — — Josie, but you'll have to wait. Come on back to the ward now" — offering me her arm to hold on to, as if I would ever touch it: meaty and tight, like a sausage.

Swimming slowly back to my room through the green fluorescent air — she is asking about "bowel movements," what next — I try to remember the last time I actually reached out to touch another person's flesh. In recent years, fewer and fewer people have dared touch me, fearing, I think, to snap my bones; even my mother, who for years stubbornly offered an awkward embrace (as recommended by the family therapist) eventually gave up, sensing my panic as a mound of inflated flesh enveloped me.

Then a blurred image revisits me, as if from a home-made porno movie. Somebody did touch me, yes, more than a year ago — when I was still in the fat eighties. How could I even have appeared in public like that, let alone lend my limbs to another's touch?

He was a fellow grad student, a runner, ostentatiously lean, drawn to me, I think, by a sense of our kindred compulsions. By the time I understood what he was after, three margaritas were braying through my blood (750 calories: two days' starvation) and I couldn't find the wherewithal to care. So we did it in the car, where I was grateful for the dark, the soon fogged windows, the cramped confusion that precluded any ritual of undressing and appraisal.

Clothes twisted awkwardly, half on and half off, we grappled angrily like gymnasts in heat. His arms were very hard — harder than mine, hairy and bony — and their unforgiving angularity unnerved me. He had my top off and was palpating me, methodically checking the tone of my upper arms, pressing my breasts with flat palms, tracing the corrugations of my ribs with a downward finger. After a while, he whispered, "You feel good," and I relaxed (I pass! in the dark). But he didn't: he felt tense and unyielding, no softness anywhere, no contour, no place to rest my head.

Trying to get my jeans off, he succeeded only in twisting them halfway down my thighs, so I couldn't move. He began rubbing briskly at my sex, hurting me with the dry friction of hair on delicate tissue. Although I was somewhat aroused, it was mainly by the feeling of his feeling me, and by knowing, from my own obsessive explorations, exactly what his hand encountered. But he carried on with his scratchy, uninflected rubbing, and I grew bored, then self-conscious, despairing of pleasure.

As a diversion, I dived into his lap, unzipped his pants, and took his cock in my mouth, almost gagging before I got it in, gagging at the very idea. To my surprise — and embarrassment — it wasn't very hard. Nor was it very big — somewhat small and gnarled, in fact, with a strange kink in the middle. Nevertheless, I sucked away dutifully, trying to ignore its salty taste. He panted but seemed to be having trouble coming, and

31

my jaw was aching and my throat gaping before he let out a little moan and filled my mouth with viscous slime.

The bitter, metallic taste made me heave, bringing tears to my eyes. I couldn't swallow. (I'd done it before, yes. But that was before, when I would swallow anything.) Without raising my head from lap level, I pushed myself across his knees, feeling for the door handle in the dark. The door opened so abruptly that we both almost fell out. But I held on to the edge of the seat with both hands, stuck my head out, and half spat, half vomited, my mouthful into the gutter.

Now, back in my room, I feel the same gag reflex thinking about the tubes. The tubes: if I don't eat these flakes. (How do they make them, I wonder — each one, if you look carefully, as rugged and pitted as a rock face.) I will eat them, I decide (five pounds and out), one by one, with my fingers, without milk (a whole enormous bowl of sodden mush is out of the question). By the time I reach flake number fifty-one, I feel sick, distended, filled with a dry, choking nausea. That's it; that is *it*. Surely I must be on my way to — god, seventy pounds, perhaps even more. My heart is racing, my gut obscenely tight; a silent wail of panic wells up in me. Placing the tray on the other bed, I close the curtains around mine, roll over on my side, curl up, and yield to a black paralysis.

My toe shoes are very shiny, my mouth blood-dark. Attired as a nymph, I pick my way delicately over the shattered glass — no, they're only snowflakes, ice crystals (but beware, they can travel to the heart and lodge there). The aroma of rosin intoxicates me; the lights are blindingly hot and white; beyond them, a velvet murmur. With a flourish, I unfurl a long, pale leg; my arm swims through space to hold me up. I could stay there forever, my being poised upon a single point, but the music tells me it's time to come down, to gather for the final leap. This time I know I can do it. The audience seems to sense something, too; the darkness draws in its breath. I coil, I spring, and it happens: I'm strong and spare enough to soar, to keep soaring, my arched front foot slicing space like the head of an arrow. Up, up, buoyed by the air, buffeted through the flies, past the startled stagehands, and out into the infinite night, while the audience, amazed and then afraid, waits in vain for me to reappear.

"Would you like to take a look at today's paper?" she's asking brightly, rustling it in a way that scrapes all the nerves in my brainpan.

"No thanks," I say (what do I care, people dying and killing each other) though perhaps I should glance at the business section for Macro. I ask her what day it is (the day nurse versus the night nurse, blue now behind bars).

"Tuesday," she says, "the seventeenth." I don't ask of what month, in case she reports me to the doctor.

Tuesday: the food section.

"OK, hurl it on over."

I turn immediately to the restaurant review.

Translucent slivers of scallop have the texture
of firm custard,
with a frothy oceanic flavor.
The veal chop is tempting, too,
thick and tender.
Try the juicy breasts of squab,
the succulent grilled quails
brushed
with hazelnut vinaigrette —

or a sole's
snowy, crisp-skinned flesh.

It's poetry; the only kind I read, tasting each word on my tongue.

The saltiness from the ham plays
seductively
off the sweet cognac.
Don't miss the silken artichoke mousse,
boosted by a lusty black truffle sauce;
or the brittle lid of sautéed potatoes
atop
melting tender fruits de mer —
a rousing combination.

No, it's pornography.

I read it again, then one more time, then throw the paper on the floor. Perhaps I should try to study instead. I haven't even looked at the books I brought with me. I can't concentrate: it's the drugs, it's the fear, it's my belly swelling up and drawing blood from my brain. It's bad enough trying to study at home, where constant restlessness agitates my bones, but there at least I can stay up all night. Here they make me go to bed even though I can't sleep, and during the day they wheel me around, prod me, puncture me. Even when I'm alone, I can't think straight because anticipation of the next meal tray gnaws at my mind.

Time to weigh myself down with heavy books, arrange them around me on the bed cover so they will hold me down, keep me in place, prevent me from expanding sloppily, yeastily, over the edges. The Topology book has a glossy red cover, like lipstick, like lollipops: I would like to put it to my mouth and lick it. But I open it instead. Topology: the study of those properties of figures that remain unchanged even when under distortion, so long as no surfaces are torn. No surfaces are torn, but there are tiny pinpricks all over my arms and a hole in my heart, where a thin wind whistles through.

"Psychotherapy is not useful to starving individuals," says Dr. Frog. "So I'm just here to see how you're doing, to chat."

I say nothing but stare into my Topology text, as if the marks on the page meant something to me. I have no desire to converse with anyone, least of all a frog. It seems ironic that those trying to regulate my diet are themselves in need of a little self-control: this doctor, for instance, has quite a belly erupting over his belt. I focus on that and try to imagine him naked, with this mound of pale flab jiggling as he moves. I wonder if he's married — of course he would be, to some lumpy middle-aged lady: I envision their doughy coupling, his tired dick poking into her wobbly thighs. The image makes me giggle; for comparison, I caress my own elegant limb, nothing but muscle and tendon and bone.

He seems to be waiting for me to say something, so I inform him: "I ate my breakfast. I ate fifty-one flakes."

"Good, Josie," he says, "it's a start. But we still have a long way to go."

I still have a long way to go — no excess baggage, no deposit, no return — but I'm not going to talk to him about that. He wants to drag me down, bury me in flesh, obscure the clear, sharp lines of my self. He wants to take me back to the days when, driven by a ravening restlessness, I would roam the streets looking for something to devour. The nightmarish days, before I learned control.

"Maybe," I say.

"What?" he asks, confused. (How much time has passed?)

"Maybe we have a long way to go still." Or maybe I'll just vanish before your eyes.

"I'm not sure what you mean by that, Josephine," he responds, carefully.

No, you wouldn't, would you. How could a person like you understand a person like me? Perhaps, like the rest of them, you would like to whip out your dick and probe me with that, thermometer-style, to find my core temperature, the deep, red heart of things. Everything else is cold and blue, betraying nothing.

Dicks I have seen in my day: let's take them out, boys, and line them up on the examining table. A blunt-headed, bluish thing, shifting and drifting in response to the bathwater's private tidal system ("Next time, please knock"). Then something like a tusk nudging my thighs; an insistent, perpetually engorged one; a broad one with a bruised mushroom head; another one I never saw, and barely felt; the small, serviceable one, veering slightly to one side; the gnarled one, with a kink.

From all of them, though, the same slime (9 calories per teaspoon).

Halibut
(with cream, of course)
on baby vegetables.
Linguine coupled with sweet young clams
and tender squid.
Bite into the plump shrimp-and-scallop dumpling
and watch the juice spurt out.
The chocolate cake is hauntingly rich,
(so dark and sweet)

with a lingering
afterglow.

Time to run. I cannot lie here any longer and listen to my body decompose; run in place, fast, faster, until nothing matters but lifting the next foot, filling the burning lungs with air, fighting off the urge to drop like a stone.

Think of nothing: keep going, keep going, keep going, keep going.

Just in time, I hear the clattering food cart stop outside my door, and throw myself, panting, back onto the bed. This time I am not going to eat anything at all. (But the tubes.) On the menu card, I asked for a tomato, knowing they wouldn't give it to me, so I'm curious to see what she has brought instead.

"Hi, Josie," she beeps, "lunchtime."

I don't respond, staring instead at the cover of my Topology text (how I'd love to lick it, so candy-apple sweet).

"And after lunch," she continues, "I'm going to introduce you to our art therapist."

It's hard to suppress a snort. "I don't need 'art therapy,' " I tell her. "I have plenty to do here" — indicating the Topology text. "Besides, therapy is not helpful to starving individuals."

She looks at me sharply but says nothing.

I look at the tray, merely for the record, as I have no intention of eating anything. Some scarlet soup, with archipelagoes of oil. A big glass of milk.

What would your reaction be if you were driving down some country lane and you happened to see a well-dressed man or woman down on his or her knees suckling from a cow? Would you make your way through the droppings and go right up to a cow and take the milk directly from her udder? No? But you would let some one else get it and bring it to you in a glass, right?

37

An orange (50 calories) and a banana (100 calories). And a GRILLED CHEESE SANDWICH. *Cheese is the hardest food to digest and it contaminates everything you eat it with.* Enough grease and fat and cholesterol to kill me. That seems to be the plan: to choke me with food, to fill my veins with waxy death.

"I want a Tab," I tell the nurse.

"We don't allow Tab, Josie, as I've already told you. The dietician doesn't think artificial sweeteners are good for people. Also, as we explained, the idea is to eat a normal diet."

"I want a Tab," I say.

"Sorry, Josie."

"I want a Tab."

She's not going to play, I can tell. But I'll win, when she comes back for the lunch tray and finds it untouched (though maybe I could save the orange, just in case; no, I don't want to give her the satisfaction). In the meanwhile, I'll just lie here, flat on my back, fingering my perfect bones.

I think of all the things I will never eat again. All the flavors so fragrant on the tongue: cinnamon and coffee and clove; apricot, raspberry, nectarine, and rye; ginger and chocolate, nutmeg and pear; almond, guava, sorrel, and plum; butternut, hazelnut, tangerine, thyme.

Tangerine, thyme. Time to tango. But the air is too thick and it's hard to tango lying flat on your back. Besides, it takes two.

Raising my robe to thigh level, I turn my legs out at the hip sockets, in ballet's first position, and lie there, a dancer on my back, like the magician's spangled, air-suspended accomplice. I lift one leg in the air, the foot elegantly arched, and admire the tense tendons, the sharply etched shinbone, the long, fibrous quadriceps. With a flat palm, I hit the back of my thigh and something quivers; I hit it again and again, harder and harder, watching it quiver, hitting and hitting until my palm stings, hitting and hitting, harder and harder. I'm panting now and my throat is choked; why not just run to the tray and devour everything on it, cram it in, shove it down this spiraling tunnel, keep shoveling to prevent the wail from making its way out? It's not fair, after all I've done, that this body, this bag of blood and blubber, should so insidiously soften, so stubbornly refuse to hold firm.

This is what happens when you think about anything else for a moment: the body seizes its chance and sags.

But I can stop it. Down on the floor again, hands beneath my lower back to protect my spine, I lift both legs off the ground, turn them out, point my feet, and open and close them slowly, repeatedly, like scissors. Two hundred of these, at least, maybe more, since I haven't taken ballet class in a week. Three hundred.

This is, after all, *my* body.

"So you just take it like this and squeeze," she says, manipulating the ball of clay in a big, broad hand. "Go ahead, squeeze."

She must be kidding, this large woman in a grubby smock (even such a loose garment can't conceal her fat belly, sectioned by her belt and bulging out under her bra). She wants me, sitting up in bed with a battered wooden tray over my lap, to take a ball of dirty-looking clay and squeeze it.

"What for?" I ask. I cannot imagine taking my dry, brittle hand from under the blanket, putting it on a ball of clammy earth, and squeezing.

"It's fun," she says. "It feels good. You soften it up a bit and then you can make something with it."

"I don't want to make anything."

"Sure you do."

I just lie here, looking at this ball of dirt, pitted like a planet. If I squeezed it, it would squeeze back; it would ooze between my fingers; it would insinuate itself beneath my nails. I could stuff it all into my mouth and be full forever, like someone buried alive whose intestines are later discovered filled with dirt.

I cannot bring myself to touch it. She squeezes and kneads it some more, and then slaps it down against the tray, her eyes inviting me to try, as if I were a dog that must learn through mimicry. I'm afraid that if I don't do anything, she will reach over, take my hand in her clayey grasp, and force it on to this lump of matter. So I take out my left hand and with the index finger pick off a tiny piece, about the size of a dime. Not knowing what else to do, I roll it, like snot, under my fingertip; it makes a thin strand, slightly thicker in the middle, about an inch long. She's watching me, but I don't want to meet her eyes. With my fingernail, I sever the strand in two pieces so that one is about twice as long as the other. Then I take the shorter and place it across the longer, about a third of the way down.

"What's that?" she asks.

"It's a person, can't you see."

"Only one leg and no head?" she asks, teasing.

"It's an abstraction," I reply, wanting to cry. I pick up the ball of clay — it's warmer and grittier than I expected — and smash it down on my person. Then I hand her the tray and say, "Thanks, that's enough now."

When she's gone, I pace, rubbing my filthy hands together. I'm suddenly afraid that all my hair has fallen out, so I alternate rubbing my hands with touching my head to assure myself that it's still there. Then I'm afraid that anyone seeing me would think me deranged, but the rhythm has taken on a life of its own: I can't stop rubbing and touching and pacing.

I need a mirror. I have no idea what I look like, because what I look like depends on which mirror I'm looking in. In the ballet studio, all four walls are paneled with mirrors, but each is slightly

40

different, so I always stand in front of the one that elongates me, Modigliani-like. The next panel, which I avoid, compresses me into a troll.

In class, at the break between barre and center, when we're supposed to be stretching, I always sit in one particular corner, where the mirrors meet. The other women use this time to gulp water, wipe sweat off their rank bodies, gather on the floor to gossip and to strain, grunting, as they reach for their feet. I'm cool, immaculate, without a drop of sweat. Sometimes, yes, there's a speedy, shaky dizziness, an acrid dryness in the mouth, but I won't even take a sip of water until class is over, until I'm home, until I've showered. Then I've earned it.

When someone opens a window, I pointedly close it; the others are always hot because they're swathed in fat, but I'm always cold. I don't ask anyone, I don't look at anyone, I just get up and slam the window shut.

I sit in the corner where the mirrors meet, my back to the rest of the class, the soles of my feet meeting like hands in prayer. And I stare, without blinking, straight ahead, as if meditating on something mysterious. (I could never bring myself to join their idle chatter: how would I ever break in? what would be the "natural" thing to say?) Aloof, on a higher plane altogether, I stare straight ahead — at my reflection, at the reflection of my reflection, at the reflection of that reflection.

I haven't seen myself from head to foot since I got here: all I've seen is a haggard, grayish face in the bathroom's institutional glare, which etches deep grooves around my mouth. I know that can't be me: my own mirror tints me hazel and ivory and rose. On the streets, anxiously scanning store windows and parked cars, I don't always recognize the waif peering back (such a sharp frown, such black shadows under the eyes). Three-way mirrors in department stores offer shocking glimpses of unfamiliar, puckered flesh — someone else's, surely, left behind by the last customer? And the hall closet, which I hate, stores a bulbous dwarf, my jeering Doppelgänger.

I pick up a knife from the dinner tray and examine my eyes in its blade, then my lips (mauve, with mulberry scabs where the skin's chewed off).

How will I ever know what I look like?

I can't eat another mouthful until I've weighed and measured myself, until I've looked at myself in all the positions I've developed, like an inverse bodybuilder, to display each part. Only I know what kind of shape this body is in, only I can appreciate its various perfections. What lover, in his urgent rush to ram himself into me, could properly appreciate what I have created here — the lean skid of the flank, the poignant ridging of the rib cage, the tiny bones of the feet?

As the diet book says: *"Make your scale your best friend and your lover."* Its cold metal embrace and — in emergencies — my own apprenticed hand: no need, ever, for the lewd rubbing of one corpse against another.

4

SOMETHING is eating me. Gnawing away with tiny rodent teeth, nibbling blank spaces around the edges of my consciousness, making it impossible for me to think a whole thought, one thought at a time, all the way through. She's wheeling me to be weighed, but I can't focus on what she's saying: there are lapses, blackouts, as if someone is playing with the sound on a remote control somewhere. Perhaps it's something to do with the acoustics of this corridor, airless and muffled, a seemingly endless stretch of shiny avocado floor and intermittent doors, some ajar, offering split-second glimpses of someone else's pain. Or perhaps it's the constant "ping" and "paging Dr. So-and-So."

Since the flakes — when was that? yesterday? the day before? — I haven't been able to eat anything. I drink everything they give me (except the milk), but nothing else seems possible; everything sits on the tray, self-sufficient, unbreachable, as if sealed in an invisible skin. I did eat two packets of mustard off the lunch tray yesterday, very slowly, dipping the point of my tongue, like a paintbrush, into the bright, burning paste. It helped counteract the sweetish taste in my mouth, but a few seconds later my gut convulsed, as if to heave. I can't stomach anything at all now, it seems.

I realize that the chair has stopped — has been stopped for some time, perhaps? — and she seems to be waiting for me to step out. But I'm very relaxed, very dreamy, my hands floating in my lap; I can't quite see the point of standing up, getting on the scale. All I want is to go back to my bed and flop down again, fade out.

She reaches for my hand, to help me up, I suppose, but, confused, I think for a moment that she wants to crush it in her strong, sausagey grasp; she must be annoyed with me, and she's going to snap my dry hand into shreds. But then her grasp feels surprisingly warm and gentle. "I can stand up by myself," I say, pulling away, pushing myself, wobbly-kneed, to my feet.

It's with a distant, fatalistic satisfaction that I watch her slide the scale's cold claw down from seventy, where she'd optimistically begun, past sixty-eight, to stop on sixty-seven. She gives a slight shake of her head and records it on the chart. I'm expecting a lecture, but it seems she's not going to oblige today. Perhaps she's given up on me, won't even pretend to care? Or perhaps she's not going to say anything but wheel me straight to the tubes, like a car to the gas pump?

Instead, she takes me back to my room and, when I'm flat on the bed again, settles herself in the molded plastic chair and says, "Josie, please listen carefully, because I need to explain to you about hyperal."

Hyper Al? Who is Hyper Al? A manic patient who has escaped from the psycho ward, perhaps, and is roaming the corridors with rape on his mind?

"What happens is this," she says. "We have to put a catheter into the subclavian vein — that's a big vein right under the collarbone, above the heart." She taps her own chest briskly; it doesn't make the hollow sound mine would, I notice. "Then there's this bottle that drips the total parenteral nutrition solution through the tube right into the vein."

Parental nutrition, right into the heart? Perhaps I could have used that, once — but not now, not like this. It's too late.

"To get the catheter in, Josie, we'll numb the area with an anesthetic, so you won't feel anything while it's being inserted. We sort of tunnel the catheter under the skin for a few inches to keep it in place and then put a sterile dressing on it. You'll need a chest X ray to make sure it's in place properly."

This is worse than I had imagined: an incision directly into the heart.

"Then of course we'll need to keep track of your blood sugar with ear pricks and urine tests . . ." but I'm not listening anymore, imagining myself lying helpless, incised with sugar dripping into my heart. The idea is terrifying — I can see it all building up, bagging out into fat — but at the same time strangely alluring: no choice at all but to take it all in, become a sweet-heart.

Realizing, finally, that she's lost me, she gets up to go, promising me a visit soon from Dr. Frog and leaving me a couple of booklets — "Care of Your Central Venous Catheter," "Nutrition Support Service Patient Information." Fascinated, I page through them, passing at crude line drawings of a stoic-looking man (neatly coiffed but naked, cut off at the waist) with a tangle of roots and bulbs in his chest and a jar of colorless fluid levitating above his right shoulder.

One end of the administration tubing has a white plastic spike. Am I a vampire, then, who must have a spike driven into my heart? But no: *This sterile pointed end is used to enter into the bag of solution.*

The solution consists of dextrose, amino acids, lipids, electrolytes, vitamins, and minerals (as if that could solve anything). Plus something called "fat emulsion," which provides calories and — they say — essential fatty acids. Fat, they lie, is "necessary for normal growth and functioning."

So they're going to mainline fat right into me, right into my veins.

You may notice that the pump normally makes a soft humming noise. It beeps when something goes wrong. Things that can go wrong: air embolism, clotted catheter, blood backup. Blockages of various kinds.

When the lunch tray arrives, I decided I have to eat something. But I feel guilty just having so much food in my possession. From the load of thick, oil substances — soup, slice of quiche, salad swimming in slime — I choose a green apple and a cube of nondescript yellow cheese. I put these together on a separate plate, which I remove from the tray, pushing it as far away from me as possible on the other bed. Then I climb back on my bed with the plate and knife, and draw the curtains tightly around me. Within this pale greenish space — the air tinged and watery like a sea cave's — I confront the food, my heart knocking strongly against the bones of my chest as if to be let out. First I slice the apple into quarters, then eighths, then sixteenths. With delicate precision, I slice the one-inch cube into sixteenths, too, each slice as transparent as skin. I arrange the apple pieces in a perfect ring around the plate and then place a slice of cheese on top of each piece. Then, very carefully, I consume each piece, first nibbling around the edges of the apple segment so it is the same shape as the cheese slice, and then biting delicately away at the resulting square, one side at a time. It takes about four minutes to eat each piece this way, and I wait three minutes between pieces. To discipline myself, I leave one piece on the plate, one perfect white wedge of apple, edged with a nail paring of green and topped with its skin of cheese.

When it's over, I lie back in fear, feeling stuffed and bloated, anxiously palming my belly to gauge the swelling there. I'm pregnant already, pregnant with matter that will soon be me.

As she's wheeling me for another blood workup later that afternoon, a hurried, self-important doctor stops her in the hall and engages her in an abrupt discussion of some missing test results. Because they're talking about another patient, I know I'm supposed to act as if I'm not there: I'm deaf, I'm invisible. Blind too, if you like, except that while they talk — argue really, politely but insistently — I'm looking across into an open door.

It appears to be a dayroom of some kind — TV, armchairs, magazines, card table — and two women are sitting there on a sagging couch. A frenetic game show is blaring from the TV, but neither is paying it any attention. One, strikingly beautiful, with an artfully painted face, is paging through a *Cosmopolitan*. The other, a skeletal-looking Asian, who could be anywhere from fifteen to thirty, is staring at herself in a mirrored compact, applying ice cream-pink blusher along her cheekbones. When she's done, she continues staring at herself, fixedly. Neither looks towards the open door nor acknowledges in any way my captive presence.

She's very thin, the Asian one, certainly thinner than me; I see I have a way to go. She is a mere skeleton (which they falsely say of me), as frail and lanky as a Halloween toy loose-jointed in the breeze. She's frightening, too: there's something otherworldly about her as she stares hypnotized into the mirror, her gaze fixed already on some far distance.

The other one, perfectly slim, doesn't strike me as sickly: I wonder what she's doing here, among the skeletons. She weighs about 108, I'd say, at five feet four inches, and is gorgeous by any standards, with her honey-coloured hair, her almond eyes, her long legs, and — it hurts to see it — a tiny, chaste waist.

There's a jolt, and I realize Miss Squeak has concluded her debate with the doctor — he seems disgruntled, she defiant — and is resuming our interrupted journey down the hallway's perfect one-point perspective. As she pushes me along, more energetically than before, adrenaline no doubt rioting through that solid flesh, I try to catch a glimpse of myself in the door's panels. Which one do I most resemble? I'm thinner than the gorgeous one — therefore more gorgeous, surely? — yet the Halloween toy has put me to shame, so much more perfect a skeleton than I.

I should never have come here, never have allowed myself to be swayed from my path. I was completely in control and now I control nothing, not even my limbs. Soon they are going to flood me with sugar, cut into my heart and feed it until it's plump and cushiony, like a satin valentine. Perhaps then I could offer it for them to feast on — so red, so sweet, so meaty — and make my escape, eviscerated.

"What if I just say no?" I ask.

"The medical team has made the assessment that your life is in danger," he tells me solemnly. "At this point, we have the right to take the necessary steps, with or without your consent."

"But what if I just refuse?"

"I'm afraid, Josie, you're really in no position to refuse anymore. We've tried to reason with you since you've been here, we've tried to explain your options, but you won't eat, your weight has continued to drop."

"I have been eating. I ate an apple and some cheese."

"Good, but that's only a couple of hundred calories in over twenty-four hours. Your electrolytes are out of balance, and, as we explained, we're seriously concerned about tachycardia. You don't seem to realize, Josephine, that you could die."

So could you, buddy: the odds in fact favor it.

"No, I don't, you're right. I feel fine. And anyway, why isn't *she* on Hyper Al, that girl I saw today?"

He's confused. "Which girl is that?"

"The Asian one."

He scans his memory bank, his eyes swiveling upward and rightward. "Oh, her. Well, the other patients are really no concern of yours at this point, Josie. What matters is your life, your health."

They always say they're concerned about me, about my health, when all they want is to control me. They want to pin me down and force-feed me: with lies, with what they call love. Like prisoners everywhere — like the suffragists, even — all I have left is the power to refuse.

He goes on talking, his mottled little hands working the air, but I'm somewhere else — an empty cage, a pile of straw — and I crawl back out only when I realize that the inflection of a question is hanging between us.

"I'm sorry?"

"I asked, Josephine," professionally patient, yet with a more emphatic croak than usual, "when you would say was the last time that you just ate normally, without thinking about it?"

"I do eat normally. I can't help it if everyone else is constantly stuffing themselves." Without thinking about it? Never — though there must have been a time when hunger announced itself, was satisfied, went away, came back, was satisfied again. Unimaginable now — but there must have been such a time.

If I had my things here, I could show him the photograph album: Exhibit A. (It's been edited, of course, purged, but there are a few token images of the terrible years — lest I ever forget.) Naturally it begins with a wedding, a formal portrait on thick cardboard, warped now and faded, like memory's own pigment.

The two children in fancy dress, smiling proudly, are my parents, Virginia and Michael, Ginny and Mike; I like to think I'm there too, a tadpole curled beneath the layers of tulle — though the official story is that I was born two months prematurely: a four-pound fetus, to be incubated, like an egg, in a box.

A few baby pictures follow, generic, of no particular interest (though I notice, in passing, that I was never chubby, never dimpled and fat-braceleted as so many babies are). It's the images of the growing child — sturdy, short-haired, rarely smiling — that I search carefully for clues. The wrists, I note, were always thick and strong, even on a skinny child of nine; the face has always been broad, the calves well-muscled (ballet classes since the age of four: here I am, a leotard-clad tot, with an outstretched leg and upturned nose; here I am ten years later, attired as a nymph, my toe shoes very shiny, my mouth blood-dark).

Somewhere in these images must lie a pure form, an essence of self; somewhere there has to be a shape I can recover, that's mine, that's me. Because at eleven or twelve, something happens. The mutation begins; everything turns lewd, coarse, lumpy. No more sleek, clean lines — only a self immured, sluglike, in flesh. From somewhere deep within, I — she, somebody — stares out in disbelief.

A few pages of these strangers (I shied away from cameras then, except when my disguise was exceptional) and then the ballooning begins to reverse itself. Here I am, thin-armed again in an evening gown, someone's champagne glass in the corner of the frame as if to toast my decline. And here I am baring a svelte midriff beneath the mimosa. In a dark, narrow-waisted jacket, braving a strong wind, I look as if I might snap in two. And, then, finally — before people stopped taking pictures, before they started looking away — the series I have lingered lovingly over: a body in a red bikini, each rib sharply etched (I have counted them), hips jutting hollowly, clavicles as clear as cartoon-strip dog bones. I must have been nineteen, and I stared at the lens in utter triumph.

Leave me alone, Dr. Frog, I want to replay that series, run those images again in my mind. Because somewhere in the gap between two of them is the reason I'm here now, perfecting my emptiness.

One more time: we have a sturdy-looking but basically skinny kid, hair cut pudding bowl-style, posing seriously and awkwardly with little brother, who's distracted by something outside the frame, a half smile sweetly dawning. We must have been on our way somewhere special, a birthday party, perhaps, because I'm wearing my best dress, blue and green stripes with a broad white collar (I still remember its starchy feel, its peachy smell). Small sibling, hair plastered back, looks like Little Lord Fauntleroy, except one knee sock has decided to descend.

The next one, at nine or ten, is a study in grays: eyes wary, hand touching my bare neck, my lips almost black.

He appeared one day in my bedroom with his new camera, a bulky affair with a protruding zoom, and, concentrating on clicking a dial's serrated edge into place, said, "Come, Jo, let's try this thing out."

"Ah, Dad, I'm doing my homework." Actually, I was reading an adventure novel, my favorite — four friends who were allowed to ride their bicycles in the street, who set off for whole afternoons at a time, who made sandwiches and climbed trees and solved crimes without anyone asking just what they thought they were doing.

"Come on," he said, "it's pretty fancy."

Sighing and rolling my eyes in exaggerated, movie-brat fashion, I put the book down and followed him into the garden, where, face scrunched, he realigned the same cog. To signal my boredom, I exhaled loudly and shifted from foot to foot.

"OK," he said, looking up at last, "where shall we put you?"

"Right here," I replied, grimacing grotesquely, a starlet at Cannes; when he didn't respond, I stretched the corners of my mouth with my hands, pushed my nose into a snout, and peeled my lower lids down, exposing the eyeballs in their veiny red bed.

"Josephine, please," he rebuked, "that's not very nice."

Seeking an artistic locale — the birdbath? no, empty and new — he found an unpruned patch behind the gardener's shed (the gardener had recently quit, spitting over his shoulder while my mother, in a frenzy, dialed 911; I watched thrilled from an upstairs window, hoping he'd come back and axe her). "How about here?" he proposed, steering me by both shoulders to the shed's grainy side.

"Dad," I said, striking a pose, then dropping it, "this is *boring*."

"Look up a little," he said, "and now to the left. The left, not the right."

He snapped a few times, then, ducking his head clear of the strap, set the camera down in the shade and, frowning, flipped through the manual until he reached *P*.

A portrait should reveal something about the subject.

"Look right at me."

When shooting a portrait, try to include some other part of the subject's body: the hand, for instance, or part of the arm. This helps to convey information and create a mood.

"Let's have your hand on your neck."

"Now a close-up (wait while I find the right — ah, here it is)."

When working in black and white, contrast's the key.

"You're so pale, Josephine. A little color, perhaps?"

Mother wore "Coral Reef." Before her mirror, like a thief, I stood on tiptoe and crayoned an amateur moue.

Next page, please: a class picture, seventh grade, St. Theresa's School. Now I would consider the uniform rather chic — white shirt, blazer, tie — but at the time we all hated it and tried to imprint it with individual flair: collar turned up, socks rolled down, skirt surely a little too short (though that tactic never survived the quarterly inspections, when we had to kneel, penitent, for a teacher to tape the inches between patella and hem).

Look closely, because something has gone awry.

All the same parts are there, but different somehow, coarsened. I'm in the second row, behind Amanda Jane (slouching, insouciant), where much of me is hidden, but what does show suggests the whole: the calves quite chunky now, fingers thick, the face a sullen moon. In an ill-advised attempt at glamour, I'm trying to grow my hair, so it's over my eyes and scraggly on the neck, with a few pieces coaxed forward in front of the ears. (I remember taping it at night to make it stay like that: why?) It looks oily, as does my skin. What the body can't stomach, it starts storing on the outside, as ugliness.

When I was fourteen, my father brought me back a bikini from a business trip to Paris; I wore it once, with the label dangling, so he could take a picture. He chuckled and said, "Well, *Playboy* likes them plump, I guess." It was reversible, blue on one side, black on the other, and bared a small tangle of pubic hair on the inner thigh.

Perhaps that's when I stopped going to the beach, to the pool. I didn't bare myself in public till I weighed eighty-eight. By then,

I'd had a bikini wax and was as bald as an egg. I used Nair on my armpits (rich foam, like whipped cream, but the smell of drains), I waxed my legs, I plucked my brows, I even shaved my arms.

Now, I've discovered electrolysis: the stinging prick, the tiny shock that kills the root, the burn that subsides, the pit where nothing ever grows again.

5

I'ts GOING TO BE a long night: Dr. Frog has gone, Ms. Squeak popped in to say good night on her way out, wearing a beige plastic raincoat (it's raining? true, my window is teary). They've left me alone here, staring into the dark, afraid to close my eyes.

"I'll be back tomorrow, for another chat," he promised.

"What are you going to do, ask me about my unhappy childhood?"

"That might not be a bad idea," he responded, humorless as ever.

Some people remember their childhoods. I pity them.

I remember something involving a ladder and a broken window when I was three, doctor. I remember the high hospital bed at nine, doctor, alone and afraid and bleeding from the throat. (Or was that much later? Or was it my own bedroom, and not blood after all?) I remember a man at the school bus stop, who asked me if I wanted to see how to clean a corroded car battery — a pan full of fizzy stuff, I recall — so I followed him trustingly to the darkest corner of an underground lot. And I remember Amanda Jane, after all these years, a fictional character like myself.

Everyone has a childhood friend. Why shouldn't I have?

Let's say we were inseparable, spending every minute of our summers together, sun-toasted, at the beach and the pool. In the winter, after school, we, let me see, staged elaborate dramas in her long, deserted dining room, awaiting our cues behind sage velvet curtains. Naturally she played all the supporting roles so that I could be the star (Sylvia Bubble, a movie queen, arrayed in her mother's old pearls and silk slips).

When we tired of the theater, we concocted dream sagas for Barbie and Barbie — and later, Ken.

Barbie, you were so slender and firm, with a tiny, jointed waist that never spread. Your breasts pointed up and forward, perfectly symmetrical, unmarked by the rude red eye of a nipple, and your straight thighs met in a demure beige plastic Y, smooth, sealed, and uncleft. Your little feet were so beautifully arched, ballerinalike, that you had to stand on tiptoe all the time, and your clothes fitted perfectly, every day of the month. You had a permanent blue stripe painted above your almond eye, and your little mouth was puckered and painted like a persimmon. And you lived in an elegant black vanity case, shiny plastic that, to my eye at least, resembled patent leather, where you inhabited a modest cubicle (coffin-shaped, now that I think of it) surrounded by your sumptuous wardrobe.

The only part of you I didn't really like, didn't covet or caress, was your hair: a dry black puff, chin-length, disappointingly like the generic round do's of everyone's mother. I would have preferred pure silk, I think, down to the back of your knees, nut-colored or roan.

But it was your wardrobe that really mattered, Barbie, that collection of fantasies for which your hard little form was merely a pretext. They came alluringly displayed in flat, frontless boxes, each tiny garment spread-eagled under plastic, wisps of dreams promising a life of endless possibility: Garden Party, Scuba Diving, Mediterranean Cruise, Wedding Day. My favorite, I think, was Guinevere: a purple velvet robe, floor-length, with a full skirt blossoming from a fitted bodice. It was richly brocaded at hem and sleeve — the sleeves silk-lined and flared, like purple arums with a slender arm for a stamen — but the best part was the gold chain looped around the waist, as if for large heavy keys to secret doors.

I loved Garden Party, too: a ladylike gown, rose-sprigged and demure, with a gusset of lace in front and little white gloves on the side. In other moods, though, Cowgirl caught my fancy. Or did I prefer the black lamé gown, strapless, that clung like a skin to the ankles, where it erupted in a puff of tulle? Luckily, Barbie, you didn't have to walk, because you couldn't have; you had merely to pose, slinky and shimmering, on bejeweled black sandals, with a scrap of pink chiffon clutched in one hand.

Amanda Jane had a Barbie, too — exactly the same as mine, except blond, like her — and we spent a couple of years in passionate involvement, inventing elaborate scenarios that would allow two miniature plastic women to change clothes as often as possible. Just as our interest was beginning to wane, someone gave Manda a Ken doll, and we knew just what to do: sniggering and giggling feverishly in the long grass out by the vegetable patch, we divested Ken of his dinner jacket and brought out Barbie, bare-assed, to be laid on the ground. Supine, her plastic arms pointed straight up, like the pugilist position of someone who has died in a fire, but we maneuvered Ken between them and carefully aligned his blank plastic place with hers. Then, at a loss, we glanced at each other, and Manda pushed me over, playfully, from my squatting position, and I chased her around the garden, both of us screaming and chortling wildly and wrestling like boys when we finally met, our contorted embrace echoing Barbie and Ken's.

*

I came to know her body as well as mine: its toasty-golden odor, the vaccination mark on her long thigh, her flat brown belly, the navel that popped out a little, where mine curved in. She was lanky and lean and stayed that way: puberty merely lengthened her, adding demure breasts and a ladylike curve to the haunch. Meanwhile, I mutated overnight into a pimply, potbellied, pendulous-breasted sow: as if offended by the sight of me, Amanda Jane left for boarding school.

Enough. Some kind of wave surges through me and I sit up and switch on the light, looking around for something to look at myself in (because in the dark, alone, how can you be sure where you are?).

I need a mirror. If I had one, I could take out my make-up (if I had that) and create a face, turn this featureless balloon into something that looks like someone. I could inscribe a self: paint on a porcelain skin, pencil in some eyes, brush contour into these cheeks, blend three colors to make a mouth.

The very shape of the human head is a result of evolutionary changes associated with eating: the jaws and the teeth became smaller, as did the brow ridges of the skull, and an increasingly large brain gave humans a superior ability to process information, much of it originally having to do with the availability of food and the best ways to obtain it.

How long it took to learn, though, — how many hours in front of the mirror, how many magazines with shaded diagrams of where and how to paint according to the shape of your face: round, square, oval, — but what shape was a heart?

Bulbous, with tubes sticking out.

The tubes.

Think about something else.

58

Fat little tubes of eye gloss; fragrant, sticky pots of lip color. Cyanotic pink. Menstrual red.

That's all over now. I discovered how to make it stop. It was mainly the smell I couldn't stand, the sweet, meaty smell of menstruation.

What crime had I committed, to be punished every month?

In other cultures, they wrap you up and suspend you in a hammock, between earth and sky, until the seepage stops.

Two A.M.

2:07 on my digital watch, the biggest, ugliest, clumsiest black plastic one I could find, because it makes my wrist look so delicate by comparison.

2:13 A.M.

Will I ever be able to sleep through the night again?

I awakened to the sound of a key fumbling in the front door downstairs, then a creak as it swung open and a muffled bang, followed by an exclamation of pain. I could tell by the darkness that it was late, very late; my mother was going to be furious. Anxiously, I lay straining to hear their bedroom door open, her voice questioning at first, then rising, sharper and faster. There'd been a lot of that lately: middle-of-the-night mumbling, rumbling, doors slamming.

But I heard nothing, though I lay there with my whole body tensed into an ear. Then a creak on the stair, barely audible: I realized that he was creeping up the stairs on tiptoe, since I heard not the usual singsong squeak but a different timbre — tentative, hushed. I pretended to be asleep as I heard the footsteps coming over the thick bedroom carpet; I could smell the whiskey before I could even make out the shape, a denser dark. He sat heavily on the bed and whispered my name. I did a mediocre imitation of waking up.

"Just came to kiss you good night."

The whiskey smell was stronger now, sickening in its smoky sweetness; an uncharacteristically high-pitched giggle seemed trapped somewhere at the back of his throat.

"How's my girl?" He leaned over and kissed me on the cheek, sloppily, giggling.

"Where've you been, Dad?"

"Working late." And he kissed me again, leaning over me so that his loose, rough suit jacket brushed my face, his bristles sandpapery and harsh, unlike the clean-shaven, soap-smelling cheek I pecked good-bye every morning. "How's my girl?" he repeated, folding back the sheet from my shoulders. I lay rigid, hoping for a voice from downstairs: "Mi-chael?"

"How's my girl?" he repeated, giggling again.

"Dad . . ." I said.

"Just came to kiss you good night," and he leaned unsteadily over, kissing me again where the neck begins.

"Dad . . ." I repeated, a chill coming over me. "Dad, it's cold."

He giggled again, and I felt the gooseflesh creeping down to the back of my thighs.

Just then, the mantel clock downstairs chimed three times. It seemed to cleave the fog around him and, as if retrieved from a trance, he pulled the sheet back over my shoulder, got awkwardly to his feet, and, with a final pat, crept out, knocking his shin on the antique rocking horse.

3:27 A.M.

I can't stay here alone anymore, pacing, throwing myself down on the cold floor for another set of sit-ups, pacing some more, throwing myself on the bed for a second before leaping up to prowl, to peer through the glass (diamond mesh, like chicken wire: am I a chicken, then, to be cooped up?). Some effervescent emptiness is fizzing inside me, beginning just under the sternum, swirling through the lungs, mounting dizzily to the brain, its tiny bubbles popping and scrambling, its silent hiss drowning out all thought. If there were any food in this cell, I would be driven to cram it in, to quell this fizzy panic (let the corrosion remain, let the connectors stay encrusted).

3:54 A.M.

I ring the bell next to my bed, expecting an immediate, anxious response. Instead, after four long minutes (I could have been dying all this time, a tiny hand spitefully squeezing my heart), the night nurse, a large, leisurely-looking black woman, puts her head in the door.

"Ye-ah?"

"I could have been dying," I say.

"What's the problem, miss?"

"It's lucky for you that I wasn't."

"What can I do for you?"

"I want some water."

She looks at the covered carafe next to my bed. "You got water, gal."

"It's dead," I say. "Don't you see those bubbles?"

"Looks like water to me, ma'am."

"It's dead," I say.

She doesn't react, just purses her lips.

"I don't drink dead water. Bring me a glass of fresh water."

She folds her fat, glossy forearms over her belly and looks at me, eyebrows raised, head tilted to one side. "Yes, *ma'am*," she says. I know she's not going to do anything. Now I wish I'd waited for Squeaky, at six-thirty.

A wan gray light begins to delineate my cage, etching dark

diamonds against the pane. The rain seems to have stopped, but what difference does that make to me?

There was a jeweler's bill that came to the wrong address: home instead of the office. Muffled voices behind the closed bedroom door (her high, whining tone, rising and falling like a dentist's drill; his low, placating rumble), then doors slamming later that night, many nights. But dinner was served punctually on the stroke of seven, soup from a silver tureen.

There was no way of knowing whom to believe, so I decided not to believe her. But I also had another, parallel line of reasoning: she was mistaken, and, even if she wasn't, he was justified — look at her, a mountain of blubber, her body irredeemably ruined by two children, a double purple gash across the blancmange of her belly.

Your husband, I am sure, would like to have you attractive, lean, and pleasant.

Through closed doors, from aborted conversations, from hushed, tearful calls to her friend Miriam, I picked up a few phrases: jeweler's bill, plane ticket. So it was someone airborne, diamond-bedecked: who could blame him? Someone slender, spangled, poised for flight.

Trapped in her private padded cell, my mother could never have bared her body to a strange man. Once I overheard her and Miriam, another large, unhappy housewife, snickering over the éclairs at tea.

"But can you imagine — actually taking off your girdle?"

"And standing there, with all your *rolls*?"

A researcher asked women what three words they like most to hear. Instead of the expected answer — "I love you" — the consensus was "You've lost weight."

*

62

Something was happening to me. Standing in front of the full-length mirror in my parents' bedroom every morning, I drew my nightgown tightly across my chest, grasping it behind so that it clung to the bumps in front. Yes, they were growing bigger, my hips, my waist, my breasts. Past the bee sting stage now, they were bandaged by a stretchy white training bra: training them to be well behaved in public, to make their point but to know their place.

My mother said I was "developing."

Into what? If only I had recognized the danger then, if only I had nipped this burgeoning in the bud. But somehow I had confidence that this body, transforming itself, would end up looking less like me and more like them, other bodies. If it didn't, there were measures, I knew, that I could take. One could always take measures, to measure up.

I studied the magazines.

When it comes to be being beautiful, half the fun is learning how.

Keep yourself in check.
Be Some Body.

Get frequent trims.

Stand tall, glance down. If you see your navel, you need tummy firming.

You can look flat-chested without a brassiere and still have a sizable bust that doesn't project.

If you're insecure about applying false eyelashes, practice.

I followed all the instructions, took all the measures, every one — painting, plucking, powdering, steaming, soaking, shaving, spraying, scenting, smoothing, straightening, oiling, creaming, curling, coloring, conditioning, toning, tanning, bleaching, blackening, moisturizing, abrading, exfoliating — but still failed to transform myself. Even the make-up I so laboriously applied ended up askew, like the lapsed color in the Sunday funnies.

Remeasure, reweigh. Try harder.

The tip-tops of your thighs: are they wide and fleshy (a typical female tendency)? They were. My mother told me that was the way I was "built." I wanted to be rebuilt. I wanted to wear miniskirts over long golden legs.

Do thigh-reducing exercises diligently to solidify them — there's still time for tightening up.

Eat sleek.

A sleek one-piecer is the answer to some of the common flaws and figure problems that can beset a girl: superfluous hair, a scar in the wrong place, blemishes, a midriff that's too maxi, a navel you're not proud of. Mine was a tight, involuted knot; Amanda Jane's popped softly out, like the tip of a tongue.

Experiment — strive for perfection.

Ask yourself: am I mature enough for the discomforts of surgery? For a receding chin. For a jutting jaw. For breasts, big and little. I put socks in my brassiere, then took them out. They only made things worse.

Will a new nose make you happier?

Or is it time to banish that untimely bulge?

Keep the refrigerator well stocked with bunny food — for that frantic hunger that sets in after school. Fill a scooped-out tomato with cottage cheese. You lose!

Notice that clear-cut lines divide angel cake into slim slices for girls, big slices for boys. And make drinks diet-sly by sipping, sipping. It's ladylike, too!

Those three o'clock hunger pangs hitting you hard? Worried about stuffing yourself at supper? It's the "fat time of day," when you're starving, and your appetite is telling you to overeat. You're as hungry as a bear.

Resist temptation!

You may be brighter than you think. I had won a scholarship to the Deerborne Academy, an elite school for young ladies of academic bent — for bent young ladies, for bending them. They all had thick, well-cut hair, slim ankles, smoked salmon sandwiches for lunch, which they picked apart and didn't eat.

Be Some Body.

Can you enjoy college in the fall — or start work — if you're overweight? You can, but it's hard, say authorities. They point out that the slender, supple girls are the ones most likely to achieve more in classrooms and offices.

Don't forget Mother's Day!
- *Do the dishes.*
- *Polish silver.*
- *(Watch nails.)*
- *Smile a lot!*

Everything she did exasperated me, especially the way she occupied space, her squat frame hauling its huge belly and behind around like a life sentence. And I, increasingly sullen and self-absorbed, unable to pass any reflective surface without a shameless, anxious consultation, jarred equally on her. In my hormonal fug, I could spend hours stretched out on the chaise on the patio, one arm across my dreaming face. Recognizing my languor, unable to endure it, she would call me inside, sharply, to unpack the groceries, to pick my clothes off the floor, to go down to the store: "Immediately!"

Sometimes, I succeeded in provoking her into a frenzy. Once she walloped me in the face, but the bruise disappointed me, so I touched it up with purple eye shadow before school the next day. Nobody noticed. Then she hit me smack on the back of the thigh with a tennis shoe; surprised, I stumbled, and she grabbed my arm, pinching the skin, dragging me, half kneeling, screaming and gasping across the floor, the rug burning my skin, screaming and gasping, burning, lunging.

I hoped that the neighbors would call the police.

Try harder.

The secret word is body.

Is it normal for teens to think about death and suicide?

66

The secret word is body.

For that frantic hunger that sets in.

The secret word is body.

There'll be long, lean days ahead.

6

AT PRECISELY SIX-THIRTY, she bounds in, as usual, swishes the curtains back (how the metallic screech scores my ears, how the light pokes my dry eyes, lidless after the long night's lonely straining). I'm still pacing and I make no attempt to hide it: I couldn't stop even if I wanted to, so it's lucky I don't. From the corner of the cell around the foot of both beds to the other corner is twenty paces, I've discovered. Figuring each stride as a foot (conservatively), that means I have to make the same circuit, there and back again, one hundred and thirty-two times to complete a mile. I'm on my third mile and I'm not going to stop until I finish it.

"Morning, Josie," she says, standing by the window, where I have to make a detour around her, pacing and counting.

"Morning," I mutter, without stopping.

She stands there while I complete three more circuits, but she is making me self-conscious. I can't stop, though, I won't, I have to finish three miles, otherwise . . . Otherwise what? Otherwise something terrible will happen, my muscles will turn to mush, I won't know what to do next, I'll spiral through space, yielding voluptuously to dissolution.

"Josie, could you just slow down a moment, please? I need to talk to you."

"When I'm done," I mutter — she's making me lose count.

"No, now, please, Josie, if you don't mind."

I do mind, you freckled cow. "OK, OK, just one more."

I do two more and then throw myself sulkily on the bed, one arm flung over my face so I don't have to look at her. Also, the room is spinning.

"Josie, the doctor is coming to talk to you about insertion."

Insertion? So it's not even a secret; even the nurse knows he can stick it to me whenever he wants. "Insertion?"

"For the tube feeding, Josie — I explained already."

"I don't want any fucking tube in me," I say. "You can't make me do this. I won't." Someone always trying to force something into you, make you swallow something, pump you full of it.

No response, just a slight petrification of the professional smiley face.

Then I notice something is missing. "Where's my goddamn breakfast, anyway? You want me to eat, I'll eat."

She looks a little confused, begins to make an explanatory gesture (offering the absent tray on flat palms), aborts it, and says, "We need to talk to the doctor, Josie. Let me see if I can get him in here."

"Just bring me my breakfast. All you ever do is try to make me eat, and then when I ask for food, you won't bring it."

Now she's definitely annoyed. Her fair, freckled skin is helplessly legible: a wash of blood travels over it, like watercolor. "Josephine, I must ask you please not to speak to me like that. I'm not your servant." And then, unable to contain herself: "And would you please look at me when I talk to you? It really gets on my nerves."

Coldly, victoriously, I remain precisely as I am. She really should have more control.

Later, we end up in a conference room, myself and four strangers: Dr. Frog, the nurse (still miffed), a "social worker," and the alleged dietician, a sporty-looking woman in her early thirties, I would guess, with a runner's utilitarian body and sun-dried skin. These aliens are gathered in this glassed-in, stale-smelling room (there are ashtrays on the wood-grain Formica: in a hospital?) to discuss what will and will not go into my body.

My body is there, too, chilled by the hoarse air-conditioning, unable to dispose its bones comfortably on the metal-frame chair; the seat's padding, like mine, is meager and connects nowhere with my spine. My body is there, but I am not; this is something that you learn, early on.

Across the table, in the dark glass, I catch sight of a face, haggard in the harsh fluorescence, its dull, wispy hair like that of a cheap doll (rows of little holes in the plastic skull where it comes out in chunks). With shadowy, sunken cheeks and deep grooves around the mouth, it's the face of an old woman. After a while, I realize it's me. Automatically, I adjust the tilt of my head, so the light catches the chin and cheekbones differently; now it's a face of exquisite delicacy, ethereal, haunting.

My body is here, crucified on this cold metal chair — even the arms, all edges, cut into my bones — but I am not.

Washing my face over the bathroom sink, with the white noise of the water drowning out all thought, if I were to feel a sudden presence behind me — just a change in the pressure, the density of the air — it would be safer to believe I was imagining it. Because how can you really tell if someone is there or not?

*

"Are you listening, Josephine?" someone is asking. "This is your health we're talking about here, you know."

Slowly, reluctantly, I lift my head, blink rapidly to refocus. There's no one there, just Dr. Frog, animated across the table, an annoying insistence in his hunched shoulders. I notice that he is (unconsciously, as he would say) stabbing at an empty Styrofoam cup with a pencil. When the pencil point goes through the cup, it makes a disproportionately loud ripping sound. I snort, an involuntary echo. He's not amused; he looks embarrassed, guilty, and squishes the cup in his hand, looking for somewhere to dispose of it. But the more hunted the expression in his hooded little eyes, the tighter the line of his lips, the more I feel compelled to snort, to chortle into my hand. The chortling begins to take on a life of its own, arriving in escalating spasms.

"That's enough, Josie," the nurse says sharply, glancing at the doctor to see if she's exceeded her authority.

"Yes, that's quite enough," he says. "Calm down now."

Hilarity drains out of me, as if a plug had been pulled, and I slump back in my chair, spent. My head is lolling; I really don't have the strength to hold it up. My bones are weary, deeply weary, weary to the core.

The social worker (what is she really, I wonder?) is taking notes on a yellow pad. I can just imagine: "Patient laughs inappropriately when doctor impales a cup. Patient picks her cuticles compulsively, refusing to meet anyone's eye. Patient seems inexplicably resentful of flabby, decaying strangers gathered to prescribe her diet." The dietician has forgotten to change the tensely bright expression on her face for quite some time and seems to think that inclining her head, birdlike, makes her look alert, engaged.

"Josephine, please pay attention for a moment," the doctor says.

"I am."

"I want to show you something, a picture."

He takes what looks like a black-and-white photograph out of a folder and passes it across the table to me. What is it going to be this time, I wonder: a mouth and a dick, a woman and a Great Dane?

It's entitled "Fig. 8" and shows a naked woman (I knew it), front and side views. She's very thin: in fact, I feel a stab of envy. I didn't know it was possible to be that thin and still live.

This woman is a skeleton, not I. Her arms, splayed at her sides, seem abnormally long, with the elbow joints at least twice as wide as the upper arms. Her knees, likewise, are much wider than her thighs, which, to my admiration, she has reduced to pure bone (but even they must flare, to fit the unseemly pelvic socket). The ribs score the skin so deeply they seem ready to burst through, a violent eruption beneath two minuscule, shrunken dugs (interesting that they never disappear altogether). Every cord in her neck is visible, even the corrugated tube of her trachea. A discreet black slash blanks out her eyes, reducing her face to the caved-in cheeks and lipsticked scar of a crone.

From the side, she is even more frightening, a hunched gargoyle on a stick. Her knee is about the same size as what's left of her buttock; as in an X ray, her long, straight tibia is visible all the way into the socket. Her chest is hopelessly collapsed.

Yes, I did know it was possible to be this thin and still live. I have seen photographs of them, too, the survivors. No black band slashed out their hopeless, uncomprehending, already other-worldly eyes.

"What do you think the woman in the picture looks like, Josie?" Dr. Frog is asking, invading my inner vision.

"A little on the thin side."

"Do you think you are as thin as she is?" he asks.

"Of course not," I respond. And it's true: I know I don't look that devastated. If I did, I couldn't go out in public. Everyone would know immediately what the problem was.

Their eyes meet across the table, Dr. Frog's and the nurse's, and an immense weariness re-enters me. I'm sure I just failed some crucial diagnostic test, but I don't care; I just want them to leave me alone, let me be.

Leaning over the bathroom sink, it begins again. As the rush of water rises in intensity, so too does the panic — the certainty that, as I bend over, blinded by the water, deafened by it, somebody is coming up behind me. No, not coming up behind me; that's not quite it. Someone is already there, close behind me, less than a foot away. I know, in a rational part of my brain, that no one can be there, because no one was in the bathroom a second ago when I looked, and the door is closed, but this knowledge means nothing in the face of the panic, the terror, the other kind of knowledge. Blood speeding and pounding, eyes stinging with soap, I reach blindly for a towel and swivel around to discover, as I already knew, that no one is there.

Yes, doctor, every time.

New regimen. New regime. Last chance. (Wasn't there a best seller a while back called *The Last Chance Diet?*)

The dietician here, Miss Sparrow (she bobs her inclined head, grimacing reflexively at the mention of her name), will draw up a program of regular, balanced meals for you; we're not going to let you choose your own menus, Josephine, but you may name a maximum of three foods you dislike for exclusion. (Meat, fish, eggs, and the opaque white or bluish white liquid secreted by the mammary glands of female mammals for the nourishment of their young.)

The nurse will sit with you during meals, encouraging you to eat. ("Eat, you bitch, or I'll eat you.")

Three-day trial. If you don't cooperate, we'll be compelled to begin hyperalimentation. It's up to you, Josephine.

When has it ever been up to me?

Last week, for instance (I think it was last week, though months seem to have passed), there they were when I got home, large as life. Perched on the burnt orange Salvation Army couch, they were sipping tea from some misshapen pottery mugs made by a friend of Jane's; evidently they'd debriefed her and were filling the time with awkward small talk. My shock at seeing them — I thought them three thousand miles away in the snowy east — was nothing compared to their shock at seeing me. My mother leapt off the sofa as if stung by a bee; my father slumped backwards, as if poleaxed.

"What are you doing here?" I said. "I mean, hi."

Unable to speak, my mother burst into tears, which Jane — the Judas — took as her cue to slink out. I remained unmoved by the door, my bicycle helmet under one arm, feeling something in me begin its familiar decampment to a cool, untouchable place just under the sternum. My only thought was: I hope they don't expect me to skip ballet class this evening just because they're in town.

"Oh God, Michael, look at her," my mother sobbed, smearing mascara on the pouches under her eyes. My father, as usual, said nothing, but permitted himself his unconscious gesture of worry, a catching of his lower lip between his teeth, which gave him the look of a pained bunny rabbit.

"Jo, you're not looking at all well," he suggested.

According to script.

"I'm looking perfectly fine, for God's sake. So anyway, what are you guys doing here? Do you have a business trip, Dad? I wish you'd given me a bit of warning because things are pretty hectic at the moment. Even tonight, you know — I have plans."

Their eyes met. Who was going to do the dirty work? She, of course, once she'd retrieved a powdery tissue from her capacious handbag, stuffed with salt and pepper packets scavenged from the airline (an ineradicable habit). After a few juicy blasts, she smudged her mascara once again, threw the balled-up tissue back into her bag, breathed deeply, and said, "Josie, sit down, we have to talk to you about something."

I stayed where I was, merely setting the bicycle helmet down so I could fold my arms, feeling myself hard and capable, lean and spare under two oversized sweatshirts.

"Josie," she began, tears welling up again, "you look like something from Belsen."

"That's what you always say, Ma." Just because I'm not fat like you.

"No, this is by far the worst we've seen you, isn't it, Michael?" He nodded, opening his palms in a placating gesture. "You're just skin and bones, I don't know how you can even be walking around." More tears.

Surreptitiously, I glanced at my watch: ten past five. I had to leave in twenty minutes and hadn't even changed yet, let alone stretched. I'd missed the first ten minutes of the news. And I needed my can of Tab if I was going to make it through class. It was time to get going.

"So did you fly all the way out here just to start this again? I'm really not into this, Mom. And I have to change for ballet. Maybe you guys can go out for dinner while I'm in class, and then we can go to a movie or something."

She couldn't speak, so he took over. "Josie, Jane called us."

"*Jane?*" At this moment, I did feel a twinge of annoyance, a slight leap of disbelief. "*Jane?* What the hell for?"

"She thinks you're killing yourself, Josie. She feels so helpless — she didn't know what to do, so she called us."

Where did she get their number? The bitch must have gone through my drawers, handled my things, thumbed through my address book.

A deep, familiar fatigue soaked into me, and all I wanted was to go into my room, close the door, turn on the radio, and begin stretching — slowly, deliberately, holding on to my bones, feeling each tendon resist, then relax. As if from a great distance, sending my words with effort through space, I told them: "All I really want is for everyone to leave me alone. I can't believe you flew all the way out here because of some flaky roommate. And I don't have time for this now because I have to go to class." And if I injure myself by not warming up properly, it will be your fault, I added, mentally.

"But *look* at you, Josie," my mother blurted, "have you *looked* at yourself?"

Have I looked at myself? What else do I spend most of my time doing, sometimes, trancelike, for an hour at a time? I see myself very clearly: somewhere between fat and thin, but not yet perfect.

I shrugged. Recognizing this conversation as the same one we'd been having, off and on, for eight years, my father intervened, a reflex developed through a lifetime of placating miserable women. "OK, OK, Gin, let her be. Jo, how about if we let you run off to ballet now, and your mum and I check into the hotel and have a bite to eat" — only then did I notice their suitcase next to the couch — "and then how about if we meet for breakfast tomorrow, when we've all had a good night's sleep, and decide what needs to be done?"

"I don't eat breakfast."

Even he allowed himself a soft, exasperated explosion of air. "OK, then, we'll meet for coffee. What time is your first class?"

"Not until ten. But I have to work out first."

The next morning, when we met at nine — at the Elysée, typical transparent ploy, to meet in a pastry shop, hoping I'll be tempted by the warm, fragrant air, by the mounds of airy dough, snow-dusted, dark-hearted (but I don't even notice, note) — everyone seemed calm, myself to the point of apathy. Mother's face was freshly painted on, her hair firmly glued; in a blue jersey suit with sensible pumps (like the Queen of England), she looked determined not to cry. Dad, redolent of shaving cream, with comb marks still in his hair, was ruining the effect with a haze of cigarette smoke. He didn't appear to have had much sleep, and neither had I, studying, as usual, until three. (Studying and pacing, reading a few lines and then jumping up to prowl the silent flat, to consult the dark glass.)

I sipped my iced tea. They troweled butter and jam on to their croissants (300 calories apiece).

There's this hospital, Josie — well, not really a hospital. More like a private rest home. Specialists. Rest up. Take care of you. Just a month. Gladly pay. Won't make you do anything you don't want to do. Break from the routine. What do you say, eh, love?

I say, fuck off and leave me alone.

I say, what the hell difference would it make? I can starve anywhere.

I say, it's becoming too much work to decide what to do next. Just to move my hand through thick, resilient air to this glass of iced tea — the lemon slice has begun to molt, the rim is sweating, how can I put it in my mouth? — requires all the energy I have. To move my hand back again and decide where to put it, somewhere it will look natural — so bony and blotchy, so cracked and fissured in the cruel morning light — takes all my attention. I will rest it here, beside the blue napkin, parallel, and line up the knife so they're all parallel, equidistant: hand, napkin, knife. Knife, napkin, hand.

Why is everyone looking at me like that?

Are they still waiting for me to say something?

She's staring at me from the foot of the bed. I refuse to say anything, won't even meet her eyes. Why should I give her the satisfaction of fathoming my fear?

This is the New Regime. She stays with me through the whole meal and I may not even close the bed curtains around me. I must eat at least some of everything selected for my dining pleasure. There is a huge glass of orange juice (150 calories), two pieces of wheat toast with four pats of butter (200 calories, plus 185 for the toast), a slice of cantaloupe (about 40 calories: it's the only legal food on the tray), and an enormous bowl of oatmeal, clumped and congealed like mucus (at least 200 calories, without milk or . . . merely to think the word *sugar* makes me feel unclean). If I ate all that, it would amount to over 800 calories, more than I've eaten in an entire day for years.

Perhaps the tubes would be better, because then I would have no choice.

She's watching me.

I can't eat with someone else watching me.

"I can't eat with someone else watching me."

"I'm not *watching* you — I'm just here. And one of the things you have to relearn, Josie, is how to eat in public."

I won't. I can't. Eating is private; only the body is public.

My hands — purple, pitiful, the way I like them — are shaking as I pick up the spoon. The psychology student ought to be here now, the one who wired me to electrodes to measure my "anxiety level" when confronted with food. She (earnest, sallow, smelling of stale coffee and unwashed hair) placed electrodes on my forehead, my chest, my leg, my thumb, and my stomach, where I'm softest, most vulnerable. These black probes, jellied against resistance, are supposed to measure heart rate, skin conductivity, blood flow, sweatiness, and such: this is, of course, how a lie detector works. Also sexual intercourse. Naturally I was tense: I was afraid to breathe in case one of the attachments came loose. Then she gave me a questionnaire about how I felt at that moment. Rate your feelings of tension, satisfaction, optimism, dread, hunger (ennui, apathy, absence, despair, numbness, vacancy, void). Write down your most prominent thought. My most prominent thought: why am I being asked to write down my most prominent thought?

Look at these landscape paintings and rate your response on a scale of 1 to 9. Look at these cartoons and rate your response. Look at this Snickers bar and rate your . . . ha! fooled you. Your heart leapt (see the graph). Now eat it. Yes, right now. See, she can't. She's too anxious.

My hands are shaking and I cannot pick up the spoon. The nurse is pretending to be absorbed in a *People* magazine (how Liz lost it, how Oprah did), but I know she's really watching me. I want to start on the cantaloupe, to show good faith, but I can't. I picture my stomach, a tiny, fisted pouch: these substances, these chunks of alien matter, don't belong in there. They belong out in the world, where they are — other.

"I can't," I say.

"Yes you can, Josie — just take one bite of the oatmeal."

It's mucus, it's slime, it's snot. "It's cold by now."

"No it's not, just give it a try."

I dip the spoon into the slime — one spoonful, maybe 15 calories. How reluctantly the glaucous mouthful pulls away, adhering to the rest in glutinous strands. I open my mouth, but something fails, some neuron doesn't fire, and I remain frozen, agape.

She's starting to get annoyed, I can tell. She puts the magazine down decisively and says, "Josie, cut out the nonsense now and just eat."

"I can't," I say, which is the truth. And then before I realize it, I have said the next sentence: "I want you to feed me."

Among the Bemba, mothers squeeze the red juice from certain fruits onto their breasts; the juice looks like blood and frightens the child. Tonga mothers in southern Africa wean a child by covering their breasts with pepper; in Iran, children are told that a witch has eaten the mother's breasts, which by way of proof are shown smeared with a black substance.

"Don't be silly, Josie. You're not a baby."

"Please."

"Josie, I can't."

She's dragging me across the carpet; with my teeth and nails I flail at her ankles, missing and screaming, screaming and screaming. Only one desire consumes me: to rend her flesh. She's panting with exertion, perhaps she'll have a heart attack, her face is flushed and oily, her teeth clenched; with her free hand she's whacking in the direction of my face: "Think you're . . . so . . . smart, don't you . . . Think you're . . . better . . . than everybody . . . else . . . Think you . . . can do whatever . . . you . . . like . . ." I manage to get back on to my feet, my knees skinned and bleeding, yelling and sobbing breathlessly. "Let me GO you cow let me GO you fat bitch I'll kill you let me GO." There's a soundless roar all through my body, a pounding, vertiginous abandon, and I launch myself toward her, embracing her cushiony flesh, obscene in its damp plenitude. Wherever I can reach, I dig my fingers in — the pads of the upper arms, the rolls of the back, even the puffy wrists — and twist and gouge and rend, grunting and sobbing, choking through my spastic jaw. She's flailing but she's too clumsy to connect; she's off-balance, screaming, and I'm going to push her over. With vicious, delirious fear — what will happen next? can I really kill her? — I shove, and she lands beetle-style on her back, the air escaping in a sound somewhere between a whoof and a wail. I'm too far gone now to stop — a violent electrical swarm buzzes through me, from somewhere deep between the ribs — but part of my brain still registers, appalled. I'm going to kick her, hard, wherever I can reach, kick and kick until she shuts up, until she disappears, until she leaves me alone, I'm kicking at her resilient haunches, working up courage to go for her face, it's not much fun, she's screaming and trying to curl up, I'm hoarse and dizzy, my throat hurts, every muscle aches, I'm not sure how much longer this frenzy can sustain itself.

Obesity never made it easy to take care of a household and a bunch of screaming youngsters.

"There. I knew you could do it."

It was sickening: three spoonfuls of cold, gluey porridge. But I did it — slowly, with a pounding heart, with something squeezing at my throat, I did it.

"Now try some of the toast, Josie."

"I can't eat that . . . butter."

"Just a little — look, spread it on and then scrape most of it off if you like, but just try a little. A small amount like this can't possibly hurt." With her strong, freckly hand, she butters the toast and then scrapes efficiently, but I can still see white grease in the blackened pores. Then she holds it out to me, a whole piece, an enormous tilted plane (about 100 calories, counting the — grease; for some reason, even to think the word *butter* seems obscene, lewd and oily on the tongue).

"I have to cut it up first."

"OK, but only halves or quarters."

I cut it into quarters, diagonally, and then pick up one of the resulting almost-equilateral triangles by one point. Can I really eat this much? A quarter of a hundred is only twenty-five, but I've already eaten all that oatmeal, and she's going to expect me to eat the melon and drink the juice, too. I nibble at one point, rodent-style, and then put it down. She's still looking at the *People* magazine and has even slowed her brisk noisy page flipping — she seems to have found something she wants to read: I wonder what — but I can feel that the force field of her attention still includes me. So I nibble some more, mainly for show, but a larger chunk than I had anticipated breaks off in my mouth, which I then find myself compelled to chew. To *masticate*, another obscene word. The chewing seems very loud and crunchy, embarrassingly so, so I stop. She looks up, eyebrows lifted. I put what's left of the toast triangle back on the plate. That's it for today.

"Are we going to have to go through this every meal from now on?" I ask.

She nods matter-of-factly, scrunches her mouth. "Yup."

"Don't you get bored?"

"Nope. It's my job."

"Pretty boring job, if you ask me."

A shrug. "I like it."

"Why?" I'm stalling, but I'm also slightly curious about why anyone would do this — wheel sullen people around, try to stuff food into them, pretend to care whether they live or die.

"It's good to help people get healthy again."

"Even if they aren't sick to begin with?"

She looks puzzled. "What do you mean?"

"Oh, forget it." I'm tired of explaining. In fact, I'm just tired, I realize, terribly tired and increasingly nauseated; all I want to do is flop back on the pillows. I start pushing the tray away, but she puts her hand out gently to stop it.

"Uh-uh, Josie. The deal is you have to eat at least some of everything on the tray."

"Oh, for Christ's sake. I can't. Leave it here, and I'll have some more later."

"Josie, don't be a pain. Just have a little of that melon, a few sips of juice, and then I'll take the tray away."

"Haven't you got anything else to do with yourself?" I say petulantly, playing up my pique, playing for time. I don't want to eat, but I don't want her to go away either.

"As a matter of fact, I do," she says, sharply. "You're not the only patient on this floor, you know."

"Who else? Who else is here?"

"Well, you might meet some of them, in group therapy, once we get you up to a functioning weight and out of here. Group therapy's part of the outpatient care."

"*Group therapy?* You must be out of your mind. There's no way, no way in hell — "

"OK, OK, we don't have to discuss that now. You're still a long way from that. Now have a little melon, Josephine, please."

I don't respond, but a few minutes later, when she's absorbed in *People* again, I scoop myself a teaspoonful, very deliberately gouging the vivid flesh.

7

SHE WANTS ME to eat straight glucose, one hundred grams of it, mixed with egg and milk. I tell her I will vomit, that the very thought of it makes me retch. She says, "No you won't dear, just give it a try." I'm back with the shriveled endocrinologist, whose own hormones seem to have quit on her, leaving her dry, grasshoppery.

"I can't possibly."

"Sure you can. Go ahead and try."

It's white, sticky, revolting-looking stuff. I take a tentative sip and gag: it's sweeter than anything I've ever tasted, putridly, chokingly sweet.

"See, it's not so bad."

This is the kind of talk that makes me sick. Why does everybody have to be so condescending, as if I were a child? Why don't they recognize my strength: how much it's taken to make so little of myself?

But the nurse is there, and I want to demonstrate my new cooperative attitude (otherwise, the tubes), so I try to force more down, fighting my throat's convulsive closing. I manage about half the beakerful before I yield to nausea, a raw, sickly thirst.

Sinking back in the chair, eyes closed, I shake my head, afraid even to begin calculating the number of calories I just swallowed.

Then she has to take blood, struggling again to find a vein, manhandling my fragile, hairy arms. I don't look, I keep my eyes tightly closed. At first the sting comes every fifteen minutes, then every half hour, then every hour. I'm afraid to lose so much blood, I'm dizzy, but she assures me in her patronizing way that the amount of blood drawn is minuscule: "Not enough to make anyone's head swim, I promise you." Then why is mine swimming?

The purpose of this vampire feast is, allegedly, to measure the levels of a hormone that makes one feel full. I can feel full of emptiness, satisfied with nothing: what hormone determines that?

"Absolutely not. She's only thirteen."

"But Michael — "

"It's out of the question, Virginia."

"But Michael — "

"The answer is no."

"*Michael!* Will you listen a moment? All the other girls are going to be there. Carol's parents will be there. There'll be supervision, it won't be just — "

"Boys. She's too young to go to a party with boys."

"No she's not, Michael. All the other girls are going."

"Well, she's not all the other girls. There'll be plenty of time for boys later."

But later that night, behind the bedroom door, my mother won on my behalf. She wanted me to be "normal." She wanted to buy me a new dress.

I wore something short and frightful, with bright yellow shoes. In this floral ensemble (daisies everywhere, sprouting even at the ears), my legs were short and stubby, leading nowhere. My hair was tortured into a ponytail; thick monochrome make-up threw pores and pimples into pasty relief; chalky blue-pink coated my lips like an unhealthy tongue. My eyes were ringed and spoked with black, a doll's painted sockets with fearful blank orbs.

It had taken me three hours to achieve this effect.

Carol's basement had been transformed — ruby light bulbs, piles of cushions in corners, and posters that glowed black-green in the dark — but as soon as I walked in, I knew I had not. Neither had the boys, who leaned against the walls in small clusters, affecting nonchalance, though (if I'd known how to read it) hormonal havoc was written all over their lurid skins. The girls, eyes roving, commented on each other's outfits, stuffing in potato chips and fruit punch when conversation failed.

As soon as the music started, these two species would pair off and spring into self-conscious, spasmodic motion, avoiding each other's eyes and disbanding again when the needle reached the blank grooves at the end of the song. Few words were exchanged, until the grappling began.

Weary of standing there — an eyesore with sore feet — I withdrew to the den, where I scanned *The New Yorker* and hoped some soul mate would find me.

Within the normal range?

Calcium and potassium levels: within the normal range.

Other vital minerals: ditto (surprisingly enough — though this proves my point about the body: how little it really needs).

Iron: within the normal range (not bleeding it away, dark and wasted, every month).

Liver: normal.

Heart: normal?

Everything normal? How can that be? Surely my survival is miraculous? Surely extremity can be read in the blood?

But then, at last, chloride level: dangerously low.

Fasting glucose level: low. This means, she tells me, that I'm producing too much insulin. "So that's why you feel hungry even after you've just eaten."

"But I don't," I tell her.

She looks at me.

"I don't," I insist.

She shrugs.

I never feel hungry, as I've already told her, nor do I ever feel tired, thirsty, or cold. Above all, I never cry — though I used to. It took me a short, stormy detour, between numb childhood and now, to become untouchable again. Now I know nothing can harm me, that I can withstand any kind of want.

Most women live their lives in a state of starvation. Why should I be any different?

I'd had my suitcase packed for three days, smoothing and refolding its contents (colorful shorts and halter tops; a new white bathing suit, consisting mostly of holes), but when the car crunched into the driveway, shyness overwhelmed me. I heard the doorbell, followed by a falsely animated adult exchange, and then my mother's voice: "Josie! Josephine! Where is that child? I swear, she's been ready all morning, driving me crazy, and then the moment you arrive, she disappears. *Josie!*"

Yelling, "OK, OK, I'm coming!" I clattered down the stairs, bumping my case behind me. There she was: a taller, somehow stretched-out stranger. Her hair was longer, her face thinner. We made as if to hug each other, then stopped, shy.

It was her first summer back from boarding school. Picking

up, perhaps, the radar of my longing, she had invited me to spend a month at their beach house.

In the car, under her father's jovial chatter, we stole sidelong glances at each other. She wore no make-up, except for a touch of rose on the lips — but then she didn't need to, with her flawless golden skin. She wore a cotton skirt and soft-washed sky blue blouse that made my outfit, fresh from this month's *Seventeen*, seem garish all of a sudden. She rolled the car windows all the way down and leaned out into the restless, sparkling air; I held my hair down with my hands.

At the beach, we shared a bedroom, a bungalow, really, away from the main house. While I was unpacking my snazzy vacation wardrobe — even more incongruous in this summer house atmosphere of faded bed linens, mismatched chairs, and dresser drawers that stuck, swollen with salty damp — she disappeared into the house with her mother, who'd been down for a couple of days, "opening up."

It had been a long drive, and I was hungry, headachy.

I sat down on one of the beds (it sank alarmingly), thumbing through an old *Reader's Digest* from the bleached-out pile beside it. I didn't know whether she was going to come back out to get me, or whether I would have to wander over to the house and look for her. Everything suddenly seemed a problem in etiquette. It never had before, when, flushed and giggling from some private game, we would stampede through the house, or yell for each other across cool, darkened halls.

Unsure what to do, I consulted the mirror, mottled and yellowish, eating away at my image from the edges. I took out my tweezers and plucked a few hairs, though I'd already given my brows a good going-over before leaving home. I squeezed at an incipient pimple, bringing tears to my eyes. I combed my hair again, parting it dead center, taking three tries to get it perfect. I applied another coat of pink lip color. She still didn't come, so I put on my sandals and went out to look for her.

I found them in the big, slate-floored kitchen, she and her mother, setting out olives and cheese on toothpicks, to be nibbled with drinks on the porch before dinner. Amanda Jane had two brothers, eighteen and twenty, who occasionally put in an appearance at this hour, sun-flushed, freshly showered, and crisply dressed for their evening's foray into town. Otherwise, we hardly saw them: they inhabited a parallel universe (cars, girlfriends, private jokes), sleeping late and spending their days on a different beach.

I sat down at the kitchen table, where Manda was chopping smoked Gouda into cubes. Without thinking, I scooped up a few in my palm and stuffed them in my mouth before she had a chance to impale them. Then I picked an English digestive biscuit off the cheese plate and crunched that as well. She looked at me oddly.

"Those are for the guys," she said, "for later."

"I know," I said.

Her mother, who'd had her back turned, rinsing radishes at the sink, looked over and said, "It's nice to be slender, dear."

"I know," I said, shrugging, a hot tunnel of dismay opening up in me. Until I had violated it, I hadn't realized that there was a rule: women prepare the food but mustn't eat it. Why hadn't my mother taught me this?

Delight him, but don't undo your diet.

How?

Pack a bilateral lunch.

His	Hers
2 slices baked ham: 290	*1 slice baked ham: 145*
1 cup barbecue beans: 220	*2 dill pickle wedges: 30*
1 dill pickle wedge: 15	*2 teaspoons mustard: 20*
2 tablespoons creamy	*½ cup coleslaw: 55*
mustard sauce: 115	*1 7-inch bread stick: 50*
½ cup coleslaw: 55	*8 ounces diet soda: 1*
1 buttered roll: 125	
3 spiced crab apples: 85	
8 ounces lime soda: 105	

Total calories: 1,010	*Total calories: 301*

Back in the ward, I'm torn between the desire to flop down on the bed, yielding to seasickness (motion, glucose, needles, blood), and the desire to pace endlessly, to use up the excess, to fill the head with one thought only: the next step, the next count. I'm still on an hourly watch, but in fifty-nine minutes I can pace a few miles (I think — my calculations may be wrong, I'm having a hard time keeping track of things, fixing my mind on a single thought). Every time I think of the glucose, a chilly panic speeds over me: *how* many calories could I have swallowed? More than a milk shake maybe (350 calories), more perhaps than a plate of fettuccine Alfredo (650 calories), more even than a — it's hard for me even to think the words — a huge hot fudge sundae, slathered with whipped cream (cold, sweet, dark, hot, melting, orgiastic).

She had become cool and self-contained.

On the beach, she wore a large straw hat, as did her mother, who was sensitive to the sun and sat fully clothed under a beach umbrella, custodian of the lunch cooler. (Pâté, shrimp, grapes.) I wanted to irradiate my pimples, so I lay face up, frying my skin in its own grease, with a white dab, clownish, on my nose.

Amanda Jane wore a pale blue bikini that was much more demure than my one-piece (which required a constant pubic hair watch and a quick dash out of the water, where it became rudely transparent). She read, much of the time, beneath her shady hat; I lay all day in a sun-drugged stupor visited by vague erotic dreams.

She shaved her legs every morning. "It doesn't take long," she said, eyeing my slothful black stubble.

She washed her silky underwear each evening by hand.

She read *Vogue*, not *Seventeen*.

She didn't "date" but was assembling a hope chest. She had already decided to marry her younger brother's best friend.

She never, ever ate dessert.

Dessert was "for the men," as well I knew, but at every meal that summer I held out my plate anyway, blankly. I stuffed in everything, whether I wanted it or not — apple pie with heavy cream, pineapple upside-down, vanilla custard, waffles doused with syrup, chocolate mousse, cookies of every kind (especially the tender shortbread that was served with tea), rum raisin ice cream, which I hated; something foamy and orangey, made with chunks of pure ginger, which I hated, too. The more I hated it, the richer and more sickly it was, the grimmer the pleasure with which I consumed it, silently, dourly, defiantly.

Naturally, I grew plumper and more hideous by the day.

"You've grown," he said. "You're becoming a big girl."

Buttering my bread, I didn't reply. What was there to say?

"It must be the sea air," said my mother.

"And the good food," said my father. "Those people certainly know how to live."

"Well, they can afford it," she said, a little sharply. He looked up briefly from his pork chop, eyebrows raised, his knife poised where it had been paring off the gelatinous rind.

I folded my slice of bread in half and stuffed most of it into my mouth. That should exempt me from further conversation. Hadn't I been told never to talk with my mouth full?

When I got back from my trip, after my mother had waved off Amanda Jane and her parents with effusions of thanks (I was surly, lumpen), she had taken me aside. The last time she had drawn me into her bedroom like this, with an air of abashed secrecy, with the yellow afternoon light filtering through the shades, it had been to inform me of "the facts of life" — which Amanda Jane had been trying to get me to believe for years. Surely there weren't more of them?

"Jo, I have something to tell you."

"Yeah?"

"It's about your father: he's decided to quit his job."

"Oh?"

"Well, you know, since the merger, he really hasn't been happy working for AminCor. They've been messing him around with this . . . you know, management restructuring and stuff."

I nodded.

"So he decided to leave."

"Does he have another job?"

"Not yet, but they've given . . . I mean, he's taking three months' pay . . . in lieu of . . . well, he'll have three months' pay when he leaves, so that should given him plenty of time to look around."

I shrugged. Three months seemed like a long time. I didn't really know what my father did anyway — "management" conjured no image except that of his deserted, gray-carpeted office in a glass tower downtown, which, as a child, I had occasionally visited on weekends, entertaining myself with the magnetic paper clip holder. Since I didn't really know what he did, it didn't make any difference to me if he did something else.

I sensed a presence behind me and swiveled around.

"Oh, I'm sorry," he stammered, "I didn't know you were here."

"Try knocking next time," I said, as I reached, too late, for a towel, shoulders bare, eyes smarting and blinded, the water still hissing and pounding, a violent wet din.

Some time later (a gap: I somehow found myself on the floor again), she comes in with a bowl of tiger lilies, adorned with an orange bow.

"For you," she says. "They just arrived."

I have absolutely no interest in these alarmingly vivid blooms, these alien, freckled creatures crowded menacingly in a glass tube.

"Here's the card, Josie. Don't you want to know who they're from?"

"No. What difference does it make?"

"Come on, Josie, they're lovely."

"I don't want them. They'll just die."

"But — "

"Take them away. They're only going to die."

"Aren't you being a little unreasonable, Josephine?"

"Take them away, they'll die, they'll die, they'll die, they'll die," I find myself repeating, with increasing desperation, my voice rising out of control, breaking and croaking.

She says nothing, but after a few seconds carries them out, her eyebrows raised significantly (except I'm not looking, I'm not reading her). I lie on the bed, rigid, with my eyes shut and my heart hammering, trying to control my breathing, which seems blocked by something at the back of my throat, so I can't get a lungful of air.

When I can inhale again — hours later, it seems — I pick up the little envelope she left, with its elegant gray florist's insignia. I rip it open. A small white card, inscribed in an unfamiliar hand, reads: "To our darling daughter — Hoping you'll soon be well and strong again. With love from Mum and Dad." Ordered over the phone, evidently. "Our darling daughter"? Don't make me puke.

Lunch: Half a salad (with the egg slices and raw onion hidden at the bottom; dressing, since she insists, sprinkled on with a fork). Lettuce, tomato, green pepper, carrot, a few drops of oil (50 calories). One quarter of a roll (25 calories). One sliver of a wedge of Cheddar (25 calories). About half a glass of apple juice, diluted with water (50 calories). There are also two oatmeal raisin cookies (100 calories), but, new regime or no new regime, I can't bring myself to take a bite. *Cookies, cake, chocolate, and other sweets — avoid them like Satan!* She refuses to remove the tray until I do, so I just break them into smaller and smaller pieces, hoping I'll arrive at one tiny enough to put into my mouth without tasting. *To a sugarholic, even a taste can start a binge.*

Looking up from her newspaper, she says: "Don't play with it, Josie, just eat it."

"Cookies are unhealthy," I say. "Sugar, fat, white flour. This nutritionist doesn't seem to know much about nutrition."

No response.

"I said, this nutritionist doesn't know shit about nutrition."

She ignores me. I look down at the tray, suppressing a wild

urge to hurl it across the room. The longer it stays here, the more powerfully it works on me, compelling me to yield and cram myself full.

To make her take it away, I pick up a cookie crumb (less than one calorie, surely?) and place it on the middle of my tongue, away from the sugar receptors. Then, terrified, I start adding up the calories I've consumed.

Grand total: at least 200. Total time: 53 minutes. That's it: I'm not eating again today.

I feel bloated, sickened, miserable, my belly bulging tightly.

Suddenly, in a panic, I ask her, "Tell me the truth: am I fatter than the normal person?"

8

"STEP RIGHT UP," she says. "Uh-uh," she says, "facing *me*."

I turn around on the platform, more like a drunk than a dancer, and confront my audience (of one). Something is fizzing through me: stage fright. I try to step down, but she blocks my exit, stranding me there, visible, alone.

Something is going on behind my back.

Dr. Frog has decreed that I am to be weighed facing away from the scale; they'll tell me, he says, when I have reached the middle of the "target weight range."

"What's that?" I bleat.

But they won't say. "Trust us," they say.

So I stand here paralyzed, blind to the news behind me, my bare feet cadaveric on the metal slab. I'm shivering; I hug myself and dig my fingers between the ribs, reassured by how bare they feel, as if there were nothing but bone beneath this robe.

Then I hear the nurse slide the marker along the scale. Fear ascends hydraulically in my throat and, without planning to, I spin around. Too late: anticipating me, she's already pushing it back toward zero. Then she makes an annotation on a chart, shielding the file with her writing arm (she's left-handed, a crab writer, I notice for the first time).

"Tell me," I say.

"Josie," she says, "you just have to trust us."

"But I don't," I say. "Why should I? You're a total stranger, like everyone else. Tell me," I whine. *"Tell me."*

But she won't. I start to whimper. What right do they have to withhold this vital information: how much space I take up in the world?

I used to know: from weighing myself twenty times a day, from measuring myself in the morning and at night, from the mirrors at home, in the ballet studio, at the gym. At the gym, we all — men and women alike — moved mesmerized among our multiple mirrored selves. We stared at our reflected images with equal longing and despair. The only difference was that, on one side of the room, where the free weights were, the men were striving to make themselves bigger; on the other — where the racks and iron maidens were, the bicycles and stairs leading nowhere — the women struggled to become smaller.

They towered above me, the overextended adolescent boys, and when they asked me to dance they stared out over my head, as if scanning the room for a better deal. Was this because I was a "dog," as I had overheard them call another (plumper) girl? Or would I ever be like my friend Carol, sexy and thin, in a glossy, athletic way, with limbs as hard and well turned as Barbie's? I tried to read their gaze, to tell me where I stood.

At first they seemed interchangeably tall, sweaty, blotchy, loud. But then one of them began to detach himself from the others in my mind, take up residence there. He was more compact, less knobbly, than the rest of them, his clothes dark or faded or baggy in interesting ways. His expression was one of chronic ennui, and he never asked anyone to dance, alternating between bored lounging and cryptic, snorting conversations with some of the rougher guys.

I began to find him intriguing.

He had oily dark hair and ice blue eyes, penetratingly cold. At odd times (walking around, sitting at my desk at school, just before sleep), those eyes would visit me, causing a strange pang somewhere in the solar plexus, similar to the sensation of stepping on pebbly ground with tender bare feet.

On the way to the bathroom, walking haltingly along with the nurse, who is humming something that sounds like "Qué Sera, Sera" (who does she think she is, Doris Day?), we pass an open door, which I recognize as the same one that was open a few days? weeks? ago. The beautiful honey-haired girl is there, exquisitely made-up as before, with the TV blaring and her attention flickering between it and a magazine. She's alone: the skeletal Asian girl, whom I'm interested in seeing again, is gone.

We pass the door, and then the nurse does a quick double take, stops, and touches my arm (I cringe instinctively, imagining the flab she must feel). "Hang on a sec, Josie." She turns to the door and says, "Cathy, there's someone I'd like you to meet."

Cat eyes look up.

"Cathy, this is Josie. Josie, Cathy."

"Hi," she says, "I'm bulimic. What are you?"

"Oh," I say. "I'm a . . . I'm a grad student in economics."

She looks me frankly up and down, the way women do. I try to imagine what she must see; I still haven't been able to see myself whole, only that same sickly face under the same stark bulb. I haven't washed my hair in a couple of days because the nurse said I was washing it "compulsively," making it fall out even more. My skin is red and scaly from scrubbing (since I've been eating so much, I never feel clean), my arms covered with

98

bruises and pin-pricks, my legs like twigs in hospital-issue scuffs: turquoise terry cloth, ludicrously festive, as if for the beach.

"Shouldn't she be on hyperal?" Cathy asks the nurse, as if I weren't even there.

"That's really none of your business, Cathy," the nurse says briskly but with a phony professional kindness. "That's for us to decide."

"Yeah, well, maybe if Amy had gone on hyperal sooner . . ."

There's a charged silence, which I try to decipher. A thrill rises in me, but I play dumb, look blank.

"That's enough now, Cathy, don't try to second-guess the medical team."

"So how long have you been here?" she asks me.

I begin to answer, then realize I have no idea. "A . . . a while," I improvise, shrugging as if to suggest that time is no big deal to me.

"I've been here for two months already," she says, almost proudly.

"But why?" She looks fine to me. A little too much flesh by my standards, perhaps, but otherwise perfect.

"Oh, they can't let me out. I just eat everything in sight and barf it up. Once I spent two hundred and fifty dollars on food in a single day," she tells me, and I realize she is bragging. How can she? How can she admit to appetite, name that insatiable, ravening urge — not only name it but boast of it?

Never. I could admit to anything but that. Unthinkable: to say, in public, the words "I eat."

I say nothing because my throat is too tight. I look at the nurse. She looks at me, seems to sense my distress, takes my arm (very gently this time), and says, "Well, Cathy, we should be on our way. Maybe you'll see more of Josie in the dayroom, when she's a little further along."

"Bye."

"Bye."

He was leaving the party: the rest of the evening immediately drained away, holding no further interest for me (except, perhaps, the bowl of potato chips). But as they straggled out — about five or six of them, loud, dark, leather-clad — one of the lesser members of the group, a blubbery hanger-on whose name I didn't know, turned back to me and said, "Hey you? Come with us." One of the other guys made a face, but Sweaty Fatso said something to him sotto voce that made him nod, guffawing. A rictus seized me, leporine in their collective gaze.

"Where're you going?"

A snort. "Are you coming or aren't you?"

I stood up, obedient, looking around to see if any of my friends had noticed. They hadn't, so I followed the disappearing group into the suburban dark.

Their motorcycles waited in a haphazard row by the hedge — on the hedge, actually, crushing it (the gardener would have to deal with it the next day: I had a mental flash of him in a vindictive rage, hacking it into a topiary horror show). I had never been on a motorcycle before and hoped there was no technique other than hanging on like hell.

The guys were paying me no attention, engaged with zipping up their jackets, kicking down kickstands, and such; I stood to one side, wondering whose bike I was supposed to climb on and what I was going to do with my ankle-length skirt. They all mounted their machines and began revving and roaring, while I stood with my hands behind my back, picking frantically at a hangnail.

"Get on then, idiot," yelled Sweatso, over the roar.

Awkwardly, I complied, hitching up my skirt and clambering over the back of the bike, feeling for a moment the hot breath of exhaust. There seemed nothing to hold on to, so I gripped the seat behind me as tightly as I could. As the bike took off, a whack of backward momentum sent me lurching and I grabbed the leather-upholstered waist in front of me. I thought I heard him laugh.

We ended up at another, smaller party, where Pink Floyd was playing and people were passing joints around. When a joint got to me, I just passed it on to the next person. Nobody said anything. A few couples were dancing, but most of the others were sitting on the floor, stoned. Like them, I leaned against the wall and stared in front of me, wondering what I was supposed to be feeling.

After a while, the fat one on whose bike I had come stood up and went over to the one who had grimaced — a long time ago, in another life. They exchanged a few words, looking in my direction, and then came over to where I sat.

I knew what was about to happen but, in a stupor of disbelief, offered no resistance.

For dinner I eat everything on my plate: corpses, embryos, fluid from mammary glands.

If they had only been served, I would have savored the tongues of larks, the eyes of sheep, eels' spawn, whales' stomach contents, and the windpipes of pigs. Rodent fetuses, too, or the favorite dish of Emperor Vitellius, who liked to dine on peacock brain with flamingo tongue, pike's liver, and — how did they ever find them? — the sex glands of long-suffering lamprey.

For dessert, I treat myself to ground glass, delicate as spun sugar or shaved ice, taking a dainty mouthful off a pointed spoon. As I swallow, the ecstatic friction begins: blood wells warm in the throat, spreading, savory, to the tongue. I smile and a hot gush escapes, meat red.

"That's my girl," he says, watching. "Now one more time."

A common fantasy among young women, so I'm told (the motorcycle gang — how banal). Mine are all pretty classic; Herr Doktor Professor Frog, I mean Freud, would recognize the lot. Dr. Eighty-Bucks-an-Hour was armed with a list (fantasies: domestic, suburban, exotic) when, a year or so later, he labored — at mother's behest — to convince me that, of course, I'd imagined it all. (All of it, all.)

So perhaps what really happened was this: we sat around, staring into space, for the rest of the night. At first I was self-conscious, then bored, then desperate to leave. My left buttock began to hurt and then went numb, sending nasty ischemic messages down the leg. My back ached from its contact with the wall. My throat was raw from, I suppose, the smoky air.

Finally I saw Ice Blue Eyes, very stoned, searching all over for his keys. Trying to sound casual, I piped up: "Wanna give me a ride back?"

He looked at me as if he had no idea who I was or what I was doing there. "Back where?"

"To the party we were at. I have to get back there."

"Why?"

"For my ride home."

"Jesus Christ, I'm not a taxi service."

I said nothing but simply followed him out of the door.

As I was trying to climb on the back of his bike, hitching my skirt out of the way, I miscalculated and almost pushed both the bike and myself off balance. Reflexively, he put out his hand to steady me, grabbing me at the waist.

"Watch it, chick!"

With his other hand he righted the bike, and we both climbed on, more successfully this time. Just before he started it up, he looked back over his shoulder and said, "A little chubby there, aren't we?" Or words to that effect (or perhaps that's what I thought he thought when he touched me).

When I finally got home that evening — "You haven't started smoking, have you, Josie? Your clothes smell awfully smoky," my father asked, tentatively — I stood before the full-length mirror for a long time. I tried, in various poses, to see what anyone looking at me might see. I sat down in front of the glass, noting how the waistband bit into my belly. I tried to see what someone taller would see, looking down on me. I even tried to see what I looked like when I wasn't being looked at. But mainly — obsessively, repeatedly — I placed my own hand on my waist, where his had been.

It was true: above the band of my skirt, even when I was standing, there was a palpable, rubbery bulge.

9

"I'M GOING ON A DIET," I announced at dinner the next night —
after dinner, to be precise, when dessert appeared, reminding
me. (Strawberries with whipped cream — it was the season.)

*For most of man's fifty million years on earth, we have lived off the
flesh and fat of other animals. When times were hard, the women would
gather roots and berries.*

"Oh, that's ridiculous," said my mother, briskly spooning
cream over a bowl of berries, dusting them with sugar, and
passing them on to my father. "You're still growing — you need
to eat properly."

"I don't need to be *fat*, though."

"You're not fat, for heaven's sake" — squishing her own
berries with a fork, bloodstaining the cream. "Whatever put that
absurd notion in your head?"

"Look," I said, standing up at the table, lifting my T-shirt, and
grabbing a plump handful of my waist.

"Sit *down*, please, Josephine," my father interjected immediately. "What on earth do you think you're doing? We're not
interested in seeing your navel at the dinner table."

(Maybe not at the dinner table, Dad.)

She went on dishing up, as if she hadn't heard me.

"Mom, I said I don't want any."

"Josephine, this is nonsense. Strawberries aren't fattening, anyway: you can leave off the cream, if you want to. Though" — licking her spoon like a cat — "it's the best part."

You, Mother, are not exactly the best judge of who's fat and who's not.

Stubbornly she passed me the bowl, heaped with fat, dark, and, if you looked closely, slightly rotting life-forms: scabrous, papillar.

"I'm not eating these. May I be excused?"

"Certainly not. You'll stay here till you finish your dinner."

"Mom, I'm not going to eat these. I'm not hungry."

"Just eat up like a good girl."

"Mom . . ."

"Ginny, if she's not hungry, leave her be."

"Oh, sure, let's let good food go to waste. Most people would love a bowl of fresh strawberries. But no, not little madam here."

"Jo, pass your plate to Anthony. He'll eat them."

I did, and he took them uncomplainingly, crowning them with soft peaks of cream.

"*Now* may I be excused?"

"No, you wait until everyone is done. Have some manners, miss."

I stayed, punishing them with my presence.

Later, when the maid brought coffee into the living room, I took it black for the first time — no more octoroon swirls, no more fat globules floating on the surface — and doctored it with saccharin tablets from a flat blue tin, bought that day. The tablets were tiny but had a powerfully sweet taste that faded almost immediately, leaving a lingering synthetic bitterness. Taken this way, coffee tasted vile.

I sipped it proudly.

*

"But sugar's not exactly food."

"Everything on the tray is food and not up for discussion: you know you have to eat some of everything. Food is medicine: try to think of it that way."

"But sugar isn't food, it's poison."

"That's nonsense, Josie."

"No, it is. White sugar's the worst. It stresses the body, makes it produce more insulin. I read it in Pritikin. It's, like, really insulting your body to eat white sugar."

"It's insulting your body to starve it, too, Josephine."

"I'm not."

We are overeating as we slowly starve ourselves to death on American junk food.

No response. I want to keep going, keep talking, so I don't have to eat. There's an orange still to tackle: before it would have been my meal of the day; now I'm expected to chow down on it along with everything else. How can I?

"And they've discovered that junk food, which is mainly refined sugar, makes kids hyperactive, violent."

"The Twinkie defense."

"What?"

"Oh, never mind."

I have no idea what she's talking about (the word *Twinkie* carries a charge of anxiety, of shame: the sick aftertaste of a binge), and she's pretending to be immersed in the paper. I look at the tray and the two sachets of sugar that provoked this discussion. I absolutely cannot put that in my coffee. Would she eat rat poison if some fat, freckled stranger asked her to?

"It also destroys your teeth, you know."

She looks up, absent. "What?"

This isn't going to work.

*

At breakfast the next day, I started reading the cereal boxes. Sugar, high-fructose corn syrup, wheat, oat flour, partially hydrogenated vegetable oil (one or more of cottonseed, coconut, or soybean), salt, yellow dye #6, sodium ascorbate, niacinamide, zinc oxide, iron, pyridoxine hydrochloride, riboflavin, palmitate, thiamin hydrochloride, folic acid: 110 calories per ounce.

We're innocent victims of carbohydrate-itis, the insidious, invisible, all-pervasive plague of our century. What causes it? Mainly, sugar.

"I'm not eating this," I announced.

"What do you mean?" asked my mother, slurping tea into a mouth full of half-chewed toast. (Most languages use a different verb for the way humans eat and the way animals do: so they should.) "You always eat it."

"Yeah, that's probably why I'm so *fat*."

She put down the gardening catalogue she'd been studying, sighed, and looked at me with her head cocked. She was not a pretty sight, my mother, oily and bulbous and unwashed in a shapeless floral housecoat. "Josie, I don't want to hear any more of this nonsense. You're a growing girl. You are not fat: you're just developing."

Into what?

Into you?

"Well, I'm not eating breakfast today. I'm not hungry." I was, of course, but felt light and virtuous, my stomach flatter already.

The night before, after my bath, I'd stood naked for a long time in the mirror's unforgiving gaze. How had this disease crept up on me for so long unremarked? How had I failed to notice deformity's spread?

What I saw was a squat, stocky body, with short legs, a short neck, and a short waist (thank you, Mother, for those genes). The solid ankles and wrists betrayed peasant stock, as did the chunky calves. A thick aspic of fat coated everything, especially the thighs, which were curdled to boot, and the belly, bulging in three gelatinous rolls. But the breasts were the worst: pneumatic and pendulous at the same time; full, formless, and flaccid.

I took off my watch, earrings, and hair clasp, then emptied my bladder. Inhaling deeply, I stepped on to the scale and stepped right off, as if my feet had been scalded by hot sand. I knelt down, jiggled the scale, checked that the needle was indeed pointing to zero, jiggled it again, moved it a few feet, checked it again, climbed on once more. Same reading. That was it, then.

One hundred and twelve pounds, at five feet two.

It was time to take matters in hand, to take myself in hand — so that nobody else could (in handfuls).

I began to study the diet books. They gave me hope. *The instructions are simple and easy. Follow them religiously.* They also contradicted each other, so, to be safe, I decided to follow every rule in all of them. *It is time to take control and responsibility back from those who are arguing about the right answer.* This didn't leave much that was safe to eat.

I discovered that my mother had been systematically poisoning the family for years: it was a miracle she and my father were still alive, after what they had been doing to their bodies (and ours) all this time. According to my sources, they couldn't last much longer; I daily expected one of them to keel over from high blood pressure, clogged arteries, diabetes, or cancer. It was only a matter of time — but not soon enough for me.

All I had for breakfast the next morning was black coffee, a bittersweet chemical brew.

When my father dropped me at school, I made a quick detour to the garbage can before class. There I deposited the lunch my mother had made for me: a peanut butter sandwich (300 calories), two oatmeal-raisin cookies (100 calories), an apple (65 calories), a bag of potato chips (150 calories), and a bottle of orange soda (125 calories). Grand total: 740 huge, enormous calories.

Remembering that I didn't always eat all my lunch, I retrieved the cookies from the trash, for verisimilitude's sake, and put them back in the bag for her to find that night: a stale reproach.

Don't feed me. I'll feed myself.

At the dinner table, she loaded up my father's plate with steak, mashed potato, peas, gravy, and an ear of corn (an ear, a hunk of muscle, thick brown blood: something dismembered). Then she started loading up mine.

"No thanks."

"What do you mean, 'no thanks'?"

"I'm not eating meat anymore."

Animals in nature eat one food at a time. Not like us. We eat everything we can get our hands on, including them!

"Why on earth not?"

"It's unhealthy. Red meat is unhealthy."

"Josephine, what has got *into* you lately?"

"Nothing, I'm just not going to eat meat anymore."

"But why not?"

"Because it's unhealthy, it's full of fat. It's about the worst thing you can eat."

"Well, what do you suggest I do with your dinner? Feed it to the dog?"

"Yeah, feed it to the dog. I don't care what you do with it, I'm not eating it."

"Josephine, don't speak to your mother like that. If she doesn't want the steak, Gin, just give her some veggies."

She served me a huge mound of mashed potato, shaking it angrily off the spoon, as if into my face. Then she piled on the peas and added an ear of corn, cooling and frayed by now. After she passed me the plate, I simply looked at it, keeping my hands clasped in my lap. In India, the hand you don't eat with, the unclean one, must remain on the lap at all times; both hands seemed unclean to me now, as did the food.

On her plate, she piled two steaks, mine and hers, all the remaining corn and peas, and a mountain of gravy-soaked mash, which she immediately attacked.

We humans eat the diet of a lion, a giraffe, a pig, a horse, and an ape. And not only do we eat the different diets of all these animals, but we do so at the same meal!

There was a long, loud silence, filled with the sound of chewing. Then my father took a sip of water, dabbed his lips, and remarked, to no one in particular, "I had a call from C C & A today."

This accomplished what had seemed impossible: she stopped chewing and looked up, knife and fork arrested, perpendicular, in her fists. "You did? Why didn't you tell me before?"

"Well, you were busy."

"So, what did they say?"

He met her eyes and glanced away at my brother, at me. "I'll tell you about it later."

"Do they want you to come in for another interview?"

He looked down at his plate, pushed a pea around with the tip of his knife. "No . . . I'll tell you the details after dinner." From the pucker between his eyes, I already knew. No job with C C & A, a big advertising company.

It seemed to be taking him a while to find a new job, although of course the situation was never described as such. He still left the house at the same time every morning, smartly dressed in a suit. Sometimes I suspected that he simply got in the car, dropped us at school, drove around the block, and came home again.

Dad, I wanted to tell him, watch your diet. *It's the lean, strong, well-tailored person who is admired today.* My sources say, Dad, *Your business associates are going to have stomachs full of rotting food that will hold them back.*

When she had finished eating — wiping down her oily brown plate with a hunk of buttered bread — I was still picking at my vegetables, pulling the kernels off the cob one by one. My father was politely interviewing Anthony about his homework. I was hoping that if I took enough time, she'd lose patience and ring for the maid, but she didn't: she just sighed, leaned back in her chair, waited awhile, and then cut herself another slice of bread.

"How can they give me cookies?" I ask the nurse. "Cookies are empty calories. They contain no nutrition at all."

"They contain energy, which keeps you alive," she responds wearily, warily, not wanting to be drawn into another long wrangle. (Once I happened to catch sight of the staff handbook — NOT TO BE READ BY PATIENTS — open on a pile of clean linen: "Patient may not engage staff in discussion of meals, calories, or body weight. Any discussion of food will be promptly terminated.") "Now just eat up."

"Do you eat cookies?" I ask her.

"What I eat is not the issue here, Josephine. But as it so happens, yes, I do, occasionally."

"When?"

"When I feel like it. When I bake."

"You bake cookies and then eat them all yourself?" I'm flabbergasted: I cannot conceive self-indulgence so shameless, on such a grand scale.

"No, I don't eat them *all* myself. But I eat as many as I feel like."

I cannot believe that anyone would admit to this. "What kind?"

"Oh — it depends. Sometimes oatmeal-raisin, sometimes chocolate chip, spice sometimes, or ginger."

I try to imagine what it would be like to think, Oh, I feel like some oatmeal-raisin cookies today — without immediately suppressing that thought, as if obscene — and then go out and buy the ingredients (imagine standing in the checkout line: everyone would know what you were going to do), come home, mix it all up (I'd eat most of it, raw, before it even got onto the baking sheet), dollop it out, bake it, take the cookies out of the oven (the fragrance!), let them cool (I'd wolf them all down hot, blistering my mouth, tearful, tasting nothing), eat a couple, put the rest away in a tin, and then not think about them anymore. Or perhaps even offer them, with tea, to a visitor — thereby brazenly admitting that you are someone whose desire for cookies was so strong that you went out and bought the ingredients and baked them, shamelessly keeping them in your house, where you can eat them any time you want to, merely to gratify your appetite.

How could someone have so little restraint?

The sugar demon grabs you by the throat and you can't shake loose.

I ate precisely half the corn and half the peas, mixed in with a quarter of the mashed potatoes, licking the lumpy stuff very slowly off the fork. All my attention was concentrated on what I was not going to eat (the rest of the corn, the rest of the peas, the rest of the potatoes, the bread, the butter, the dessert, the cereal the next morning, the sandwich for lunch the next day).

It was simple: you decided, once and for all, that you weren't going to eat and then there were no further decisions to make.

I had learned a rule for life: *NO thyself.*

Desire, it seemed, could be quelled by a single act of will.

Only one thing matters for the rest of your life. Does what you are about to put in your mouth contain carbohydrates?

Your mind should always be on your diet.

Tell yourself: "This is forever. I will do whatever it takes. I want to be thin more than anything, even food."

DIAGNOSTIC PROFILE

NUTRITIONAL HISTORY

Have you ever been on a diet? *You've got to put away once and for all the naive idea that you can diet for a while until you've lost the worst and then go energetically back to digging your grave with your teeth. You're not weak-willed. You're not a glutton. But you are sick. Very sick. Getting well must be your first concern. You can never look forward to not being on a diet.*

Please list your usual methods of dieting:

10

I KNOW I'm not imagining it: my belly is bloated. Where there used to be hollowness, concavity, now it curves out rudely, tight as a rubber tube. *Stand tall, glance down. If you see your navel, you need tummy firming.* I need tummy firming. I need to firm my will, too, so marshmallowy of late, to stop them from doing this to me — to stop me from letting them. It's so tempting to be taken care of, to make no decisions, to be responsible for nothing. But without my will, what am I? *"NO thyself"* the book says; that's all I know.

"Look at this," I say to the nurse, pulling my gown tight across my gut. A thick pad of blubber shows clearly against the bones. Close to tears, I'm waiting for her to deny it.

But she doesn't. "Yes, there's been some gain, Josie. We're very pleased. You should be pleased, too, though it's natural you'll experience some anxiety as your body changes."

"But why is it all there, all in one place? I wouldn't mind a little on my back or calves."

'It'll take a few months to redistribute itself."

"A *few months*? And in the meanwhile, I'm going to look like this?"

"Like what? You're beginning to look a lot healthier: your color is much better, for one thing."

"Fat," I respond. "I look fat, fat, disgustingly fat" — pinching hard at a fold of belly flesh, not saying what I really think: pregnant.

There are certain things that, if you swallow them, take root inside you.

In the newspaper today: the story of a boy who fell onto a fence and was impaled on an iron spike, which went through his neck and came out through his mouth. He had to lie there for hours, emitting the silent scream of the spike, until they blowtorched him free of the fence and carried him off, spike and all, to the hospital.

I would like a spike in my mouth, filling it with cold, tasty metal, keeping everything else out with its sharp point.

From the books, I learned what to put in my mouth and what not to. I learned to substitute saccharin for sugar, skimmed milk for whole, cottage cheese for Cheddar, yogurt for cream, diet soda for regular, carrot and celery sticks for sweets, lemon juice for salad dressing, rice cakes for cookies, frozen bananas for ice cream (special treat only), clear bouillon for dinner, black coffee for breakfast, shopping for lunch, exercise for tea, air and club soda (but watch that sodium!) for food of any kind.

Keep a food diary. (Dear Diary, today I had a bite of birthday cake. Please forgive me.)

Eat in only one room of the house.

Use smaller plates so your meager portion looks like more.

Use fine table linen and silver to make your half grapefruit and dry toast an occasion: pamper yourself!

Put your fork down and allow a full minute to elapse between bites.

Don't do anything else while you eat: concentrate entirely on mastication. Few overweight people really know how to enjoy their food. Chew! Chew! Chew!

If all else fails, get dysentery, staple your stomach, wire your jaw; try a spike through the mouth.

Weigh yourself: if you don't weigh yourself, you may not lose weight.

Two days later, after my morning shower, I unwrapped my towel (several ounces), peed (several more), unpinned my hair, aligned the red needle precisely with zero, took a deep breath, stepped up, and opened my eyes.

111 pounds.

It was working. I could do it.

My resolve redoubled itself.

But on the third day, late in the afternoon, after nothing but black coffee for breakfast and Tab for lunch, a frantic, shaky ravenousness overcame me. Almost before I knew what I was doing — part of me was trying to take advantage of this attack before the rest caught up — I found myself feeding a vending machine in the school basement and wolfing down the Mars bar that it whelped. It tasted sickening and wouldn't fill my mouth, melting before I could sink my teeth into it. Cram as I might, it filled me only with disgust. So I immediately ate another.

Sugary bile rose in my throat, bringing tears to my eyes.

I was hopeless: I'd never have the slightest control.

There was only one thing to do: start again, tomorrow, this time forever. Whose body was this, anyway?

In the shower, with the nurse waiting outside, I squeeze and pinch my belly in panic: this has to go. I lift my leg and shake, watching the flaccid flesh quiver on the femur. This has to go.

My whole body has to become frugal again, minimal, without a hint of excess (every fat cell the visible deposit of desire).

In the body, as in art, perfection is attained not when there's nothing left to add, but when there's nothing left to take away.

If I had a full-length mirror, I could go through my posing routine: naked except for underpants (I won't stare at that scar, shaven or not), I bend over to touch my toes, seeing, in profile, the scalloped vertebraic crest. Then, facing the mirror, I reach upwards to examine my arms, as streamlined and schematic as the elastic-jointed wooden figures that artists use. I can see every fiber of the small, perfectly defined deltoid, below which the upper arm reverts to bone. Traveling up and down like an elevator on its cable is the mobile, compact biceps — a muscle I'm proud of, responsive, nervous, ready to flinch like a small mouse, its namesake.

The parts I like best are the shoulders, sharp as wings, and the collarbone, which I can wrap my hand around. Their names, *scapula, clavicles,* are poetry to me. Across my chest, the body's infrastructure is most obvious, and I even like the ugly violet maze of veins which traverses it: like the Visible Woman (that lurid kit I couldn't bear to look at in the toy store), I'm approaching transparency.

But today, if I continued my routine (inhaling, counting the ribs, clasping my hands around my waist until the fingertips touched), all I would feel would be thick, rubbery fat. No wonder they won't give me a mirror: I'd kill myself.

As the diet book says: *Death means the body no longer has the energy to deal with its situation.*

Starvation is fulfilling — at first, anyway. That is why, I suppose, mystics go in for it. Colors become clearer, sounds sharper, as if some kind of fuzz had been scraped off perception, as if more of the body were available to attend. For the first few weeks, I was in a state of sustained exhilaration: speedy, powerful, unstoppable.

The clinical term, I imagine, is *manic*. Mania has its uses; it gets things done.

At first, I didn't tell anyone at school about my diet. (It wasn't a diet, anyway, it was a life plan. *What becomes really important is maintaining your state of perfection and the freedom that accompanies it.*) When we'd gather at lunchtime on the landscaped lawn and open up our offerings from home — some in humble waxed paper, some in aluminum foil, and others in bright plastic containers — we'd show an open, envious interest in each other's food. Since I'd already thrown most of mine away, I took to saying I had eaten it during the morning: "I couldn't wait."

After a week or so of this, my father dropped me late one morning at school (he seemed slower, more lethargic, every day), and I hadn't time to void my lunch bag. So I opened it in front of everyone and headed straight for the garbage can: "I'm on a diet," I announced, dumping everything except a container of strawberry yogurt (210 calories). This caused an immediate buzz.

"A diet?" said Carol. "Which one?"

"Well, not any one in particular — just a kind of adaptation of my own."

"What can you eat on it?" asked Nicola Talcott, through a mouthful of cake; she was effortlessly lean and horsey, with an appetite to match. (Sometimes, out of sheer distractibility, she would forget what she was eating and leave it, picked apart, to be gathered carelessly and tossed out on the way back to class: I noted this because it was an attitude I was trying to cultivate.)

"Well, I just have black coffee for breakfast." To me, this sounded like the height of sophistication.

"And then?"

"Maybe a yogurt or an apple for lunch, if I feel like it. And some vegetables for dinner, because my mother makes me."

"Vegetables are fattening," pronounced Sarah Rosen, who fitted snugly into her pleated skirt already and was really going to have to watch those hips.

"Nah," said Carol.

"No they aren't," Nicola drawled, at the same time, while I listened, stricken. What if I had been mistaken, misinformed?

"They are," Sarah insisted. "Potatoes, cauliflower, rice, squash — they're all starchy, I read it in a magazine."

"Rice is not a vegetable," Nicola said.

"Of course it is," scoffed Sarah. "If it's not a vegetable, what is it?"

None of us could answer, so we had to cede the point.

To show that, despite the vegetable blunder, I was serious, I ate my yogurt very slowly, in half spoonfuls, licking the spoon clean after every taste. Long after the others had stuffed down their sandwiches and moved on to the next stage — pelting each other with balls of foil — I was still working on my yogurt. Finally, someone noticed.

"Is that really all you're having?" Carol asked.

"Yes, I'm stuffed," I said, putting down the container, which was still about a quarter full.

"Well, I don't have the willpower," Sarah said, sucking her ripe lower lip and looking around for something else to eat.

I did, it seemed. It became my claim to fame.

"I won't," I say.

The "art therapist" is back, with her ball of clay. How much longer do I have to put up with this? She has the yellowish brown eyes and hangdog smile of the family pet; like that dim creature,

119

always bounding hopefully back with the stick, she refuses to take offense at anything I say. I say: "Take that crap away."

I say: "I'm too old to make mud pies."

I say: "For Christ's sake, leave me in peace. If you're so keen on playing with dirt, go play with it yourself. Go play with yourself, for all I care."

None of this seems to work. She just sits across from me on the bed, with the tray full of variously sized clay lumps, fingering them suggestively. I close my eyes and throw my arm petulantly over my face, but when, bored, I open them again, she's still there. Is this what they teach them in art therapy school?

I sit up against the pillows and look around for something to read, so I can block her out, but they've taken away all my books this week, as "punishment": turns out rereading Pritikin is a sign of "backsliding." ("But it's not a diet book," I explained to the nurse. "It's about nutrition." "Nutrition, my foot," she said to me. What's that supposed to mean?)

For want of anything better to do, I pick up one of the clay lumps — clammy, resilient — from the tray. A powerful urge to cram the whole thing into my mouth seizes me: what it most reminds me of is cookie dough. (And suddenly, a scent of long-ago afternoons: wan winter light outside, fragrant and warm within, the kitchen windows beginning to fog.)

Cookies, cake, chocolate, and other sweets — avoid them like Satan!

Using the edge of my hand like a rolling pin, I flatten out the dough on the tray and then mark out four small circles with my forefinger. She's watching me proudly now: what a good girl. With my fingernail, I pare each clay disc loose and line them all up, painstakingly indenting their surfaces until they're rough and irregular.

"What are those?" she asks me.

"Can't you see?" I respond. "You're supposed to be the artiste."

"Buttons?"

"Buttons? Are you out of your mind? These are cookies."

"But why so tiny?"

Why do you think?

I'd forgotten that we ever baked cookies together. (Or maybe we didn't and I'm just making it up, to create a plausible past for myself: the present is such a high, lonely place to be beached, with such thin air.) Other girls, I've noticed, do things with their mothers. Maybe I did, too.

All I really remember is going shopping. Shopping was my mother's main pastime, an end in itself, something she did to kill a morning or afternoon — as if the time wouldn't be killed, wouldn't kill her, soon enough. Often she took me along, in a prim frock and shiny shoes: she believed that you had to dress up for the salesladies (thin, frighteningly made-up middle-aged women in navy blue), otherwise they would treat you with contempt. They did anyway. That was part of the thrill of shopping, to feel you were unworthy of the merchandise.

We'd meet Miriam for coffee in a department store's pink and beige lounge, as padded and pouffy as the inside of a chocolate box, a place for ladies to indulge in genteel gluttony. While Mother and Miriam dithered coyly over the pastry cart, I ordered a Coke and toasted cheese sandwich because I liked the way it was served: a quartet of crisp triangles, ranked upright on shredded lettuce. After a cream puff or two, Mother and Miriam — in concert — would dab their lips, take out their compacts, frown into them, crayon their mouths back on, snap their purses shut, and rise, stuffed and wanting.

The department store was a magical space, a perfumed maze

with no EXIT signs, through which shoppers swam hypnotized in the aquarium light. Time was suspended there, and an overwhelming appetite possessed you: not to buy but to become, to become as perfect, as immaculate, as the objects displayed jewel-like in their glass cases.

We could spend the entire day shopping, coming home befuddled with little bags: a new lipstick, a pair of earrings, pantyhose in whatever the saleslady assured Mother was the season's latest color (mulberry, almond, peach). Often she folded them away and never took them out again. "They looked different in the store," she'd explain.

For me, there'd be a new hair ribbon or an outfit for Barbie, a pair of socks or a pen that wrote in five different colors. There'd be gingerbread men from the bakery for tea.

It was so easy to buy things then. So easy to believe you were entitled to anything you wanted.

"This is getting ridiculous," she exploded, gesturing toward my dinner plate: a tablespoon of rice, twenty peas, and a large pile of diced carrots that I was trying, without success, to dice smaller.

"What is?" I asked, primly.

"This . . . this stupid diet you're on."

"It's not a diet" (my habitual response). "And anyway," I added self-righteously, "I'm just eating the way most people on this planet do."

"What's that supposed to mean, miss?"

"It means that I'm just eating the way most people on this planet do. It's not my fault if everyone around here is always stuffing themselves." This always made her angry, which is why I said it. But it was clear to me that she — occupying so much space already, gobbling up so much more than her share, so crassly exceeding bounds — did not have the right to eat; nor did I, as long as a single fat cell remained.

The waistband on my school uniform skirt had definitely become looser: if I sucked in my stomach, I could slide my hand, flat-palmed, beneath it. On the outside of my wrists, a small bump began to emerge. Gradually, too, a faint bony hollow appeared at the base of my throat, scaring me at first (I thought it might be a goiter). But the most gratifying change was to my face. From a formless, pudding-like mass, I thought I could see a chin, and perhaps even cheekbones, struggling to assert themselves. Buried in this blubbery disguise was my true form, the sharp but delicate articulation of a self.

I had lost three more pounds.

I was transformed.

My wrists look thick and puffy; I hardly recognize these hands as mine. When I touch them, especially where the thumb folds on, little dents remain. My feet too: "Elevate them," says the nurse. My chin feels as if it's developing a little pad, right under the point, though she says I'm imagining it. But I can feel it, I can even see it, so familiar from its former residence on my mother's face. On the outside of each thigh, a pinchable piece has pushed out (bruised rotten from my pinching it, hard, all day). No amount of leg-lifting — dog-at-the-hydrant-style — seems to help, though I have flapped both limbs till they seized. What's happening is that my true nature is re-emerging, inscribed in fat for all to see: corrupt, slothful, insatiable.

I lie on the bed and turn to the wall. I can't deal with any of this anymore: this room, this gross body, these fat cells silently swelling, the nurse, the food, the talk, the effort to impersonate a human being. I can't, I can't, I can't, I can't. I curl up as tightly as I can, a loud, silent wail ricocheting inside me.

In the bad days, the out-of-control days, I knew how to induce coma: eating, cramming, stuffing, ramming it in desperately until, sickened by sweetness, bloated beyond recognition, moribund with self-loathing, I could flop onto the bed and invite extinction. But why resume consciousness at all, when inhabiting a body is such hard work?

A person who had died and been given proper mourning might then be butchered in much the same way as a pig, or else buried and left until the flesh decomposed. In either case, the corpse was ordinarily dismembered by kin, who first removed its hands and feet, then cut open the arms and legs to strip out the muscles. The torso would be opened to remove the viscera, and finally the head was cut off and the skull fractured to extract the brain. Little was wasted.

Out of sheer spite, my mother was trying to make me eat three times a day. But I steadfastly refused "junk food," so after a week of my black-coffee-for-breakfast routine (how sophisticated it made me feel, how world-weary; how nauseated too, and how weak), she switched tactics and brought home some Special K (rice, wheat gluten, sugar, defatted wheat germ, salt, corn syrup, whey, malt flavoring, calcium caseinate: 110 calories per ounce). Because it declared itself "lo-cal," I was prepared to concede: the words "A Diet Delite" were magic enough. But the magic worked only if you prepared it a certain way: half a cup of cereal, exactly (or was it two-thirds, in the early, less-disciplined days?), with a quarter cup of skim milk, diluted with water up to a third of a cup, sprinkled with a teaspoon of sugar substitute. This watery, synthetic-tasting mush helped protect my innards against the coffee's acidic assault; through its sheer unpalatability, it also primed me for another day's abstinence. Its message to the taste buds every morning was "You're out of luck — again."

We're prisoners. Prisoners! That's right. We're prisoners of our taste buds.

Lunch was easier, because I could throw most of it away and because, eating with others at school, I had a reputation to uphold. Gradually, my apple or yogurt dwindled to half an apple or half a yogurt, then a third, consumed excruciatingly slowly, with frequent protestations of how full I was. It became the daily spectacle — how little I would eat, how strong my will, how few my needs — and I, the hunger artist, rarely disappointed my audience. For three days, Sarah Rosen tried to emulate me, but on the fourth, she gave in to greed, tearing with hands and teeth at a hunk of dead fowl. I never yielded — not in front of them, anyway. (And I wished for another witness, but she was a lazy letter writer and never, after that surly summer, asked me back to the beach.)

Dinner was the constant struggle. At first, I tried to excuse myself altogether, but there was no question of that: the family had to gather every night, nuclear, its charged particles within a single field of force. (My father tense and abstracted; my mother chewing vehemently; my brother playing with his meal and trying to keep his head low, out of range; myself painted like a ghoul, sullen and pouty, picking ostentatiously at my food, cutting it into smaller and smaller pieces until I provoked the desired outburst.) Since in those days I felt compelled to eat "normal" food at dinner (but no meat! no butter!), I saved most of my calories for the evening meal.

Peas were good, because you could eat them one by one, spearing each on a single tine. Brussels sprouts were good, because you could unwrap them leaf by leaf and make them last forever. Corn could be nibbled, a few kernels at a time, but carrots tended to pop off the plate if you tried to section them any smaller. Beans could be diced up to a point, but then the fibers would resist athwart the knife. Salad was bad, because the maid saturated it with oil before bringing it to the table. Potatoes were evil. I would never eat one, no matter what.

It's sitting on the plate, looking back at me. (They have "eyes," don't they — they have skin, too, in which, wrinkled brown, this one has been baked.) It's plump, complacent, daring me to eat it. Eat me, it commands, silently, so that only I can understand. Go on, I dare you. Eat me for the sheer pleasure of stuffing your face, you pig.

If you make a pig out of yourself, you will become one.

Why can't she hear?

I pick up the knife to puncture it — it's the only thing left on the plate that I haven't at least touched — but it's completely sealed in its papery skin. I cannot decide where to slit it, stab it, spill its mealy guts.

"Josie," she says, from the foot of the bed, where she has been filling out forms (my chart? does the graph plummet off the page, as in a cartoon?), "time's almost up. Eat your potato."

"I can't," I say.

"Sure you can," she says, "just half."

"I can't," I say.

"Josie," she says, "it's a plain baked potato. It has about the same number of calories as an apple. You'd eat an apple if I asked you to, wouldn't you?"

"Yes," I lie, "but I can't eat this."

"Why not?" She's not supposed to be doing this: the handbook is clear: "Any discussion of food will be promptly terminated." I should report her to Dr. Frog.

"It's alive."

If you want to be vibrantly and vigorously alive, you have to eat food that's alive.

She looks up with an irritated grimace, but something about the expression on my face wipes it away. She comes over to the chair next to the bed and sits down beside me. Hunching up, I let my hair fall across my face so I don't have to look at her. Frantically, in my lap, I'm ripping away at a cuticle that I've already chewed until it's raw. The smarting brings tears to my eyes.

She has the gall to put her hand gently on my forearm, where it feels unexpectedly warm. I let it stay for a little while before I shake it off, muttering, "You know I don't like to be touched."

The potato has calmed down now; it offers no resistance to the knife. Strangely, its white flesh soothes me.

11

AT 105 POUNDS, I began to see what I might look like when perfect. *Once you are perfect, you have your choice of anything. Once you have reached your ideal weight, you no longer have to deny yourself anything.* People — schoolmates, friends of my parents — started complimenting me on my diminished self, and on the street, men's gazes, scanning routinely, snagged a moment longer. But I knew that I still had much to lose. There was still fat on my stomach, a handful above the navel and a roll below. I pinched it hard several times an hour to remind myself that it was there, that nothing mattered more than getting rid of it.

There was also the thigh problem. My thighs were — to use one of the most obscene words in the language, but how else can I say it? — they were flabby. I developed a habit of hitting them hard, underneath, to watch the flesh quiver, to inspire me with disgust. For some reason, this habit provoked my mother more than anything else I did.

"Will you *please* stop doing that, for Christ's sake. It's driving me crazy."

"I will if I feel like it." (Sullenly, giving my right thigh another whack from below.)

"Well, go and do it somewhere else, then. I can't stand to watch you doing that every five minutes."

But I followed her around, examining myself minutely in every reflective surface (the toaster, the kettle, my knife at the dinner table), kneading my calves and upper arms, pinching the soft excess at my waist, whacking my thighs. I also spent hours inspecting my hair for split ends. When that failed to enrage her, I would do jumping jacks in the kitchen while she cooked.

"Will you get *out* of here before I go nuts!" No response, just heavy breathing and the thump-slap of my stubborn perseveration.

"You've got to be the most self-obsessed person on the face of the earth," she would yell, throttling her dish towel as she dried her hands. "Do you ever think about anything except what you look like?" I wouldn't respond, thinking only: What about you, all of you, who do nothing all day long but gratify your desires? What about you, who just take up space?

"My, we are looking better, aren't we," he says, putting down the stethoscope, crinkling the bags under his eyes to simulate a smile.

My heart speeds up immediately because I know what he means: fat. In that instant I decide not to eat again for the rest of the day. This has gone far enough; they won't be happy until I look like everybody else — solid, unexceptional, resigned to being plain. I see them all the time, women hauling their carcasses around as if that flesh were somewhere they just happened to live, real estate they had merely to maintain. As if janitorial services were enough. As if they had no choice but to live in that particular, imperfect form.

Not I, though. Anyone looking at me would know instantly

that I was an artist: my medium myself, my materials air and bone and will.

Lunch causes a little contretemps, a little brouhaha. (The manual, surely, bans brouhaha: "All brouhaha will be interrupted by the staff"?) Since Dr. Frog told me I looked fat, all I've done is pinch myself frenziedly: belly, thighs, cheeks. I slap my thighs to feel them shiver (they do), I slap my face to see if the flesh feels loose (it does). If I had something hot — an iron, a match, a curling rod — I would touch it to my skin: just a touch.

When she brings me the lunch tray and sits at the foot of the bed as usual, I look at the dense matter heaped on the plate — hummus with pita bread, only the finest international cuisine for us inmates, penned in for plumping like battery chickens — and something in me revolts, as it should have weeks ago. With a convulsive heave of my knees, I send the tray crashing to the floor.

It hits the tiles with a satisfying boom; apple juice arcs across the wall; the hummus plops into a pile like shit; chips of china and shards of broken glass spray sharply up. I'm exhilarated by this sudden surge of power — why didn't I do this a long time ago? I look around for something else to destroy — but part of me is appalled, stricken. Look at the mess I've made: brown liquid and lumpy stuff smeared everywhere, broken glass.

She saw it coming, saw me shove, and sprang up with a small grunt but couldn't get near the tray in time. For a second she stood arrested in mid-gesture, mouth agape, hands poised for the catch. Now, exhaling, she caves in, spine slumped, arms flopping to her sides. She shakes her head slightly, and color — too much of it, she's mad — floods back into her face.

"What the hell was that for?" she exclaims, but then catches herself and switches into professional mode. "OK, Josephine, I want you to clean up that mess, right now please, and then I'm going to get you another lunch tray, exactly the same, and I'm going to sit here with you while you eat it calmly."

I say nothing.

"When you're calmer," she adds, "we can discuss why you did that."

"I am calm," I say, though my heart is pounding.

"Good," she says. "Now get down there and clean that up."

"*You* clean it," I say sullenly, without much conviction; I feel I should sustain this over-the-edge behavior for as long as possible, get as much mileage as I can from being out of control, though the initial impulse has long passed. It's a cold urge — old news, light from a distant star — that I recognize from binges.

"I most certainly will not," she snaps.

I say nothing, concentrating on my cuticles, letting my hair fall over my face. She looks insistently at me for a moment and then walks out of the room, leaving me deflated: that was too easy. But within seconds she's back, clutching a wad of paper towel. She holds it out to me but, chewing frantically on a hangnail, I refuse to meet her eye. She takes a step closer and rips the bedcovers back, exposing my stick legs, which pucker purple and ivory.

"Get up now and clean up that mess," she says, articulating each word very distinctly, as if at elocution school.

"The rrrain in Spain falls mainly on the plain," I respond, in a haughty British accent. I think this is hilarious and snicker with half-suppressed glee while she stares at me, disconcerted.

She stands there for a while, holding her wad of institutional off-white paper towel like a shield, then half drops, half throws, it onto the bed. "Boy, am I sick to death of you," she mutters, and picking up the empty tray and an unbroken plate from the floor, makes her way gingerly through the debris to the door. I notice that her fat white shoes, normally immaculate, are spattered with sticky brown.

Once alone, I feel the spasms of hilarity phase out like hiccoughs. Emptiness flows in again. What does she mean, she's sick to death of me? She can't be; she has to put up with me, pretend to care: it's her job. Is she going to ask to be transferred to another patient, someone sweeter-natured, someone without a vein of black, violent evil inside her? I would if I were her; I wouldn't be able to stand being around me either.

I climb out of bed but have to lie down again immediately because standing up so fast makes my head soar, sending the room jiggling and lurching about. After a few minutes, I try again, cautiously uncurling, tensing my abdominals to force the blood upwards. It works and I stand wobblily for a second, making sure everything has stopped. Yes, even the mess of food on the floor is back where it was, as if it hadn't been spinning around seconds ago (as if it weren't spinning right now, as I am, with the earth's relentless rotation).

Penitent with my paper towel, I kneel down and start sopping up the juice, the yellowish mush, the limp remnants of a salad. I put an intact orange on my nightstand and retrieve a fork and spoon from under the bed (the dust balls! it's a disgrace). Then I start collecting the shards of broken glass, one by one, placing them delicately in a cupped palm. I'm using my forefinger and thumb as pincers, but a splinter so small I can barely see it pierces the skin, causing a tiny shock of pain. Squeezing the fingertip's fleshy pad, I force out a single, perfect bead of blood, and then, watching closely, fold my fist tightly, deliberately, over the entire handful.

At first there were only a few drops of blood, which I expected, both from the dry, searing pain that had made me cry out and from what I knew of folklore — the nuptial sheets draped over the balcony, displaying the red petals that had bloomed overnight. Then, as I walked stiffly up the stairs to my bedroom, having sent him on his way (satisfied but abashed), I felt a sudden hot wetness between my legs. It wasn't until I went into the bathroom and pulled down my underwear — cautiously unsticking it from myself, where I was tender and raw — that I realized what it was.

A slight thrill of fear went through me, but I focused on the nuisance value: underwear to rinse out and conceal from my mother at this time of night; a wad of toilet paper to stuff between my legs while I waddled to the bedroom and found another pair of panties, and, just to be safe, a sanitary pad, though I didn't really expect more bleeding. The toilet paper was soon saturated; when I pulled it away, red, it conformed to the shape of the space it had plugged. Staunched by the pad, I went back to the bathroom and blotted a few dark splotches from the floor.

The pad turned meaty and sodden within minutes; growing giddy, I removed it and a scalding gush pulsed down my leg. Panicking — none of the books had said anything about this, about hot, unstoppable seepage — I grabbed a towel (the stains! too late, this was an emergency) and pushed its entire rough bulk between my legs. I realized it would stay in place only if I sat down, so I closed the toilet lid and pressed myself on the bunched-up towel, my feet on the edge of the bathtub and my head between my knees, watching in disbelief as the dense wetness crept through the jungle of tiny loops, which sucked it in, I recalled from science class, through capillarity.

By the time the towel was almost soaked through, I was still sitting there, hunched, staring, my mind empty of anything except the word *capillarity*. Slowly, almost abstractly, it occurred to me that if I stayed there I might bleed to death.

*

"Oh, Josie, what have you *done* to yourself?" The resentful mask she's wearing when she walks in with a fresh lunch tray — exactly the same as the first, pedantically so — crumples immediately and, dumping the tray on the nightstand, she crouches next to me on the floor.

I'm sitting cross-legged, my fist still clenched in front of me, watching the blood trickle out through the runnels in the folded palm flesh (even now, there's fat there, otherwise it wouldn't pleat like that). The course the blood takes illustrates some of the basic laws of physics.

Taking my brittle fist in her warm, living one, she gently unfurls it. We both regard the mutilated palm with interest: in most places, the shards have barely pierced the skin and are hanging in precariously by their narrowest point. Others, though, have wedged themselves in well, opening up purple-edged mouths.

She gets to work with tweezers, making little sounds of compassion. Before she applies antiseptic, she warns, "This will sting," but, even so, I can't help a sharp hiss, some hot smarting tears. Looking up, she blots one with a pad of gauze.

Leaving the sodden towel where it was, I climbed off the toilet seat; where a corner hung down, it was starting to drip. I took the matching bath towel (sorry about ruining the "designer" set, Mother) and bundled that between my legs as best I could. I realized that I was light-headed (whether from fear or blood-letting, I couldn't tell) but completely calm.

For decency's sake, I put on a short nightgown, though I knew it would soon be ruined, and, with the word *capillarity* still running monotonously through my mind, made my way down the stairs, clutching the towel with one hand between my thighs.

My parents' bedroom was dark and I bumped into a lamp table

near the door, which immediately woke my mother, a light sleeper. My father, I knew, was on a business trip (he had a new job at last, putting the best face on it); perhaps that had nudged me to choose this night, for no other particular reason.

"What? Who is it?" she barked, fear roughening her voice (burglars, murderers, rapists, black men: she knew they were out there, she knew it was only a matter of time before they got her).

"It's me, Ma."

"Josie? What's wrong."

"I'm bleeding, Ma."

"Bleeding? What do you mean?" she asked, sitting up and turning on the light.

We both shaded our eyes, blinking and watering, against the sudden brightness. What she saw was her sixteen-year-old daughter clutching a bath towel to her crotch.

"Mom, Peter and I tried to . . . have sex. And now I'm bleeding."

It was obvious that her brain was failing to process this information. She stared at me. I tried again.

"Mom, I'm bleeding a lot. I think I need a doctor."

"Bleeding? Peter . . . did he . . . " (whispering) "rape you?"

Would that have made it more acceptable?

"No, no. I'm just . . . bleeding, I don't know why, but it's a lot."

No response.

"Mom, I need a doctor. I'm afraid I'm going to bleed to death."

She was becoming more alert now, rubbing her eyes and temples distractedly. "Josephine, I can't possibly call Dr. Arnold" — our family physician. "What on earth would he think?"

I knew I had to stay calm. "I don't care what he thinks, I'm bleeding to death."

"But where did you . . . do it?"

"What difference does it make, Mom? I'm bleeding."

"How *could* you? Oh, Josie, I wish your father was here." Her voice was rising in plaintive, helpless panic.

"Mom, please call Dr. Arnold."

I don't know why it never occurred to me to call him myself: somehow, my sole object was to convince my mother to help me. Stand there hemorrhaging wasn't enough, it seemed.

"He was kind of cute," I tell her, "but nothing really special. Certainly nothing worth almost bleeding to death over."

"What did he look like?" she wants to know.

"Tall, lean, wiry, the way I like 'em," I say, trying to sound like a woman of the world, though it's been so long since I felt the faintest flicker of sexual interest that I don't know if this statement is still true. Is this how I like them? I don't think so: any body at all seems repulsively alien — just matter, meat on legs.

"What color eyes?" she asks. I wonder why she's so interested in this minor character, this gate-crasher long gone.

"Green, with dark hair. And rather thick, sensuous lips. I thought he was gorgeous. I think I even wrote a poem about his skin, if you can believe that."

He was a college student who seemed to spend most of his time getting stoned with his friends and the rest taking me to the movies. In between, he worked hard to convince me to have sex with him. I never wondered why he wanted to date a high school kid instead of a woman his own age: at 105 pounds and losing, I felt powerfully desirable, my newly naked ribs and hipbones all the explanation I needed. When I met him, through a friend's brother, I was impressed mainly by how wild he looked, how feral and uncombed. Older people, I noted, did a disapproving double take on seeing him; he took LSD, read Hermann Hesse (or carried the paperbacks around), and practiced transcendental meditation (when he had time). He showed me how to make an origami swan.

"Were you in love with him?"

"Whatever *that* means. I convinced myself that I was, I guess, because I wanted a boyfriend."

Even at sixteen, I knew better than to believe him when he sighed passionately and breathed "God, I love you" into my ear. But it conformed to my sense of the way the dialogue was supposed to go.

I enjoyed prompting his passion and was proud to feel his hands urgently outlining my new bones. (But there was still too much softness there, in the belly and the thighs: I wanted to be perfectly hard, offering no purchase.) Sometimes, after prolonged kissing, I would feel myself growing weak and slippery; mostly, though, I just put in my time.

Sometimes, if he touched me the wrong way — pressure in the small of the back, hot breath on the nape — everything would be drowned out by the sound of rushing water, white noise rising to a pitch of panic. I'd have to stop, open my eyes, look wildly around — because how can you know for sure who is there?

"Did he force you to have sex with him?"

"No, not at all. After we'd been going together for about nine months, I just decided it was time. It hurt like hell."

I can't believe I'm telling her this.

Finally, when I showed her the ruined towel, she seemed convinced. Shaking her head tearfully, she called the doctor's answering service and, hardly able to choke the words out, whispered that her teenage daughter had been "fooling around" with her boyfriend and was now bleeding from the, er, private parts. Fifteen minutes later, he called back and instructed me to lie with my legs crossed, feet elevated on a pillow. If the bleeding didn't stop, I should go to the emergency room. I lay with my legs crossed, feet lifted. After a while, the bleeding stopped.

I spent the next day in bed.

She sent my father up for a little chat when he got in from the airport. I was lying with my feet on a pillow under the covers, working through a pile of magazines, stupefied and headachy from staying in bed too long. It felt odd to see him walk into my bedroom in daylight, in his suit.

He sat on the edge of the bed — a familiar creak and list — but then changed his mind and moved to the wicker chair. He laid his arms carefully on the arm rests.

He asked me how I was feeling. I said fine. He asked about the, ah, bleeding. I said it had stopped. He said, "Your mother has asked me to talk to you."

I said, "Oh."

He said, "I don't quite know how to say this, Josephine."

He said, "You're very young."

He said, "Your mother and I are a little worried about your relationship with Peter."

He said, "We wouldn't like to see things continue this way."

I told him not to worry, that I never wanted to have sex again.

He said, "Oh, you'll feel differently in a while."

He said, "Your mother has asked me to talk to Peter, too."

I snorted.

But a few days later Peter was summoned to my father's study; it was hard to tell who looked more uncomfortable. For the fifteen long minutes they were in there, I hid upstairs, writhing on my bed, clutching the blanket into me as my gut contracted with humiliation, cackling into a pillow as I tried to imagine the dialogue.

Afterwards, Peter and I strolled around the garden, taking the long way, by unspoken accord, to avoid a certain spot. My father had suggested that I was perhaps a little too young for sexual intercourse on a regular basis and it would probably be best if Peter didn't see me anymore. Although Peter had earnestly promised to keep his appendages out of my sixteen-year-old orifices, that didn't satisfy my father. He required that we "take a break" from seeing each other. I didn't really care, because I didn't want anyone's insistent purple organ near me again, but I was annoyed that Peter had so flaccidly assented.

That was the end of Peter.

I decided instead to concentrate on my schoolwork and on perfecting my body.

Amanda Jane married (intact) at eighteen, with a half-hearted half year of French Lit behind her. Bruce, her brother's friend, cast long ago as romantic lead, stepped from the wings on cue, in morning attire. Months earlier, at my dorm, I had picked up the mail: a cream envelope adorned in her curly round hand (it wasn't my birthday, with Christmas long gone . . .). Something jolted inside me, but I soon sobered up. Join the wedding party, Miss A, are you out of your mind? Some obscure rule of etiquette, I supposed, that she knew but I'd missed: *Former intimates, even if no longer such, should attend the bride — unless, of course, they're on their Grand Tour.*

As I stared at the note, its implications unfolded. I'd have to wear some kind of dress (showing my arms, perhaps: how long did I have?). I'd have to be photographed, over and over, ruining each pose, a toad that had somehow crawled into the frame. And

— fear rising now like a tidal wave — would I be expected to eat wedding cake?

I starved for two months to wear rose crêpe de chine, no sleeves, fitted waist. The other bridesmaids, slim cousins, had necks like swans. In ivory silk, she looked fragile, antique. I waltzed with her brothers, who winked over my head.

It was the last time I saw her.

She moved, so did I.

(Of Bruce, all I remember is a silly cleft chin.)

It all seemed so simple, at sixteen. If I could lose enough flesh, I could have any body I wanted, look like anything, anyone. I remember an ad for some kind of mineral water which showed an array of lithe, muscular types lounging around a locker room, and invited you, in effect, to pick the body you wanted. Perfection was easy: it equalled not being fat. *The same way a plant will reach for the light source from wherever it is located in a room, so your body will forever strive for perfection.*

Studying those clean, articulated limbs, I decided that I had to eat even less and, more importantly, begin exercising — I, who had always been too lazy to walk to the end of the driveway to check the mail, who had, mostly by lying, exempted myself from sports at school. But my body cried out for motion (*Motion is a magic potion,* the magazines told me): it was becoming increasingly difficult to sit still for more than fifteen minutes, and I woke up every morning at five, shocked into anxious wakefulness.

Since I was awake, I might as well get up and do something. So I put together an elaborate repertoire of calisthenics from magazines, brutally punishing to every muscle, especially the abdominals. This ritual I had to perform in complete silence, and, in the winter, in darkness, because I didn't want anyone else to know. My mother would have taken it as evidence of my increasing lunacy — she who never walked when she could drive, who was in such sorry physical shape that she tore a ligament hopping over a puddle.

Amanda Jane had once shown me a waist-trimming exercise that she did every day, swiveling purposefully left and right. I began doing it, too, but for a long time my waist stayed at twenty-five inches. In the historical romances I borrowed from my mother, eighteen was the norm. I hadn't heard, then, of corsets worn since childhood, of deformed inner organs, of crushed, useless lungs.

But if I'd had such a corset, I'd have worn it without complaint.

Instead, before I began, I wrapped those parts of me I hated the most (my waist, my belly, my breasts, my thighs) in plastic sandwich wrap. This was supposed to melt the fat away. The plastic didn't adhere, so I had to tie yarn around it, in large bows, to keep it on.

There was something comforting about the silence, the cold, the dark, the stubborn, will-driven repetition, the mind empty of everything except the next count.

Get down on hands and knees.

Donkey kick. Pussy Cat. Inchworm. Doggie at the Hydrant.

Lie on back as shown.

Decline Dumbbell Fly. Chicken. Compromise Curl-Downs.

Stand with knees unlocked.

Dumbbell Shrug. Bent-Arm Fly. Slow-Motion Jumping.

Almost Kneeling.

Hanging from a Bar.

12

DIAGNOSTIC PROFILE

MEDICAL HISTORY

Have you ever had any serious medical problems? No
Have you ever suffered a serious injury? No
Do you engage in regular physical exercise?
If so, describe your habitual mode of exercise: Going too
far
Are you currently on any medication? Yes
**Do any members of your immediate family suffer from
the following ailments?**

Heart disease	Hypertension	Diabetes
Epilepsy	Breast cancer	Obesity
Scotoma	Scleroderma	Gargoylism

Is there any history of mental illness in your family?
List all family members who are still alive:
Childhood diseases: The usual
Age of menarche: 11
**Have you ever ceased menstruating for more than two
months?** Whenever possible

Average length of cycle: No cycling allowed in the hospital

Current height: Five feet two inches

Current weight: Don't know

Ideal weight: Zero G

Highest weight since age 18 (excluding pregnancies): 122 pounds

Lowest weight since age 18: 67 pounds

How long did you maintain your lowest adult weight? 3 days

Are you engaged in an occupation (e.g., dance, modeling, wrestling) that requires you to maintain a specific weight? Yes, the occupation of maintaining a specific weight.

How does a 3-pound weight gain affect your sense of well-being? *Excess fat creates attitudes that can actually work to keep you unhealthy. If you believe that you are fat and unhealthy, you will stay fat and unhealthy.*

How does a 3-pound weight loss affect your sense of well-being? *In reality, you are a different entity every time you lose a single pound.*

Have you ever sought psychiatric help? No

Please indicate how often you experience the following symptoms:

Anxiety

Depression

Loss of appetite

Fatigue

Irritability

Insomnia

Fear of heights

Fear of enclosed spaces

Fear of open spaces

Fear of running water
Difficulty getting up in the morning
Difficulty making it through the day
Difficulty making it through the next day
Sense of floating through dark interstellar space

Have you ever made a suicide attempt?

All information will be kept strictly confidential, available only to doctors, nurses, endocrinologists, dieticians, social workers, psychiatrists, psychologists, art therapists, physical therapists, fellow patients, parents, significant others, readers of professional journals, insurance companies, and/or whoever pays the bill.

Have a Nice Day.

"That's not funny," she says, looking over the form, though I can't tell whether she means the places I answered or the places I didn't. "And you're *not* on any medication, though we might consider some lorazepam for the anxiety."

"What anxiety?" I say.

They tried to have me fill out this form during the intake interview — that's how they put it, "fill out this form" — but I just stared at it, so they took it back, muttering something about "inanition." Now here it is again, for the record. But whose? and why?

"None of this is anybody's business," I tell her. This is where all my previous experiences with "psychotherapy" have foundered: whenever the therapist (the high school counselor, the family therapist, the cut-rate psychoanalyst, Herr Doktor Frog) asks a question, something in me shrinks up, shuts down. Primly, as if the issue were one of etiquette, I tell them, "It's none of your business."

("I don't pay eighty bucks an hour for you to tell this man, this expert, this *Ph.D.*, that it's none of his business," my mother ranted, when the family therapist finally admitted defeat.)

The therapist and the rapist — a matter of spacing, but the approach is the same. The psychology student with her jellied probes. The endocrinologist with her vampire prick. The doctor with his insistent tube.

"It's none of your fucking business," I repeat.

"It is if we're trying to help you," she replies smugly, "to understand you better so we can help you."

I permit myself a dry laugh.

"Your mother and I," he said, avoiding my eye, obviously obeying orders but with no stomach for this discussion, "are a little concerned about you."

"Why, for God's sake? I'm getting straight A's, all I ever do is study, I never go out anymore, I haven't had a goddamn *boyfriend* in six months . . ." I let that idea hang in the air between us, shaping space with the unspeakable, using it as a shield. It had been six months, more or less, since the public blooding; after Peter made his exit, none of us ever mentioned it again.

"Yes, but," he said, addressing the floor, "we're a little worried about your, uh, eating habits and the hours you spend exercising. Mom thinks it's all got a little out of hand. And she thinks she hears you moving around upstairs at odd hours of the night — I don't know, you know how she is . . . ?" — almost pleading now, but trailing off into silence, as a similar image visited us both.

None of this was anyone's business, none of this was even up for discussion. This particular block of time (5:30 to 6:45 P.M.) was scheduled for studying, and I couldn't afford to lose the ten minutes this "conversation" had already cost me. Other people wasted so much time, volumes of it, letting it expire unspent, unredeemed. But since I had put myself under production, I practiced economies of scale. I made each second count: I jogged from 6 to 7:30 in the morning, swam laps from 4 to 5, and worked out with hand weights for an hour before bed; around these fixed points (and, of course, school), I had to schedule homework and my nightly command performance at the dinner table, which left only an hour for leg waxings, brow tweezings, facials, manicures and weekly extravaganza involving egg yolks (for the hair), cucumber (for the eyelids), and lemon halves, like small mouths, sucking on each elbow.

I fidgeted and felt my left triceps. It was 5:43. "Yeah, well," I said, "I need to do my homework."

The desk in my room was a slender white secretary, which opened to reveal an array of dainty niches designed for a lady's correspondence. Nothing I needed ever fit into those elegant red-lined innards, so I left them empty, piling books and papers on the floor. If, while writing, I pressed too hard on the hinged lid, it shuddered, reminding me to go lightly.

The way I did my homework was to write everything out three times and memorize it. Later I could summon up anything I needed — Latin, Chemistry, Poetry, Math — by reading it off my mindscreen, never betraying (I hoped) that it meant nothing to me: black traces over a void, a code to which, staring at the page from a distant star, I had somehow lost the key.

Studying like this, I made straight A's. Studying like this, I won scholarships to three major universities and chose the one farthest away from home. I had reached an important goal — cracking one hundred pounds — and immediately set myself a new one: cracking ninety-five by the time I left for college. There, a thousand miles from jealous surveillance, I could begin to perfect myself.

"I won't eat it," I say. "It's a garnish."

"Josephine," she says, "you know the rules. You have to eat some of everything on your plate. Now eat that orange slice and quit stalling."

"But, Suzanne," I say, mocking her tone, "to eat that would constitute a gross breach of etiquette. Didn't your mother ever tell you not to eat the garnish? It's very gauche, very déclassé, very *je ne sais quoi*. Look it up in Emily Post if you don't believe me."

"I don't need to look it up in Emily Post, miss," she says, with the emphasis, the edge, that tells me I'm winning. (Next she'll flush, showing that I've insinuated myself under her skin, riding the blood tide like a surfer.) "I don't need to look it up in Emily Post because I know what our rules are: lemon slices don't have to be eaten but orange slices do. So just eat up and let me take your tray. I've got work to do."

"Come on now," I say, "do you mean to tell me that you don't know the difference between food and garnish? For instance, if a lettuce leaf is served *under* something, as a mode of presentation, you're not supposed to eat it. Likewise with parsley, though some people seem to think it's good for them and munch it right up, not stopping to think that the chef may not even have washed it."

I'm rambling, stalling, improvising, because while we've been talking about it, the orange slice — the garnish on my sandwich plate — has mutated, moving almost imperceptibly out of the realm of the edible. This happens. (Sometimes permanently — as in the case of meat, fish, eggs, and the opaque fluid excreted by bovine mammary glands.) This . . . slice now seems as grotesque, as alien, as a paper parasol in a glass of punch (would you eat that, nurse, gagging on wood pulp, drooling cheap dye?). The more I look at it, with its scaly, reptilian rind and colony of pustular sacs, the more it looks like a section from the dissecting room. It should be sent to the lab for staining, not served on my plate.

I cannot put that thing in my mouth.

I'm not playacting anymore.

But she doesn't understand, she's still irritated by the Emily Post routine, she's just standing there with her hands on her (not insubstantial) hips, waiting for me.

"I can't," I say.

"You have to," she says.

"Well, I can't."

"For heaven's sake, Josie, you just managed most of a peanut butter sandwich, a glass of juice, and half a banana, and you're throwing a tantrum about a slice of orange! Give me a break! Just take a small bite out of it, and I'll walk you to the bathroom." (She knows I always want to go to the bathroom, so I can wash and wash, scour this greasy, seeping skin.)

"What if it were an olive?"

"What if it . . . what the hell's that got to do with anything?"

"Well, what if it were an olive? Would I have to eat it then? Olives can be either a garnish or an hors d'oeuvre, depending on how they're served."

"WE DON'T SERVE OLIVES HERE! THEY'RE TOO HIGH IN SODIUM!" she yells, for the first time really shouting at me, really losing it, flushing beet red, grabbing the tray off my lap and sending everything sliding, clattering, to the edge as she stomps out, bumping the door open with one tray corner, the other braced against her hip in a slovenly, violent manner that terrifies me.

*

She's dragging me by the hair, my hair is coming out in handfuls, the tiles are searing the skin off my elbows, she's trying to gouge my eyes with her other hand, with my teeth and nails I flail at her ankles, missing and screaming, screaming and screaming, the ambulance is at the door, false alarm, yes, but what is that smell? It's the roast, doctor (my patient, skinned and burning), sorry to have bothered you. Next time, drug her and gag her as well. I will, doctor, I will.

I crawl under the covers (though this is forbidden, until bedtime) and curl up tightly, like a shrimp. In this position, my bloated belly presses against my thighs, reminding me, in a wave of loud despair, that I'm ugly, ugly, inside and out. Just ugly — ugly, ugly, ugly, ugly: nothing can change that.

STAFF MANUAL
FOR PROFESSIONAL USE ONLY:
NOT TO BE READ BY PATIENTS

- Patient may not choose her own food. This is the task of the dietician.
- Patient should achieve nutritional rehabilitation at an average rate of 3 pounds per week.
- Meal trays should be attractively presented, with real china, glassware, and linen, to recondition the patient to normal social eating patterns. Staff person is present at every meal to monitor consumption and to interrupt inappropriate behaviors.
- Patient must consume all food prepared for her (meals and snacks, flamingo's tongue). If patient exceeds the one-hour time limit, staff person must stay to provide supervision and support until the meal is finished.
- Patient may not engage staff in discussion of meals, calories, or

body weight. Any discussion of food will be promptly terminated. Manipulative and/or stalling behavior must not be reinforced.

- Patient is entitled to one cup of water and, in summer, one cup of ice in addition to the nutritive fluids on the meal tray. No artificially sweetened beverages or colas are permitted; fruit juices may not be diluted; milk or cream must be added to coffee.

- Patient is expected to consume the syrup that comes with canned fruit, but may leave the liquid from cooked vegetables (exception: melted butter).

- Patient is required to eat chicken skin.

- Patient is *not* required to eat ground glass.

- Patient must eat every item on the plate, even if it is served primarily as a garnish (e.g., lettuce leaves, grated carrot, orange slices). Lemon wedges do not have to be eaten, but must be squeezed. Note that, due to their high sodium content, olives are no longer a menu option on this ward.

- Staff must guard against countertransference reactions. A firm, professional, but humane demeanor should be maintained at all times; research shows that an irate or authoritarian approach increased resistance and jeopardizes the therapeutic alliance.

"I'm sorry," she says, standing at the foot of the bed, clasping one elbow behind her back with the other hand. "I let myself get excessively annoyed. It's what we call a 'therapeutic blunder.' "

Still curled shrimplike in the bed, my head touching my knees, I say nothing. She says nothing either, and a vast loneliness overwhelms me, as if I'm zooming back into space but can still see myself on the bed, becoming smaller and smaller, with ever more vacancy around me.

Seconds pass and space continues to expand. I feel I may never make it back from this emptiness where sound doesn't carry. But then I hear someone speak.

"Well, it wasn't very therapeutic, was it?" It's me, muffled, unfurling. A stricken look crosses her face, but then she realizes I'm attempting a joke.

"Well, nobody's perfect," she says briskly, unclasping her hand to smooth out the cover at the foot of the bed, then bending over to pick up a pillow I had tossed overboard in pique.

"Except me," I say.

"Except you," she says, and we both smile.

13

"GIVE ME SOMETHING to *do,* for God's sake," I say. "I'm so bored I could die."

"You could read," she says. "You could write letters. You could listen to the radio. The art therapist will be by later today, too."

"Don't make me laugh," I say. But I don't feel like laughing. I feel like emitting the sound that would come out of Munch's painting, out of its black funneled mouth — a sound that perhaps does pour out, inexhaustibly, at a frequency too high and too horrible for the human ear.

What's killing me now is time — as I lie here and listen, as I lie here and wait, paralyzed in its thick, stupefying sludge. I am allowed out of bed, but the chair is so hard that it leaves livid dents on the backs of my thighs. I'm allowed to watch television, but I don't understand what's going on, what the characters are getting so worked up about; their faces are alarmingly orange or blue, and every few seconds some kind of lurid food zooms into the foreground. I requested a novel from the library, but I'm having trouble making sense of it: "Getting to his feet, Vernon walked over to look through the window above the kitchen sink" — what's that supposed to mean?

So there's nothing to do but lie here and feel my body bloat and rot, rot and spread, spread and deliquesce, decompose. My ankles are enormous ("Elevate them," she says), and I'm sure my thighs are becoming thicker than my knees. I can't bear to look down at my belly, engorged like a giant tumor, sucking substance from the rest of me. But even if I don't look at it, it occupies my mind with its vile inner life: violent growlings and eruptions; vicious pains, as if something had perforated; terrible sewerish smells.

"I'm dying," I whisper.

"It's gas," she says briskly. "All part of the process. Perhaps we'll cut back on the lactose for a few days."

Because there's all this putrefaction, fermentation, and resulting acid, what actually is in the stomach is a mass of spoiled, rotting, foul-smelling food.

I gave up Biology after the first two lectures, stricken with squeamishness, and decided to seek understanding on a larger scale: Economics, History, Cosmology. I stuck with Math, too, because there was something reassuring about its rule-governed universe, one that wasn't even supposed to reflect what human beings did, in their blundering way. (Poetry alarmed me: did those people really feel all those emotions, or were they only faking? And if they weren't faking, how could they make such a spectacle of their sniveling need?)

I lived in the dorm, where my parents mistakenly believed I would be well supervised and well fed; instead, no one paid me the slightest attention. I was assigned a double room, but the designated roommate — Miss Ellen West from East Hampton — never materialized, as if repelled from afar by my self-absorption, like the field of dark force around a collapsed star.

So I lived with a missing person — which gave me all the more space to make myself scarce.

Every night I ate lavishly, discovering a drawerful of strawberries and cream in my file cabinet, or opening door upon door until I happened upon the right one, which disclosed an endless buffet. Its centerpiece, an ice-carved ballerina, was the sole witness as I strolled along, using both fists to scoop up and stuff in whatever caught my fancy: avocado mousse, crème caramel, fettuccine Alfredo, sherry trifle, vichyssoise, Sacher torte. I stuck my tongue lewdly into éclairs, probing the cream filling with grunts of lust until, appeased, I moved on, leaving the pastry shells vacant and violated on the plate. Sometimes, I wept as I ate and wept as I woke.

After a while, I began jolting awake as the dream began, just as the door was opening.

"I was an outstanding student," I tell him. "I made straight A's all the way through college." Not surprisingly, since I was awake much of the night, driven to pace and study, perform sit-ups in the dark, pace some more, study some more, consult my double in the dark pane.

"Yes, I see that," he says, shuffling papers in a file, holding one at a distance, head cocked, in the middle-aged, presbyopic way of one too vain to wear reading glasses. (What does he have to be vain about, with his age-spotted, amphibian features, I wonder?)

"What's in that file?" I ask. "Can I take a look?"

"Uh, no. This is confidential — medical records and such."

Once, when he was paged during one of our sessions and had to leave, I waited until he reached the door, and then, riding a wave of sheer desperation, leaned over and flipped open the file he'd left behind. I hoped to find, reduced to a few lucid sentences, the knowledge that he was withholding from me, that they were all withholding: the words that would explain me to myself.

Instead, the first page was in code, with letters and numbers cunningly scrambled — Heme-7, SMA-6, SMA-12, LH, FSH, T4, T3, RU, EKG, MMPI, IQ (WAIS), EDI — and, finally, this jeering annotation: ZING (or was it ZUNG?). I didn't read any more because my own daring had terrified me and I had to sit back before my heart battered its way out. But when he returned, I slyly dropped a clue. "Quite a ZING-er, huh, doc?" I added casually — and, admittedly, inconsequentially — after some trivial remark. He showed no reaction at all, except perhaps a flicker of puzzlement.

Now he's looking at me, eyebrows arched.

"I'm sorry?"

Rueful grimace. "I asked, Josephine, what else you could tell me about your college years."

"Well, I made straight A's."

"Yes, I know. We already talked about that."

"Well . . . that's about it."

"That's it? Surely not. What about boyfriends? Extracurricular activities? Were you involved in politics or anything like that?"

"Please," I say.

Our laws must be changed to provide a proper way of eating for everyone. Political action can cut carbohydrates for you.

Yes, I was involved in politics — and economics, too — but not the way he meant it. I lived under an absolute dictatorship, with myself as both subject and tyrant. Maintaining this rule of law consumed all my attention, so I had none to spare for the groups of loud, ill-groomed others who registered at the edges of my consciousness. Some of them always seemed very upset about something, gathering in large crowds, yelling through bullhorns, chanting, waving signs that attested mainly to their poor spelling and worse penmanship. They scarcely seemed real to me, indistinguishable from similar images I saw on TV (7:00 to 7:30 P.M., though I soon gave that up); besides, I never had time to loiter. I strode along speedily, despising the sluggish pace of my fellow students. Attending only to the drumbeat in my head, I glimpsed their obscure agitation as if in an aquarium, through thick muted glass.

Now and then, something would catch my eye: an exhibit of photographs in the student union documenting the plight of people in Ethiopia (or was it India? Biafra? Angola? I forget — there's no shortage of famine). I studied these images intently: how much simpler life must be for them. How easy for them to attain the perfection I struggled so hard for; how strikingly pure their bodies; how luminous, how knowing, their eyes. How beautiful the bone-mother, sheltering in the sweep of her scarf her child's fleshless corpse.

There was Bobby Sands, too, whose progress I followed with interest, learning for the first time precise statistics about how long the human body can survive without this or that (food, water, salt) — but then he overdid it and died.

I was happy to put my lunch money into the Oxfam can at the cafeteria door once a year, like everyone else, and forgo my daily yogurt (or half yogurt). It was a good pretext to test my will. But I refused to give even a penny to the bulky young woman collecting for — what was it? ERA? NOW? "I'm not a feminist," I said firmly. "I've never suffered because I'm a woman. I'm tired of people using that as an excuse."

"Suzanne," I ask suddenly, as she walks in, "do you have a boyfriend?"

She purses her lips and pops out her eyes, mimicking prissy surprise. "Do I have a boyfriend? Aren't we nosy today —"

"No, but do you?"

"Nosy, nosy," she replies, pointing a finger, schoolmarmish, at me, while with the other hand she quite casually pulls up a chair.

"Ah, come on, tell me."

"Well, why do you ask?"

"I just want to know. I just want to know what it . . . what he's like."

She examines her thumbnail — it's ridged — and I can almost hear Dr. Frog's voice in her head: Inappropriate behavior. Manipulation. Countertransference. Then she looks up at me, no more mugging, and decides to respond.

"There is someone . . ." she says, eyes elsewhere, as if picturing a face.

I knew it. "I can't even imagine," I interrupt, shaking my head.

"Imagine what?"

You, naked and lewd. "Oh — you know. Boyfriends. That whole routine."

"It's not so bad," she says, "having someone around."

"Breathing your air . . ." I reply, making a strangling gesture with both hands.

She opens her mouth, then her palms, to respond, but for a while nothing comes out. I wait, hoping for some clue — how does she live? How does anyone — but then I begin to feel ridiculous: what am I, the family dog at the dinner table, waiting tensed, eyes fixed on her face?

Leaning back, I look around for something else to do. On the nightstand, where she dropped it on the way in, is my mail — a new "privilege," paid for in pounds. A letter from the university, inquiring whether I, ID number 071158, wish to extend my leave of absence into the spring (please complete this form). A membership renewal notice from the gym. A bill from the bookstore, last chance. A change-of-address card, forwarded by my mother (though I note that, of course, she's misspelled the institution's name).

Amanda Jane would like to inform you of her new address in the city; she and Bruce have decided, with regret, on a "trial separation." (But the blond babies: where are they?) I try to believe it. I try to imagine her alone after all these years; I imagine her, in the long black insomniac night, staring into the mirror as if it might tell her something (is she still lean and golden, I wonder, or has she — no, impossible). I imagine her like me now, with emptiness all around her, so independent that there's nothing left to hold her to the earth. Don't do it, I want to cry out; I've tried separation and it doesn't work.

Perhaps I might call her.

No; what would I say?

I return to the mail (how long have I been staring at that tiny noose of wire, where the window mesh has pulled away from the frame?). In the same envelope — as if merely by chance — I find five photos and a note: "To our dearest Josephine, Hoping these remind you of happier times, and that your recovery is going well. Did you get the flowers? Your loving Mother and Dad." Dr. Frog, I'm sure, requested these as part of the "therapeutic process"; they all show me at my most grotesque — two, which I refuse to look at, at over a hundred pounds.

"Is that you?" Suzanne asks, shuffling through, picking one.

"Let's see." I have to inspect it carefully because I never recognize my own face on film (does anyone?). This one shows a pale girl who bears no resemblance to me, with long dark hair and blackened eyes; she's wearing a chocolate-colored corduroy jacket over faded denims and high-heeled boots. "Freshman year, near the beginning: ninety-two pounds," I decide. "Look how fat my face is!"

"You look beautiful," she says. "Were you menstruating at that weight?"

"God, no."

It was the stench I couldn't stand, that of the body's dark red rotten interior. The exterior — with enough effort — could be kept under control.

It took me two hours to get ready in the mornings, which was one of the reasons I was grateful not to have a roommate. Blow-drying my hair so that it looked negligently windswept took forty-five minutes; forty minutes more to confront the sallow, oily gargoyle in the mirror and mask it with a perfect layer of paint; a further thirty minutes to decide on an outfit and examine myself in the mirror, with rising panic, as I dressed. Whichever way I looked, all I could see was fat — fat face, fat gut, fat quivering thighs, fat disgusting tits. How could I go outside and show myself to other people, when they'd all know, just by looking at me, how weak I was, how self-indulgent?

How could I justify the space I occupied in the world?

Only by resolving to be stronger; by thinking of the next thing I would not eat, and the next, and of nothing else.

It fills up the brain, thinking all the time of what you will not think, what you will not do. It fills up all your time, maintaining emptiness.

I don't know what else to think about.

I don't know what else to do.

I don't know how to get from one moment to the next.

*

Today they're keeping me busy with a full schedule, a series of special events presented by the "treatment team." (My whining must finally have gotten to them, my panicky weeping last night when I looked at my legs, the damage I did to my hands and nails. Now I'm required to wear these ridiculous mitts: I don't know why — there wasn't that much blood. I've done worse before, with more desperate teeth).

Quite an outfit, for this outing: a new hospital-issue robe, which, like my skin, is the wan blue of skimmed milk; these terry cloth slippers two sizes too big; these jumbo white mitts. I haven't washed my hair for days because I can't stand to watch it wad up in the drain, so it hangs over my face in limp strands. I imagine — still no mirrors — that what I most resemble is an exhumed corpse, with these sores around my mouth ("They'd heal if you didn't pick them all the time") and these "pockets of edema" below my eyes. That's why I keep pulling my hair down over my face — to hide it. The other reason is to make sure more hasn't fallen out.

"Try, Josie, please, to look at people when they're talking to you. It really makes a difference."

But I can't — what would they see? — so I stare at the floor, bumping the numb mitts together behind my back in a thwarted effort to rip at my cuticles. She touches my shoulder (she must have tapped bone — no fat there yet, at least), and we proceed slowly into the hallway, walking this time. It's too late, though, for me to take any pleasure in this meager privilege. I've given up any notion of exercise. Why even try? Everything's beyond repair, beyond redress.

The sight of a scale still sends a fizz of panic through me — it always did, even when I stepped on that miniature stage twenty times a day. But now — helpless, bulbous, and sluggish — I'm grateful to be accounted for behind my back. I have no urge to turn around and know: let her record it, let her keep the score. Suffering from this deformity is terrible enough. If I had to name it, put numbers to it, the very words would send me free-falling into the dark with a vanishing cry.

"Am I there yet?"

"We'll tell you when you're in the middle of the target weight range. You have to trust us, Josie." Trust them, when they've turned me into a moving target, stumbling blindfold across the range? Trust them, with all their sights trained on me?

Speedy with fright, I try to stuff my fingers into my mouth, but get a mouthful of padding instead. She encircles my wrist handcuff-style and pulls my hand gently away from my mouth. I refuse to meet her eye, but she doesn't let go and, warm fingers still locked around my bones, leads me to my next stop: the alleged dietician, with whom I'm supposed to have an informative chat about nutrition. I recognize her vaguely, having once seen her, I think, through some kind of haze (fog? smog? smoke? conference room!). She beckons me brightly into her office, where the prefab partitions are covered with charts featuring the Four Food Groups. (Good name for a rock band.) The illustrations, which I examine with interest, are fifties-style, flat and primitive — a crimson haunch; a wedge of something brown on a tilted plate speeding UFO-like through the air; a broad-shouldered bottle of milk. *Would you make your way through the droppings and go right up to a cow and . . . ?* I can't say I'm impressed: my dorm room, by the end of the year, exhibited a much richer array of images, culled from *Gourmet* and *Bon Appétit,* to which I subscribed.

(My career aspiration, then, was to be a food stylist: the one who, before the photo shoot, blowtorches the turkey and injects the berries with dye — thereby, of course, rendering them inedible.)

I wonder what she thinks she knows about nutrition, this dietician who prescribes chocolate chip cookies. *It's vital that you learn where those killing carbohydrates lurk.* I wonder what she thinks she can tell me, after my years of systematic study. I used to believe all the best-selling claims — *Some have lost 30, 40, 100 or more pounds while consuming 2,000 to 3,000 calories or more a day. They've lost weight on bacon and eggs for breakfast, on heavy cream in their coffee, on mayonnaise in their salads, butter sauce on their lobster, on spareribs, roast duck, pastrami, on my special cheesecake for dessert. And on this diet, cholesterol levels usually go down* — but now I know the truth.

Just don't eat.

It's as simple as that.

But she, of course, has other ideas. "Sit down, please!" she says, wrists fluttering, and continues to chirp away as I lean back in the chair, which hurts my spine, so I sit forward, but the seat slices my thighs, so I put my hands underneath me and cushion myself with the Minnie Mouse mitts. This all takes time, and meanwhile she's still chirping, unnaturally animated, like a character in a TV commercial. But the sound must be turned down because not much is reaching me where I sit, a vast distance away, raised toweringly on my padded hands.

I fix my eyes on the UFO to the right of her head. Myths, she says. Absolutism. Set-point theory. (I perk up for a moment: sounds mathematical.) Taboo.

I'm not listening. I look downward, at my naked shins, still like sticks. I look under the desk at her tight but solid calves, sausagey in their nylon skin. If you know so much, I think, why aren't you perfect?

I had boyfriends that year — why wouldn't I have? I was skillfully painted, I wore striking clothes, I made witty remarks, and I put in my time — but I felt desire only once. That was in the library, the place I liked best (NO FOOD OR BEVERAGES ALLOWED). One of the reference librarians was a large man with extremely thick glasses; whenever he had to read something, he would hold it right up to his face, caressing it with the end of his nose. Or he would bend all the way down to the book, as if grazing.

'He's legally blind," someone whispered to me. (As opposed to — illegally?) "Isn't it amazing? He has a Ph.D. and all."

Later in the semester, when I was checking out a pile of books — the Chandrasekhar limit was causing me problems — I overheard one of the other librarians congratulating him. His wife, it seemed, had had a baby.

Wife?

And a terrible pang, so unfamiliar I at first thought it sorrow, swept over me. That's what I would have wanted, could I have chosen any kind of human comfort: to be loved by a blind man.

14

THE EFFECTS of starvation on behavior: a classic study, by Herr Professor Keys, University of Minnesota, 1950. He took thirty-six "young, healthy, psychologically normal male volunteers" — as if there weren't already enough unwilling subjects, an entire planet of the slowly wasting. But, adding thirty-six to their number, he tormented them with want for six months. At the end of that time, they were no longer so healthy and psychologically normal, nor quite so young.

Robust corn-fed types at first, they soon found themselves compelled to root in garbage cans. To read cookbooks and collect recipes. To shoplift. To hoard — anything: knickknacks, secondhand clothes, kitchen utensils. "The men," wrote Keys, "would be puzzled as to why they had bought such more or less useless articles."

A new lipstick, a pair of earrings, pantyhose in mulberry, peach, almond.

One man was in such distress that he chopped off three fingers.

Another was interested in a woman but reported: "It's almost too much trouble to see her. It requires effort to hold her hand. Entertainment must be tame. If we see a show, the most interesting part of it is contained in scenes where people are eating." He had, he said, "no more sexual feeling than a sick oyster." (Note, Herr Professor, how even this image invokes the edible.)

When confronted again with food, the men lost control. One required hospitalization — for "aspiration," whatever that is. (Perhaps that's why I'm here, too: for aspiration.)

Such is the theory that the dietician has told me.

"Well, that was decades ago," I say.

She looks at me blankly, as if what I've said makes no sense.

Dinner: a bowl of lentil soup (300 calories). I manage about a quarter — *food is medicine* — until an image flashes into my mind: diarrhea. Lumpy. Then I can't eat any more.

A small tossed salad (100 calories). *Too much salad can slow you down.* It's soaked in dressing, but, shaking each leaf hard before I put it in my mouth — she looks up; is this "inappropriate behavior"? — I force some down. *Medicine.*

A huge plate of wormlike pasta, with red stuff on top. Huddled together, seeping.

"What is this supposed to be?" I ask, playing for time. She looks up again from her paperwork.

"I don't know: some kind of noodles with tomato-basil sauce?"

"Well, la-di-*da*," I say, prodding one with my fork.

"Don't play with it, Josie, just eat it."

I prod harder, impale one of the pallid grubs, shake some sauce off, look closely, and ask, "But what's this white stuff on top?"

"Parmesan cheese, for Chrissake, what does it look like?"

Mold.

She's watching me now. *The nurse will sit with the patient during meals, encouraging her to eat.* I put it in my mouth. It's OK. She looks down again. I eat a few more, in slow motion, rolling each one first to the edge of the plate, so it's not touching anything. Soon they're tepid, so I stop.

A slice of carrot cake.

Three doughnuts, a glass of milk, a slice of pizza, most of a package of chocolate chip cookies, a bag of Doritos, a glass of orange juice, an English muffin with butter and jam, another, a large dish of coffee ice cream with chocolate chunks, more cookies, pretzels, a bowl of Raisin Bran.

Two hours' work. Total calories: several million.

I wanted to vomit, but I couldn't.

I wanted to weep and gnash my teeth, but I couldn't.

This was the worst thing that had ever happened to me.

It was his fault: if he hadn't insisted we spend the night at his place, rather than mine, which I always preferred so I could kick them out before breakfast; if he hadn't had to leave so early the next morning for grand rounds (he was a med student, skinny and bright, with his head permanently cocked as if expecting to be amused by the next thing he heard); if I hadn't been hollowed-out from his enthusiastic, nightlong assault on me; if he hadn't left me alone in his bed.

If he'd only had some Special K in the house.

But he didn't, and, padding around his place alone, in one of his extra-large T-shirts (which made me feel gratifyingly tiny and frail), I was agitated, driven. Being in someone else's house when he's not there gives you a sense of license, a reckless desire to open the drawers, read all the mail.

Something lukewarm was running down my legs, but I didn't want to take a shower in a strange bathroom. So I went to the kitchen and started opening the cabinets, not planning to eat anything, just with voyeuristic intent. Canned chili, instant coffee, peanut butter (jumbo-sized, smooth), potato chips, Oreos, and — in the malodorous fridge — leftover moo shu, stale pizza, beer, milk, mustard, and a limp and exhausted lettuce. On the counter, there was a box of Raisin Bran, one of Cheerios, and an almost empty Cap'n Crunch.

I should have just dressed and gone home. But instead I picked up the box of Raisin Bran, opened it, and took a small pinch (I didn't know if I'd ever see him again, so what did it matter if I stuck my hand, still rank with sex smells, into his food?). I pushed it into my mouth, realizing, with a frighteningly ecstatic rush, that it was the sweetest thing that had gone in there for months, maybe years. Sawdusty at first, it soon turned on the tongue to a soothing paste.

Before I knew what I was doing, I had my hand in the box for another fistful.

An alarm flashed through my brain, an image of myself cramming the box's entire contents into my mouth, handful by handful. Do something, the alarm said.

What should I do, I thought, is eat something — something permissible. This is happening only because my schedule has been disrupted. Maybe if I eat half a cup of cereal, with a quarter of a cup of milk diluted to make a third, then my body, fooled into thinking it's getting the usual, will calm down, quiet itself. (But the cereal has sugar in it, the milk is whole! Never mind: I can compensate later.)

So, after searching in the cabinets for a measuring cup, I mixed the milk and bran and climbed back into bed with yesterday's newspaper. Practicing my policy of delayed gratification, I put the bowl aside until I had read the entire "City" section. By the time I started spooning it in, delicately at first, it had turned to mush — sweet, milky mush that went down so easily, so tenderly, that I found myself in the kitchen measuring, then, abandoning measure, giddily pouring out another bowlful, not even bothering to dilute the milk this time.

I had never done this before. I watched myself with appalled disbelief. Stop now, before it's too late, a stricken voice cried from deep in my brain, but a wild, deaf roar rising from the rib cage drowned it out.

I climbed back into bed — perhaps this had been my initial mistake, allowing myself to eat in bed, unwashed, undressed, amidst the encrusted sheets — and, this time making not even the slightest pretense of delay, wolfed it down. My belly felt tight but not full: I'd eaten so quickly that no chemical messages had yet reached the brain. Taking advantage of this lag, acting as if automatized, I jumped out of bed again and carried the empty bowl to the kitchen, looking around for something else to eat as I rinsed it out, sloppily. Something had opened in me like a funnel, and the only possible appeasement was to fill my mouth.

This has nothing to do with hunger. It has to do with filling the mouth so the howl can't make its way out.

Reaching up for the package of Oreos, I noticed that it wasn't properly closed, just kind of crumpled together at the top. There are two kinds of people in the world: those who carefully close packets of cookies and crackers so they won't get stale and those who don't. I have little patience with those who don't. It was becoming increasingly obvious that I wouldn't want to see this person again, so — sealing the decision, since I would never be able to face him afterward — I ate all his Oreos, standing at the counter, pushing each one into my mouth before I had finished chewing the last, thinking all the time only of what I would eat next.

No pleasure: only terrified self-witness, encroaching nausea, and the single, urgent drive to keep the mouth filled.

I put a small forkful in my mouth, but — it's so sweet, so moist — terror surges up and forces it out again: *pffft*, a soggy, brownish lump.

"No!" she says. "What on earth are you doing?"

"I can't. I just can't. Not . . . cake." The very word is difficult for me to say: obscene, taboo. *Cookies, cake, chocolate, and other sweets — avoid them like Satan!*

"It's food, Josephine. There are no 'good' foods and 'bad' foods."

I know this isn't true. But how can I convince her? There are certain . . . things . . . that, once you put them in your mouth, force you to keep going, keep cramming, keep chewing, in a frenzy of horrified craziness. How is it possible that she doesn't know this?

"And you know you're not allowed to scrape the icing off like that," she tells me, looking more closely at the despoiled plate (what once was a slice of carrot cake — 400 calories — now reduced to a mess of crumbs and mashed butterfat).

"I can't," I say, my voice rising. "I just can't. This is really going too fucking far." How can I explain to her the siren that sounds through me, the choking spasm that stops my throat? (And the image, unbidden, of three thick blubbery rolls: my gut.)

I am too frightened to put a forkful of . . . this . . . in my mouth. At this moment, I would rather die than eat. Something is wrong here, some exorbitant blockage of biology: I have seen babies at the breast, and I know, yes, how the organism is designed — to experience life through the mouth, to put everything there first and try other inlets later, as dismal substitutes. That's how we first know the world, through the ecstatic workings of lips and tongue, but now some current has reversed in me, and I negotiate the world by keeping it out.

Because if you begin taking things in, how will you know when to stop?

What finally impelled me to leave that morning was that there was nothing left to eat. After the Oreos, I attacked the potato chips (they were stale, but what did I care?), cramming them in by the handful as I stood with eyes fixed on the wallpaper (sheaves of wheat, tied with blue bows), my mind void of any thought save what to eat next. Before I reached the bottom of the chip bag, licking the last greasy crumbs from its folds, I had the jar of peanut butter ready with a spoon, so my rhythm could continue uninterrupted.

Some blind drive had taken over my brain.

I had to leave, to find more to eat. *Whereas roughly seventy percent of an ape's time each day is devoted to finding food, hunters and gatherers need spend only a few hours a day.*

But first I had to confront the damage. When I took off his T-shirt, my belly, usually concave, was swollen, as if last night's frantic insemination had produced immediate fruit. Helpless, I looked away. I dressed as quickly as I could, not looking at myself — I, who usually spent so long posturing before the glass. The waistband of my skirt felt snug; my hair was oily and unwashed; I stank of sex. I spent a scant few minutes on my face, as if it were someone else's, then, crumpling the empty packages and stuffing them into my handbag, I left the house — invisible.

This wasn't me. My identity had been temporarily suspended. Until I became myself again — empty and immaculate and controlled — nothing mattered, none of the usual rules applied.

*

"Tell me more about him," she says.

Him? I've just finished telling her the most shameful experience of my life — haltingly, painfully, leaving most of it out, admittedly — and she says, "Tell me more about him."

"Who?"

"The guy whose apartment it was — how you felt about him."

Felt? Don't make me laugh. (When did I last laugh, spontaneously, joyfully, for the sheer hell of it? A half memory flits through my brain — Styrofoam cup, dark glass, wild cackling — and evaporates, leaving an aftertaste of shame.)

Felt? How can I make her understand that I haven't "felt" anything for years, numb and vacant behind my wall of glass? I've told her everything I can remember about him — med student, skinny, head cocked (could it have been his, I suddenly wonder, the broad, bruised mushroom?). I don't recall his name or if I ever saw him again, but I can still see every box on his shelves, every stalk on the wallpaper, every last lettuce leaf.

"Felt?"

"Yes, felt," she repeats (a little defensively, wouldn't you say, doctor?). "Don't you think there might have been some connection between your feelings for him and your sense of being out of control the next day?"

I snort. "Spare me the cheap psychoanalysis, Suzanne. I get enough of it from the doc."

She stands up and starts gathering my empty glass, my crumpled napkin, so she can take the tray away. I had finally forced down three forkfuls of cake: by then, it tasted only of tears.

I don't want her to go.

"I really didn't feel anything," I say quickly (offering, for once, what I think is the truth: I have no way of knowing. I remember things as if they had happened to someone else, unfolding at a great distance on a cold, mute star).

"I know," she says, stopping, studying my face, "I know."

For a moment, I think she does. Then she takes the tray out, leaving me, as I lie back, to grip my belly's distended drum.

When I left his building (a once beautiful brownstone, ruined now beyond repair) the first thing I noticed was the word DONUTS. Suddenly the world had split into two categories: the edible, and everything else. This made it much easier to negotiate, as if, in this bipolar field, I too were magnetized. There were no decisions to make, no choices, no resistance. I found myself walking through the DONUTS door and approaching the counter, as serene as a somnambulist on the rooftop, oblivious to the waking mind that signals wildly behind soundproof glass.

It had been so long since I had bought a doughnut that the sheer variety overwhelmed me, paralyzing me in the gaze of the pink-uniformed pubescent who waited, jiggling, for my order. Eventually, out of pure self-consciousness, I mumbled the first kind listed, Apple 'n' Spice, but as soon as I named it, I knew it wasn't what I wanted (no fruit, nothing remotely natural, nothing that resembled anything I might otherwise eat), so I whispered the next item on the alphabet.

"What?" she said, loudly.

"Bavarian Cream," I whispered again.

She threw the doughnuts into a bag, I paid for them, and was on my way to the door when I realized I couldn't wait until I got home — at least a fifteen-minute walk. But could I really eat these lewd-looking pastries, powdered like a plump woman's flesh, in public? It was hard enough for me to eat anything, even a celery stick, in front of other people. How was I going to cram these obscenely sweet and oily concoctions (250, maybe 300, calories apiece) into my mouth without causing everyone to turn and stare?

I made a quick survey of the doughnut shop's other clients: a stained septuagenarian, immersed in his tabloid, and a chunky young woman with a frizzy perm and sneakers in place of the pumps she prudently carried in a plastic bag. She was smoking and staring vacantly at the wall. Neither of them paid me the slightest attention. I decided to risk it: the clamor of my mouth, my tongue, was too strong. I took a seat with my back to them and, reaching blindly into the bag with both hands, shoved the Bavarian Cream into my mouth.

The rhythmic, mechanical act of chewing helped soothe the almost unbearable anxiety it produced.

The doughnut was soon gone, untasted: all I could think about was what people watching me would think. Perhaps they would assume I was one of those naturally thin types who could eat anything and therefore did, with complete insouciance. Gobbling frenziedly, I tried to look insouciant. I moved on to the Apple 'n' Spice, preoccupied with what I was going to eat next.

Something savory: I was sick from sugar. But on the way out, afraid to stop even for a few minutes, I bought another doughnut — Choc D'Lite — and, abandoning shame, ate it as I walked, smearing chocolate on my face and hands like shit.

"We're not *going* to give you a laxative, and that's all there is to it."

"But I'm in agony. I haven't . . . been to the bathroom for days."

"I know," she says. Naturally she knows: not only does she stand outside the toilet stall while I sit there with the door ajar, vainly straining, but she's the one who flushes the toilet. No wonder I can't produce anything: my sphincter shuts down from sheer embarrassment.

Meanwhile, all this water accumulates within me and compacts: I've become a human trash compactor. My belly is hard and bloated; perhaps if I pressed hard enough, it would explode, firing its contents at her in a hail of hard, stinging pellets (I see her running awkwardly from the room, grunting in alarm, one arm raised to shield her face).

"Why not?" I whine.

"You know very well why not, Josephine," she says (my mother's intonation exactly). "You've probably used enough to last you a lifetime." *Keep in mind that pounds leave the body two main ways — bowel movements and urination. The more time you spend on the toilet, the better.*

I don't know how she knows about that. I've never told her.

There's no privacy here, none at all: I'm the Visible Woman, with all my veins and nerves and guts on display. What goes in, what comes out, even what stays inside me is everybody else's business. To them, I'm merely an intestinal tube on legs.

Maybe they're right. Maybe that's all we are, a twenty-eight-foot tube from mouth to anus, a tube of variable diameter, coiled like sausage links, but — if you think about it — "inside" us only in the sense that the hole is inside the doughnut.

The Choc D'Lite lasted me as far as Supreme Pizza, where I bought a Mushroom Slice with Extra Cheese, sprinkling it thickly with hot pepper flakes, folding it lasciviously in half, and tearing off huge dripping hunks with my teeth.

Nobody paid me any attention, even though it was only 10:30 in the morning. I suppose people eat pizza all the time. I would have ordered a second one, but I was afraid of what the pimply boy behind the counter would think.

Anyway, what I really wanted was something to drink and then something dry and crisp and sweet.

Milk.

Then cookies.

I can't go on with this.

Let me just reiterate: three doughnuts, a slice of pizza, a glass of milk, most of a package of chocolate chip cookies, a bag of Doritos, a glass of orange juice, an English muffin with butter and jam, another, a large dish of coffee ice cream with chocolate chunks, more cookies, pretzels, a bowl of Raisin Bran — which returned me, as if in an infinite loop, to the episode's starting point.

This was the worst thing that had ever happened to me.

Eventually, it had to end (if I'd learned to void myself, it could have gone on forever). My frenzied travels were over: my stomach, pressing painfully in all directions, could hold no more. I needed to collapse. Belching in rancid, vomity bursts, oozing oil from my pores, heavy and numb with self-hatred, I made my way home — if that narrow, sterile space could be called home. Avoiding the mirrors, I pulled off my clothes, releasing an unrecognizable belly; my waistband left a vicious red stripe, but I looked only once.

You may feel nauseated, mildly or enough to vomit.

Indigestion and constipation may occur.

Your breasts will probably swell.

Your feet, ankles, fingers, hands, and even your face may swell.

Your waist becomes thicker, your clothes no longer fit.

As your abdomen grows larger, the skin over it will stretch and lines may appear, pink or reddish streaks.

It becomes increasingly uncomfortable for you to lie on your stomach. You may feel constantly tired.

Throwing on an old, oversized T-shirt — the only thing that would fit — I flopped onto the bed and covered my face with a pillow, welcoming annihilation.

Perhaps that's why people do what they do to excess — drink, drugs, food, sex. All produce a brief but predictable coma.

Afterwards, how hard to resume consciousness, what hard work to be alive: everything puffy and sodden, the eyes piggish in a bloated face, heart black and leaden with self-loathing. That's when I started cutting class, canceling appointments, staying home to starve myself. I wouldn't go out in public until I could see bones in my wrists and cheeks again, until I could fit a palm between my belly and waistband.

I stopped going back to my parents' house for the summers, too, and for Thanksgiving, because I couldn't trust myself around all that food. I lied and said I had a job, an internship, a research project. They seemed relieved and so was I, never knowing what would possess me on any given day. How could I appear among people as the ravening monster I truly was — huge, with a crammed, bloated maw, hands full of food, half-chewed matter drooling from a never-empty mouth, lumbering insatiably towards everything, everyone, in my path?

Godzilla, King Kong, a mutant monster from the sewers.

After trying almost everything on the breakfast tray (except the butter), I feel, for the first time, that I could keep going, eat more. But surely I must be full by now?

"Suzanne," I ask, terrified, "how will I ever know when I've had enough?"

DIAGNOSTIC PROFILE

Have you ever engaged in binge eating, i.e., the consumption of excessive amounts of food in a short time, accompanied by feelings of being out of control? Yes

If so, where? Here

Can you describe your feelings before, during, and after these episodes? No

Have you ever purged yourself of food by vomiting or taking laxatives? None of your business

Did any particular events in your life trigger this behavior? List as many as applicable:

15

"OK, JUST EXTEND your arms all the way but don't lock the elbows. That's good."

It's ridiculous. I'm standing here with my arms out like a scarecrow. They're still sticklike enough to qualify (I think — or have I lost all perspective during these . . . weeks? months? of being fattened like a beast for slaughter?).

"Now just gently circle them, slowly now, deliberately."

So I do, as if signaling in some kind of semaphore (help me, please, help me, I'm being held against my will).

"The other way, now, for a count of eight."

This is supposed to be exercise. I used to work out with weights for two hours at a time — I could bench-press my own weight — and she calls this exercise, standing here, open-palmed like a supplicant, twiddling my deltoids.

"Excellent. Now let's move on to the next one. You start with your hands by your sides and slowly raise them as far as they'll go. Imagine you're cutting through cheese — that'll give you a sense of resistance." (Cheese: note the subliminal suggestion.)

Resist, she says. Stop resisting, says the shrink. I wish they'd make up their minds.

This morning, before we set off for Physical Therapy — our

current exercise in futility — the nurse brought me a brand-new set of gray sweats. I immediately checked the label to see what size they were.

"Size five!"

"That's the smallest size we have. Don't worry, they'll look fine."

"Size five!" Size one used to be too big; sometimes I had to shop (proudly) in the children's department. But I was relieved to see that these really were too big and that I had to fuss with them, rolling up the waistband, winding the drawstring around, folding back the sleeves. Then I was worried that my stomach looked grotesque where the pants bunched up, so I undid them, pulled them lower on my hips, and rearranged the gathers behind me, where I still feel relatively flat. Then my stomach looked even worse without camouflage, so I untied the pants again and tried to redistribute the gathers more evenly. But when I rolled up the waist, they ballooned out over my potbelly; looking down, I let out a bleat of helpless misery.

It's a familiar routine.

In ballet class every day, everywhere, the women walk into the studio, put their dance bags down, and head straight for the mirror, where they make some anxious or reassuring adjustment. Some are more subtle about it than others, sneaking a sidelong glance and a quick tug; the rest, like me, are so mesmerized by the horror of what we see that we abandon shame, turning helplessly this way and that, pulling and yanking at our practice clothes.

Everyone has her own gesture: tugging at the bottom of a T-shirt, looking over a shoulder to hitch tights up and leotard down, pressing a palm against a tummy glimpsed in profile, rearranging a neckline to show clavicles or cleavage. Everyone has her own costume, ritualistically designed, a palimpsest in whose layers you can read the history of that body's imperfections.

We know each other's bodies better than lovers do.

I used to wear a black leotard with black tights and an oversized T-shirt with the neck cut out. Over the tights I wore a set of woolen warm-ups, rolled down at the waist, and over that a pair of short, baggy nylon parachute pants and a pair of slouchy leg warmers. If I felt particularly distended, I added a sweatshirt and ballet skirt. Sometimes during class I would catch sight of myself in the mirror and want to run screaming from the room.

When she returned this morning, I was back in my robe, ripping my hair. The sweats were on the floor.

"I can't wear those," I said. "This robe is the only goddamn thing that fits." I didn't know I was going to cry until I did.

"Why won't they fit?" she asked, gently.

It was too hard to explain, so I just made a gesture, as if cupping a football, above my gut.

"But when you're wearing the sweatshirt, that part doesn't show anyway," she said.

"I know," I said, "but it does."

Somehow she convinced me to dress again, the sweatshirt first this time and then the pants. She tied the drawstring herself, so decisively that I didn't resist. Standing there with arms raised over my head while she adjusted the waist and tied a tight, crisp bow, I imagined that next she might hand me a bright lunchbox and walk me to school, holding my hand in the traffic. That might be Physical Therapy, that safe, warm grasp.

Instead she escorted me (untouched) to this pitiful gym.

We've done our Five-Minute Warm-Up on the Exercycle, our Warm-Up Stretches, our Deep Breathing, and now we're Circling Our Arms and Cutting Cheese.

"This isn't much of a workout," I say. I'm bored. I feel ridiculous. I also feel tired. The idea, explains the dykey-looking instructor, is not to overexert ourselves but to Reconnect with our Bodies.

This isn't my body. If it were, I'd be horrified at how hot and bulky it feels, how sluggish and stiff, how wobbly the thighs, how tight the hamstrings when I try to bend down. I used to press my palms flat against the floor, now my fingertips dangle helplessly six inches above.

My body is an impeccable machine. This, therefore, cannot be my body.

My toe shoes are very shiny, my mouth blood-dark. Masked like a harlequin, I pick my way over broken glass. The aroma of rosin sickens me; the lights are blindingly hot and white; beyond them, a hostile buzz. I try to unfurl a leg, but something is wrong, I can't balance, my arms flap like fins. I want to run offstage, but the music commands me to stay, to give the audience what it paid for. I know I can't make it, but, grinning desperately, I go through the motions, trying to hold out until the end. I almost do, but as I recoil for the final leap, an ankle folds under me and I stumble instead, landing on hands and knees, gravity's pied fool.

"It's OK," she says. "You'll get used to it."

"I never will," I say. "It's a deformity."

"Josie," she says, "it's flesh — normal, human flesh. It's what we're made out of."

Not me.

I wish they would leave me alone in this Physical Therapy room, with all its racklike contraptions. I could design myself a workout that would rid me of this tumorous belly, these jellyish thighs, this loose wad of flab on the upper arm.

I could, but the thought of so much effort, constantly renewed, exhausts me.

I could design myself a workout that would rid me of all flesh forever. I could do Hanging from a Bar. (A cartoon: a doctor's waiting room, a skeleton in a chair. "The doctor will see you now." No need: all aches already cured.)

The exercise session or whatever it's supposed to be is over, but the nurse is lingering to talk to the crew-cut instructor, out of earshot, in the far corner where she's putting the mats away. Perhaps, it suddenly dawns on me, the nurse is a dyke, too; that would explain a lot (the constant touching, the tenderness). Meanwhile I'm standing here propped against some kind of massage table, not knowing what to do with my hands, so I start pulling at my hair to see if it's still falling out. It is, especially when I pull at it, but perhaps not as much as before. I pull harder.

No one pays me any attention, so I start picking at the sores around my mouth, but then the phone rings, the exercise therapist goes to answer it, and Suzanne — reluctantly, it seems — comes over to me. We're on our way out when I hear someone call my name. I ignore it, a familiar hallucination (it happens all the time, doesn't it: you hear your name called, as clearly as if someone were right next to you, but there's never anyone there). I hear it again and ignore it again, but she nudges me (unnecessarily hard, startling me).

"What?" I say.

"Answer when someone calls you."

"Where?"

Climbing on to one of the exercise bikes is a pudgy blonde I've never seen before, dressed in gray sweats like mine (except hers are much snugger around her hips). She waves and calls again. "Josie! Hey, Josie!"

I glance at the nurse, unsure. Why is this stranger calling me?

How does she know who I am? Instead of explaining, my jailer tilts her chin and cocks an eyebrow in the direction of the bikes, implying that I should go over there. I don't want to but I do.

There is something familiar about this face, after all (a fugitive taste of honey, almonds). It's puffy and bloated, with chipmunk cheeks and pouchy eyes, but memory, trawling, stops at the mouth. A wide mouth, a mouth that might eat everything in sight.

She has, by the looks of her.

It's Cathy.

So this is her, without make-up, with her hair grown out to a nondescript dirty blond. Fat, grotesquely fat, deformed by a thick new deposit around her waist. Where she used to be slinky, now she's all pumped up, every part of her: her neck, her wrists, her ankles, each porky little paw.

They let her eat. They let her eat everything she wanted, and this is what happened.

This is what will become of me.

This is what could have become of me then, in the terrible years. Some mornings I — someone else — would wake up with the mania upon me. I never knew when the disease would strike, the urge to gnaw, to cram, to rend; I would only know that it had struck, as soon as I opened my eyes, as soon as consciousness infected me again. (Why? The bitter afterlife of a dream? The body's rage at being alive again?)

I knew if I ate anything I'd eat everything so I ate nothing and sat at my desk staring at words. It would be worse to go out, with the world reduced inside me to a radar display, glowing and flashing where danger lay in the form of food. Desire gradually took over — not simple need, like hunger, but a taut, elastic compulsion. It took all my energy to withstand it, this urge to ravage, to tear with the teeth, to devour and destroy, to stuff the hollow skull. I knew I was lost; the only question was how long I could postpone my convulsive capitulation.

By this time, I lived alone in a small studio apartment because it had become too difficult to maintain my regime in the dorm, where I had to eat and even use the bathroom in public, where people had begun to whisper about me.

No one ever spoke to me, and I, unreal in my glass case, never said anything to anyone. It never occurred to me, and, besides, I needed all my concentration just to make my way through space. One day the Resident Assistant, a chunky, officious girl of the type I loathed most (sporty, "bubbly," with shiny brown muscular legs) took me aside and — touching me for some reason on the triceps — asked if I was "OK."

"OK?" I asked.

She gestured in my direction, and mumbled, "Well, you know . . ."

I didn't. So I lied to my parents, telling them I'd lost my room in the housing lottery, and got their permission to move off campus. They didn't care, because it was cheaper.

Finally I could organize my life the way I wanted it.

I decorated my room with nutrition charts, collages from *Bon Appétit,* swimwear spreads from *Vogue* (lean, golden, toasty), and a hefty collection of cookbooks, though I never cooked (*The Cake Encyclopedia* was my favorite, with color photos so luscious I sometimes touched my tongue to them — feeding on images, the only food I needed).

I kept my refrigerator near-empty, so that on those days when, defeated, I abandoned my desk and headed for the kitchen, I knew exactly what I'd find: nothing. I never kept anything in the house that I really wanted to eat — only cottage cheese, squeakily repellent to the palate, lettuce (I could sometimes eat a whole head, slathered in mustard), and a carrot or two. Ranks of Tab and mineral water occupied the rest of the cold space; I'd feel unbearably anxious if I didn't have at least six bottles of each on hand at all times.

The grocery cupboard was equally sparse — Mother Hubbard's dog would have been long dead. Some coffee filters, a few cans of tomato paste (why?), and a bag of flour, alive, on closer inspection, with swarming brown specks. That didn't stop me from taking a handful and cramming it, choking, into my mouth; in this paroxysm, I would even eat weevils.

One recent estimate of the amount of protein contributed to the Aztec diet from wild sources comes to, on the average, about one slice of deer meat, two small fish, three-quarters of a duck, and a sackful of worms in a year.

But weevils couldn't feed the need, so I'd be driven out into the streets, in dread and relief, looking for something to consume. Not just anything, the right thing — but what that was, I never knew. So I had to devour everything in hopes of discovering what I wanted.

Roaming in desperate agitation, my sole purpose was to postpone, preferably forever, the moment my mouth would be empty again. Perhaps a similar hunger drives men in search of sex — the difference being that my frenzy led me to seek something to cram into myself, while they crave something into which to cram themselves.

"I don't really see that it's any of your business," I say, after a pause, and he leans back in his chair, where he had been pressed forward, tensed in the effort to probe me. My body used to be the boundary, but now that it's been taken over, I'm concentrating my self inside my skull. Today he wants to talk about sex (why doesn't he call an "adult" phone line if that's what he wants?), and

I don't have the stamina to convince him that nothing could be more beside the point. (Just as I can't make Suzanne understand that none of this is about appearance.)

"And anyway," I say, "most of the time, I never give it a thought, never did." This is intended to shut him up; it's also almost the truth.

So take your theory of transference and stick it, I add mentally, though at the moment (by coincidence) a sick sensation seeps through me that I thought I had staunched.

I don't know why he of all people penetrated the fog that enveloped me. But suddenly, in my junior year (eighty-three pounds), I was besotted with him. There was nothing — I thought — that he didn't know, and every time he looked my way, ants swarmed inside me with ticklish feet.

Twice a week, before his seminar (Theory of Scarcity), I spent two and a half hours in front of the mirror. I was always perfectly prepared but wore an air of ennui designed to unnerve him, opening my mouth only to make brilliant remarks I'd rehearsed the night before.

Towards the end of the term, shortly after I'd handed in a forty-three-page paper that even I thought was good, I passed him on my way into the library, as he was on his way out. He did a double take and turned to look back over his shoulder at me with a delighted grin. I had, it seemed, succeeded in attracting his attention — but even at my most feverish I couldn't imagine a situation in which anything might come of it. For the first time ever, I besieged my numb slit nightly before falling asleep, but my imagination, a literalist, drew a blank: it balked at the earthquake scenario, the car crash routine (his wife and children wiped out, I happen to be in his office when he receives the news), even the accidental encounter in a bar (what would he be doing there alone; what would I?).

It turned out to be so much simpler. The Economics Department held an informal wine and cheese reception for majors who were considering grad school; faculty members were there to "mingle and answer questions." Abandoning my usual prohibition against wine (150 calories a glass), I went and drank and stayed until the end. Everyone drank too much because the department secretary, overestimating the number of interested students (or perhaps in a fit of *Schadenfreude*), had ordered extravagantly from the liquor store. I avoided him all night, but by the end so few of us were left that we gathered into a single knot.

I began sending him psychic messages to glance at his watch, look casually about, and say "I should be getting on home. Anyone need a ride?" I knew where he lived (I knew everything about him that was on the public record), and it was in the right general direction. But instead an officious little adjunct instructor picked up the radar, peered at the clock, drew her crocheted shawl around her, and, looking straight at me, said, "I should be getting along now. Anyone need a ride?"

"Which way are you going?" I mumbled.

She launched into an elaborate description of her route, but when I named my street, began fretting about where the nearest gas station was and how late it stayed open and how much cash she had on her.

"I'm going that way," he interrupted. "I could take, ah, Josephine."

"Never?" he asks, his voice quavering in exaggerated disbelief.

"Never," I repeat, making a slicing gesture to illustrate my point.

He folds his hands in his lap, looks across at me, unfolds them, and shrugs. I shrug, too, blank-faced. No sex talk today, doc.

Drunk and reckless, for once, I decided to seize the moment. As his silver Toyota drew up outside my apartment building and paused, idling, for me to get out, I took a deep, dizzying inhalation.

"Would you like to come in?"

"What for?" he replied, taken aback.

"For whatever you like," I said, significantly, and then repeated: "Anything you like."

The nature of the invitation seemed pretty clear.

He hesitated.

"OK," he said, "a cup of tea would be nice."

As a rocket-burst of elation exploded inside me, my brain made a quick inventory: yes, I did have tea; the apartment, of course, was neat — so neat I wished I had a moment to run in and scatter some newspapers around for a less pathological effect; he might think the pictures on the wall were weird, but I'd keep the lights low; my underwear was passable, but my stomach and thighs were a flabby disgrace.

Too late to do anything about that now.

He settled awkwardly into the only chair, looking around for something to read while I made tea. I tuned the radio to a classical music station, and he surprised me by identifying the Bruckner violin concerto that came on. To me, music was indistinguishable noise, but other people seemed to hear something more.

Neither of us had the faintest idea how to proceed.

Should I perch on the edge of the bed and chat about economics?

Should I launch myself upon him as he sat there, looking as

inscrutable and self-contained as he did in the classroom, a slim, soft-spoken man with hooded eyes?

He resolved the problem by setting his mug down carefully on the floor, looking straight at me, and asking, in his measured way, "May I spend the night with you?"

Equally calmly, despite a seismic jolt of disbelief, I answered, "Sure." Then putting my own cup down, I added, "Just let me go to the bathroom first."

He's clearly embarrassed but decides to persevere.

"Have there really been no, uh, sexual experiences that you would describe as pleasurable?"

Her body: lean, golden, toasty.

"No, not really," I lie. "Anyway, I just don't see that it's any of your business."

Perhaps I should invent a sexual fantasy, just for him. Oh, doctor, I'm so ashamed — before I go to sleep, I dream that you cram your doughy dick into my mouth. What on earth do you think this could mean?

I found out afterwards that his wife and children were on vacation, visiting her mother. At the time, I didn't ask any questions.

We went to bed, where we performed with solemn concentration.

I was drunk enough to believe I was enjoying it.

The next morning he showered and dressed before I was properly awake, said good-bye, and slunk out looking shifty and self-satisfied. With his wet hair plastered down, he resembled a water rat.

I closed my eyes and dozed, feeling battered and sleep-deprived, as if I had been in a train wreck. Stray images from the night revisited me; a hand placing a mug, very carefully, on the floor; the slight tripping movement he made stepping out of his pants; the stretched-out elastic on his underwear; his small, skewed, but willing cock; the crumpled skin around his eyes; his graying beard slimed with my secretions.

After tossing for a couple of hours in a bed that smelled of rotten mushrooms, I got up and wandered shakily into the bathroom, not knowing what to do next. I had missed my morning run, my morning calisthenics. I consulted the mirror. A pale, unclean-looking person looked back, with wild hair, aubergine eye sockets, and dark, gnawed lips. A violent pimple was about to erupt on my chin. I looked and felt like a hallucination.

Tensing over the toilet, I took out my diaphragm. (The pill, of course, was out of the question: weight gain.) Its folded cup came out resistantly, dripping on my hand and releasing an odor of rubber and vinegar and raw meat. Mucus clung to it, some viscous, some gelatinous; I couldn't tell which was his, which mine, and which the goo from the tube. As I began rinsing it, nausea rose in my throat.

I decided to shower but instead found myself in the kitchen measuring out a bowl of cereal. After I'd eaten that, standing up, I measured out another one. After I'd eaten that, I poured out all the rest, drowned it in milk, and ate that. Then I combed my hair, pulled on sweatpants and T-shirt, hid my face behind dark glasses, and walked to the corner store, where I bought a bag of blueberry muffins, another box of cereal, several bars of dark chocolate, a bag of potato chips, and three liters of Tab.

I ate until I was unconscious and finally slept.

When I saw him in class the following day, he ignored me. He ignored me the next time, too, though I never took my eyes off his face. He pretended not to see me when we passed on the stairs.

I understood what the problem was. The problem was my body.

Naturally he was disgusted.

If you make a pig out of yourself, you will become one.

It was time, I could see, to take matter in hand.

I decided to limit myself to two slices of bread a day, one in the morning and one at night, plus a green apple every other day, at noon (though some days I would forgo that too). I increased my evening swim from forty-five minutes to an hour and added another fifteen minutes of abdominal exercises. But no matter what I did, my belly still looked enormous to me, soft and full, overripe. Despite the frantic sit-ups, I could never get warm after swimming, and my skin stayed puckered, purple and parchment-colored. Down grew all over me but I shaved it off.

Inside, an icebound emptiness opened up. I would find myself staring at something — a knot in the tabletop, the colophon of a book I'd opened — and have no idea how long I'd been sitting there, propping up my head with my hands. At night, in Arctic dreams, fierce penguins lumbered toward me with bloodstained beaks.

After a month or so, he telephoned late one evening (11:18 P.M.), unnaturally emphatic, as if he'd been drinking. He asked if he could come over, and I said yes — panicking because when I put down the phone I'd have to rip the Saran Wrap off my thighs and the ankle weights off my wrists and jump in the shower to get the Clearasil off my face and the Vaseline off my feet (cracked soles).

He arrived clutching a paper bag. It was a bottle of Scotch. We each drank about two inches without ice and then went to bed; this time, I noticed, he carefully placed his watch right side up on the nightstand. Concentrating hard, he achieved his spasm, dozed heavily for ten minutes or so, woke with a jolt, rolled over to read his watch and left, splashing around in the bathroom first to purge himself, I presume, of any whiff of me.

Thus began our two-year affair.

For the first year, the pattern was invariable. Once a week, in the late afternoon, he'd drive me home from school, drink two inches of Scotch — he kept me well supplied, I will say that for him — take me to bed, check his watch, wash his dick, and leave in time for supper. He had two children, aged eight and eleven, and prided himself on being a good father. Sometimes, in my arms, he'd repeat my name — as a mnemonic device, I assumed.

I prided myself on making no demands.

I just kept myself available and in shape.

I thought I was happy.

One afternoon several months into the affair, as we lay together after having sex, he said to me, "I know you're faking it, you know. But it doesn't matter."

Was I? I didn't even know.

DIAGNOSTIC PROFILE

SEXUAL HISTORY

Sex: Being wielded by a large, hairy person in the grip of an inexplicable frenzy

Have you ever engaged in sexual intercourse?
Allegedly

Have you ever been sexually abused or assaulted?

Sexual preference: None

16

I wake up hung over from a bad dream — dark, cavernous spaces, inexhaustible weeping — and it takes me too long to remember where I am, to reinhabit this dying animal. While I'm still trying to sink back into my skin, she bursts through the door, whistling, with a tray.

"Pancakes!" she says. "Apple pancakes!"

320 calories.

A deep exhaustion drains me out again through the spaces in my self. Every day the same story, the same futile repetition: feeding the carcass, forcing it to live, keeping it going until one day it just stops.

I'm too heavy, too blurred, to do anything, so I just roll over and curl up again, folding my hands under my chin.

"Uh-uh-uh, madame," she says cheerfully, "it's time to rise and shine."

This is how she speaks. Rise and shine.

"Sit up and eat your pancakes now, so I can take you for a shower before we do your hair."

"Do my what?"

"Your hair, honeybun." (Why is she so chipper this morning?) "The stylist is coming by, she can give you a manicure too."

These dead strands: what's she going to do, pick them off the pillowcase and make a pin-the-tail-on-the-donkey? Manicure — on these gnawed stumps?

"What the fuck are you talking about?"

"You know what I'm talking about. We discussed it with the doctor yesterday."

Yes, but I wasn't there. I may have been in the room, but I wasn't there. "Discussed what?"

"Ah, don't start this again, Josie."

"I can't," I say.

"Sure you can," she says. "It'll be fun."

She puts down the tray, but I refuse to pour syrup — pure sugar, 100 calories an ounce — on my pancakes. We argue about this for a while till I end up drizzling on a few drops and then slowly, mechanically, masticate my way through the stack. I drink all my juice and two cups of tea; pancakes make me thirsty because they're so high in sodium. I'll bloat. But what do I care; what does it matter, after all, how much decaying flesh I cart around with me?

We walk to the weighing room, but no thrill of anticipation leavens me as I step up, my back obediently to the scale. I feel leaden in a way no numbers could compute. Then I take a shower and look down at my bulging gut; yes, I'm grotesque, so what?

"What a lovely face," the stylist lies, combing out what's left of my long wet hair.

"Please," I respond, staring at the pig head in the mirror. She lifts up my hair, pulls it over to one side, then the other, bunches it up, tilts her head appraisingly, lets it drop.

"So what are we in the mood for?" she asks, busy with her comb again.

"That hurts," I say.

"Sorry!"

There's a long, empty moment.

"We're not really in the mood for anything," I say. She meets the nurse's eyes in the mirror over my head.

"Well, if you don't want anything drastic, we could keep the length but put in some layers, to give you some volume," she suggests.

"I don't want any volume."

Her comb falters, but the poor creature, over-made-up and aggressively coiffed with a fashionable cut that doesn't suit her, perseveres: she's obviously taken a course (probably a "work-shop") in Dealing with Difficult Patients. "OK," she says, verbally shrugging. "Why don't I just take half an inch off the bottom to clean up those ends and then blow-dry it for a bit of pizzazz."

Pizzazz. I don't say anything but just sit there while she snips busily, stopping every now and then to pull two limp strands for symmetry. It doesn't look any different after she's done, but then she gets out a blow dryer, like a sawed-off shotgun, and starts blasting away. By the end, I look as if I've emerged from a wind tunnel. Once, I would have thought this glamorous; now an unraveling bird's nest seems to have landed on my head. I stare at my reflection with perverse gratification.

Even she has to admit that nothing much can be done with my nails. They're too short to file and the cuticles survive only as ravaged scabs. She has me soak my fingertips in a half-moon dish filled with warm, soapy liquid, then gently pats them dry. That's my manicure.

"A little make-up?" she asks Suzanne, as if I'm not even there.

"No!" I say. I want to look as horrible as possible.

She packs up her pink imitation-leather vanity case, gives my hair a final flip, tells me I look lovely, and takes off.

"You do look good," says the nurse. "You've got some color back."

It's true. My lips aren't blue anymore. They're a kind of cracked brownish mauve, like everyone else's. I wish they were indigo with livid scabs. I wish all my hair had fallen out. I wish I looked ghoulish instead of absurd.

It's visiting day.

I'm expecting only Mr. and Mrs., but they've brought Anthony along, too, surprisingly tall and adult in a navy blazer just like my father's, with a slicked-back forelock springing defiantly forward. He's loitering by the window, the tilt of his shoulders disclaiming any kinship with us. He keeps putting his hands into his pockets and taking them out again. He's probably become a smoker since he's been at college — hell, since prep school, how would I know. He could be anything, this good-looking stranger, my brother.

Mr. and Mrs. are sitting side by side on a pair of vinyl-covered chairs in this "visitors' lounge," as if in an airport. The nurse's warm hand between my shoulder blades propels me through the door, as if she senses my shrinking, my urge to turn and run, shrieking. But once I'm in, she pats my arm, nods to the audience, and abandons me.

Here we all are, captive, waiting for our flight to be called.

"Josephine!" says my mother, rising clumsily. "You look so much better." I know what she means: fat.

"Jo, darling," says my father, also rising. He looks old.

Neither of them makes any move to touch me: my giant belly keeps them away.

"Hi, Josie," Anthony mumbles, with a shrug.

We all sit down again, except Anthony, who stays slouching by the window, staring out at the hospital lawn. I'm facing them, filling up my chair, bulging over the edges, hovering ominously like one of those looming balloon creatures in the Thanksgiving Day parade. I cannot think of a single thing to say.

"Doesn't she look better, Michael?" my mother insists.

"She looks great," he replies, nodding and widening his eyes to convey alert sincerity.

I don't say anything, I just sit there, sullen, lumpen in my gray sweats. My mother snaps open her purse, which she's holding like a shield across her lap, and starts ferreting around in it. "We brought you something . . . now where's it got to?"

She presents me with a small, elegant box, heart-shaped, held together with a blood-red bow. I untie the ribbon and pry off the lid to reveal ranks of dark truffles. A dense rich acrid aroma. I look at them as if I don't know what they are.

"The doctor said . . ." she says, helplessly. "They're hand-made . . ."

"You know I never eat chocolate."

Her face crumples, and she glances at my father, whose hand, autonomous after all these years, reaches over to pat her arm.

"Here, you have one," I say, and she does. My father takes one too but forgets to eat it, keeping it poised between forefinger and thumb. My brother shakes his head when I gesture in his direction with the depleted heart.

We seem to have exhausted this topic of conversation. I stick one of my fingers crosswise in my mouth, but it tastes soapy so I stop chewing.

"Doctor says . . ." my mother begins.

"We hear from the doctor . . ." my father says, simul-taneously. They both stop.

Catching her eye, he resumes. "The doctor tells us, Jo, that it won't be too long before you can leave here."

So that's it. I must be near the target weight range.

I've tried, over and over, to predict what they would consider "normal" for my height. They probably use the same "ideal weight" charts that I've studied obsessively for years — recognizing them, with their absurdly inflated figures, as propaganda for obesity. (Who publishes them, I wonder? The medical profession, to create more customers?) Even in the column for "petite" frame, which I always consult, though Suzanne told me I shouldn't (something to do with the width of the elbow), the minimum for my height is 107 pounds.

One hundred and seven pounds! Is it possible that I weigh that much? Instinctively, I grasp my belly with both hands. I don't think so — today — but on other days I feel as if I could weigh two hundred. People do; I have no way of knowing.

I have to get out of here.

"About fucking time," I say.

Anthony exhales loudly and shifts so he's leaning on the windowsill with his back to us. My father continues, speaking very deliberately, as if to the dull-witted.

"What we're wondering about, Jo, is where you're planning to go. For the outpatient phase. Naturally, we want to help in any way we can — "

"Back to my apartment, where do you think?"

He hesitates; the bunny rabbit look is imminent. "Well, no . . . that's not going to be possible. Jane has indicated — "

"Jane has *indicated* what?" I ask, though, in a surge of cold rage, I already know.

"Jane has indicated that she'd rather not go on with the roommate arrangement, that it's too much of a strain on her. In fact, I think she has another roommate already lined up." Turning his hand over, wrist flexed, he looks helplessly at the now melting truffle.

If I'd ever thought about it, I could have anticipated this. But I never did. I thought I was going to stay here forever, that Suzanne would always take care of me.

She sits quietly by the bed waiting for my wailing to subside. I'm vomiting up all the loud black emptiness inside me, retching it out in funnel-shaped roars. It hurts. I'd forgotten how much.

I must look a mess.

After a while the weeping exhausts itself, except for the occasional dry spasm. I roll over on to my back, and she smooths the hair out of my eyes, continuing her calm, even stroking even when the damp tangles have been straightened out. (So much for the hairdo.)

"Josie," she says.

I hiccough.

"Josie, Josie, Josie," she murmurs, singsong.

"I can't," I say, a wail ballooning in my throat again.

"I know," she says.

"I can't live with them. It'll kill me."

"The doctor doesn't think it's advisable, either."

"I want to live by myself."

"The doctor . . . well, I don't think that's such a great idea, do you?"

"Why not?" I whimper.

"Do I need to remind you?"

I didn't want to go to grad school because it would mean being separated from the man I thought of as my lover (once a week, for almost an hour). He was my only point of reference, my only reason to be in one place rather than another. But what were my options?

1959: Fashion Model
1961: Ballerina
1961–64: Stewardess, American Airlines
1964: Candy Striper
1965: Fashion Editor
1966: Stewardess, Pan American
1973–75: Flight Attendant, American Airlines
1973: Medical Doctor
1976: Olympic Athlete
1978: Aerobics Instructor
1979: TV News Reporter
1980: Fashion Designer
1981: Corporate Executive
1982: Perfume Designer
1983: Animal Rights Volunteer

Animal Rights Volunteer? What would Barbie wear?

Don't worry, he said, if you go, I could get a grant and spend the summer with you. So, cataleptic on the conveyor belt, I accepted a scholarship at a place I'd never seen, a name on the map.

Economics, why not.

I made a one-day reconaissance trip and took the first apartment I saw, a "studio" in a cement shoe box near campus. It had royal blue shag carpeting, no windows (save one, painted shut, showing a sealed air shaft), and no kitchen, just a waist-high refrigerator with a hot plate on top. That's why I chose it.

We made our farewells in my echoing room. Everything but the mattress was packed, and we used it one last time, its bare buttons boring into my bones.

"I'm sad," he said afterwards, sounding surprised.

As I drove across the country, space shimmered and sucked me in. With eyes fixed on the horizon, with the radio's static at full blast — why wouldn't it stay tuned? — I concentrated hard and thought about nothing. (At first, yes, there was pain, but then I bought an air cushion to protect my ischia from the seat.) An oily rainbow led me on; I drank Tab to stay awake and ate an orange when I felt faint.

Nine days later, a fugue-like gap, I arrived.

Other people were also moving into my apartment block that day, usurping three parking spaces outside the front door. As I wedged my car into a semilegal half space, a bright yellow van disgorged a man and a woman carrying a couch, lopsided, laughing helplessly the way people do when they try to lift something too heavy. A person alone doesn't laugh, just grunts and grits her teeth.

After carrying everything up to the second floor (eighteen trips in all, at, conservatively, twenty-five calories a trip), I unwrapped the scale and weighed myself. I had lost so much weight, six and a half pounds, that for a moment I was frightened — just a flicker, before elation set in, followed by determination to keep it off. I wouldn't buy any food, I decided; I would never have food in the house, so if I wanted to eat something, I would have to go out and get it, thereby giving myself plenty of time to reconsider. I stocked the little fridge with Tab and seltzer water, plus a lemon, presliced. (A precaution: once I watched myself cram an entire lime into my mouth and then observed, in slow motion, as my esophagus convulsed.)

I was so afraid of regaining the weight that, for the first time, I started taking diet pills (pheno-something-or-other, propane, I think), adhering for a few days to the stated dose, but soon increasing it to two and then four pills a day. They kept me in a constant state of agitation, so that the instant I sat down I had to spring up again. The skin on my scalp crept and tingled as if, chilled, it had become too tight; an electric thrill ran through my limbs while something wormlike drilled away at my diaphragm. Eating was out of the question because I had become a hologram, unreal and radioactive and empty at the core.

It was wonderful. Why had I never thought of this before, instead of relying for so long on fallible will?

The city I now lived in was strange — windy and spacious and blue — so I spent most of my time in my room. It smelled of mildew, overlaid with scouring powder, and the rug's ancient dust, deep in the pile. After a while I couldn't breathe, so I went out and walked the streets. People stared at me oddly, envious of my fine, naked bones.

I ignored them, these phantoms, finding it harder and harder to make sense of anything they said or did. In the grocery store one evening, for instance, I was waiting with a six-pack of Tab behind a woman buying what looked like a year's worth of food, when the bag boy, slinging the last few items, announced, "Chilly."

It wasn't at all — it was midsummer — and evidently she didn't think so either, for she didn't respond. But almost a minute later, counting out her cash, she replied, "Enchiladas."

"What?" he asked, startled (he'd been picking a scab on his hand).

"I thought you said 'chilly,' " said the woman, over her shoulder. "I said 'enchiladas.' "

"Oh!" he said, some kind of light dawning on his pimply face.

Every now and then, fellow students herding somewhere after class would ask me along (from pity, I knew), but how could I join them for dinner or beer? Even the movies weren't safe, so I had to decline. (The margaritas, a sick, saline memory, were my sole mistake.) Let them waste their time talking and eating and

202

getting silly with drink; I preferred to stay home. My abs needed work.

My neighbor across the hall glared at me as if I had done something to offend him, though I could never think what, and the attractive woman downstairs was clearly a call girl. I would catch her in her bathrobe at midday, getting her mail; she said she was a bartender who worked nights. Upstairs was a drag queen — or someone who sounded like one, giggling and tottering about — and in the basement, a lumpy lesbian who stared lustfully at me. At night, I'd hear my name whispered through the walls.

"I don't know what you're getting at," I say, though I do. "I like living alone. It's the best arrangement for me."

"It's the best arrangement for you if you want to persist in this pathology, you mean."

"*Persist in this pathology!* Well, excuuuuse me."

She chuckles and yanks a strand of my hair, softly. "You must be feeling better now, Miss Sarcastic."

"*Ms.* Sarcastic, if you don't mind."

But an undertow of fear tugs me back to the topic. "I'm much happier when I live alone, really."

In China, only someone living alone and in abject poverty would sit down to a solitary meal.

"Just one?" said the hostess at the café, as if she had never seated a lone customer before.

"Are you waiting for someone or should I go ahead and take your order?" asked the waitress, sweeping the previous diner's crumbs into her hand. He had, it appeared, partaken with abandon of a buttered brioche.

"Just an iced tea," I mumbled, then hesitated. "Do you make it yourself or is it from a mix?" (a mix might contain sugar).

"Oh, no" — aghast — "we make it ourselves."

Everyone in the café was staring at me as I hunched over my newspaper, awaiting my tea. Whispering and pointing, they were wondering what I had ordered, hoping, I know, to see me gorge myself on *gâteau Saint-Honoré*. In a camisole that displayed the fine architecture of my neck and arms, I felt suddenly naked, X-rayed, and pulled on a sweatshirt though it was hot. But then, after a few minutes, I took it off again. Take a look, everyone: the bare bones.

A loud party of five arrived and milled around at the next table. After a minute or two, one of the men approached and I froze: what was he going to say, this stranger, to me? But he only indicated the chair facing me (even emptier than mine) and asked, "Is anyone sitting there?" — as if I might have an invisible friend.

I looked over, hopefully. When I didn't respond, he bore it away.

Without even a chair-back between me and the world, I couldn't finish my tea; my throat closed up and I fled, leaving a handful of dollars so I wouldn't have to ask for the bill. Across the street, cool, anonymous darkness invited me in. On that late-summer Sunday, there were only three patrons at the first matinee: myself, and a sepulchral couple who dozed, in shifts, through *Funny Face*. Emerging disoriented into the light, demoralized by Audrey Hepburn's hipbones (I kept fingering my own), I yielded to sloth and took the bus home.

It soon filled up and, without meaning to, I found myself staring at a young couple who'd obviously just climbed out of bed, sensuality still strong, compulsive, around them. She was leaning against a pole and he was leaning into her, facing her, his mouth in her hair. Her hands were under his T-shirt at the back, but he didn't have that sheepish, hunted look men get when pressed by their women for a public display of affection. He looked as if he really wanted to touch her, hold her gently against him on the bus.

I studied her, her broad, rounded belly, her plump arms, her well-covered neck and chin. How could he desire her? Why wasn't he repelled, as I was, by that slovenly padding? And how could she let a man touch her — never mind (I tried to imagine) exposing that flabby flesh to his sight?

I felt for my hipbones again, beneath the newspaper on my lap. They reassured me, but not enough. Watching the couple, I felt something swell like a wave under my rib cage, ending up, damming up, at the base of my throat. I must have blacked out for a moment, because I almost missed my stop and had to scramble sideways at the last moment through the closing doors.

"Watch your step, ma'am, please," said the bus driver.

Why was everyone always trying to tell me what to do?

"The question," she says, "is not how to get cured, but how to live."

"Huh?" I respond. I have no idea what she's talking about; it sounds like a quotation. "Don't get all existential on me now."

Is that the question? I thought the question was whether to live, not how.

I cannot live with my family. (Nuclear winter.)

Other people cannot live with me.

I cannot (I'll admit, but not to her) live alone. I make myself sick.

The problem seems insoluble.

Our talk is over, and she leaves for the night, for her life in the world with other people. I remain here alone in this fluorescent cube, an organism that knows only how to eat and excrete, a dead creature trapped in a dying one. Now I wish I'd consented to the tubes, to connect me with something, to fill me with something other than my own emptiness.

I have no idea what to do next. I inspect my wristbones, I caress my clavicles, I finger my iliac edges (blunted now, blurred by fat). What was it that I hoped my skeleton would tell me? I can't seem to grasp it anymore.

Somehow I thought I could make more of myself by making less of myself. Somehow I thought I could become some body. Somehow I . . .

I: the slenderest word in the English language, the flimsiest.

I

I cannot sit here any longer.

But I can't think what else to do.

After a long while, it occurs to me to go over to the window and look out, through the mesh. A smudged moon looks back.

17

I SHOULD HAVE REALIZED something was wrong when he failed to recognize me at the airport — after only nine months, as if in that time some other self had hatched around the thin voice on the phone. Lying about it later, he said it was because I had grown so frail. But I recognized him immediately and in that instant recalibrated my inner lens, stopping it down to accommodate the dim version of him that reality presented. After a while, he looked more like himself.

I drove him back from the airport in anxious distraction — on the dark, dizzying freeway, every car seemed aimed at me — pointing out places of interest just after we had passed them. He stared gloomily out of the window. Then I got lost trying to find the apartment he had sublet for the summer, though I'd studied the map before leaving home (as if, for once, I might be able to remember directions, numbers, spatial relations). When I finally pulled up outside the right building, he was hunched in his seat like a hooded owl.

The apartment was a disaster, left in a state of chronic filth and acute disorder by a couple of grad students who had departed for South America — in a hurry, by the look of things. They had left their massage oil and marijuana next to the bare mattress, and, in the kitchen, a sinkful of dirty dishes, a half-eaten ham sandwich, and an entomological cookbook open at a recipe for chocolate-dipped ants. We looked around in weak dismay.

Putting his bags down in the bedroom and his briefcase by the worktable, he began, mechanically, to pick things up.

I had imagined that as soon as the door closed on us he would press me passionately against the wall, kissing me like a starving man until my knees buckled and only the pressure of his mouth and his body and his hands would keep me from sliding to the floor. Instead he opened the refrigerator and announced: "Well, at least they left some eggs in here. And" — sniffing it dubiously — "some cheese. How about if I make us an omelet?"

I hadn't eaten in three days. After forcing down four forkfuls, I vomited — discreetly — in the tiny bathroom. For once I was grateful for his habitual inattentiveness.

Later we did make love, if that's the word for my lying rigid and miserable while he labored over me, sweating and panting and losing his erection. Afterwards he mumbled something about jet lag and fell into a wheezing coma, while I lay wide-eyed long after my arm had grown numb beneath him.

Thus began our summer of love.

She's asked me to explain it — sitting next to the window with me, her feet propped on a second chair, using her lap as a desk as she scrawls out forms in canary and goldenrod and other names that stationers use to disguise the tired fact of triplicate — but I can't. Might as well ask the somnambulist for an account of her route, the shade for an account of her day.

Fogbound, I felt I had no choice. I never asked myself why he was there, why I was there, whether anything could be changed. He was there, like a blight; I had to live blighted until he left.

We slept together every night, or rather he slept, collapsed upon me as if struck from behind, while I lay open-eyed, burning all night with a thin white light. In the morning, he would roll off me and slide out of bed, trying not to disturb the sheets, both of us maintaining the fiction that I was still asleep, that I ever slept, that I didn't need to be warmed back to life after my vigil in deep space. Within half an hour (time for a shave, a cup of tea, a slice of toast, and a vain attempt to defecate), he would be at his desk, unspooling from his bent head the curves of supply and demand.

A couple of hours later, I too would crawl out from under the covers, avoiding any motion that might draw his attention (unwashed, unmade-up, I was a livid, oily monster that no one could look at), and shuffle into the bathroom to begin my long ablutions. Again I hoped that his self-absorption would save me, that he would think only ten minutes had passed when it had been two hours. Then, gathering my belongings (wallet, keys, notepad, pills, lipstick, laxatives, library card), I would leave for the day, pecking him on the scalp in exchange for a grunt.

The story was that I spent the day in the library, doing research. In fact I headed straight for the campus coffee-house, where I breakfasted on hot chocolate and cheesecake, piling both high with whipped cream. When I had read the entire newspaper, including the classifieds, and had reached the right degree of nausea by ordering a second hot chocolate, I would make my way at last to the library.

There I wandered stupefied through the stacks, filled with vague lust, looking for something without knowing what. Perhaps I was hoping that a book would, quite literally, leap off the shelf and save me. Instead of staying safely within the HB 3717 section, I found myself drawn to the RC 537's, and spent most of the day in a cramped carrel near those shelves, which I ravaged numbly and randomly.

This was my research. I can't say I learned much.

I didn't allow myself to leave the building because if I did, I would eat (eat: stuff myself with everything I could find that was chewy and creamy, gagging as I forced down ever more, blocking in the only way I knew how the banshee wail that inhabited me). I couldn't eat because by 10 A.M. I had already blown the caloric budget for the day — and for many days to come, but I tried not to think about that: it was the next hour, the next half hour that I had to live through.

It never occurred to me that I might go out and do something else. It never occurred to me that I had a choice. It never occurred to me that I was in despair. Since the day he arrived, I had lost the ability to activate myself, even to exercise. All I could do was wander around the stacks, suffocating in the fog of my own stupefaction.

Belatedly — I've been thinking about something else, about how I think I can feel my thighs rubbing together when I walk, though I'm not sure if it's my thighs or these sweatpants — I realize we haven't made our usual right turn to Physical Therapy.

"Where're we going now?" I ask, not intending the teakettle squeal that escapes me. My voice sounds shrill, as if I'm alarmed.

"You'll see," she says, with the fake cheeriness that means trouble. "It's a new phase of the therapy."

I grab a handful of hair above my left temple and begin dragging my fingers through it. "Why didn't you tell me?" I whine. "Why didn't you tell me we were doing something different?"

"It's no big deal, Josie, you'll see."

"Yes but why didn't you tell me?"

The room she leads me to looks like a small classroom, where all the chairs, save one, have been stacked against a wall. The lone survivor sits in the middle of the floor, facing a blackboard and a video camera. On the rear wall, huge sheets of kindergarten-quality drawing paper, torn from a roll, have been pinned, overlapping, to mask the entire surface.

Like a dog on a leash, I balk at the door.

"No," I say.

"No what?" she says. "You don't even know what we're going to do. It'll be fun."

"No," I say.

I should have known I couldn't trust her. (Other people: bodies you can't control.)

"What stupid little game is this?"

"It's not a game, Josie. It's Body Image Awareness. The doctor should be here in a minute to explain it to you."

"Body-what Bullshit? Get me out of here."

But it's too late: Dr. Frog arrives, hustling and harried as ever, a few files stuffed fanwise under his arm, his pouched eyes swiveling apologetically toward the nurse.

"Josephine!" he says. "Good to see you."

I say nothing.

"Looking well," he continues. "I take it," he perseveres, "that the nurse has explained our procedure for today."

"No she hasn't," I say, "and I'm not doing it, whatever it is."

He begins to open his hands, palms forward, in a gesture of intervention but forgets the files under his arm, which fall to the floor, spewing an arc of graphs and charts and forms. My last name is on most of them, as PATIENT.

But I'm not: my patience, it seems, has run out. I'm here in the room, the room is real, and everything makes itself present to me: the toppling stack of plastic chairs, the pulpy strips misaligned on the wall, the blind camera tilted attentively on its three thin legs, the scuffed floor where the nurse kneels, gathering forms.

What am I doing here?

After a few weeks, I feared that if I had to spend another evening on the broken-down couch watching him read, I would go into the kitchen, fetch the heavy marble pestle (what those graduate students ground with it, I don't know), and beat his head ecstatically into a pulp. I had imagined it many times: his absent gaze finally taking me in as I approached, swinging the pestle pendulum-style to warm up, my face calm and intent as I grasped what was left of his hair, and, mocking his faint puzzlement, swung at his skull with all my force, back and forth, side to side, again and again, grunting with pleasure and exertion, sobs of abandon escaping my clamped teeth.

Instead I'd say, "Should we go to a movie tonight? If you want — "

"Which one?"

"Well, what do you want to see?"

"I don't really know . . . What's playing?"

By the time he had studied the listings and I had told him, often for the third or fourth time, what each one was about, it would be too late to make the 7:30 show and the evening was effectively over because he needed eight hours of sleep so he could rise refreshed in the morning to spin out his slender, elegant equations.

I too longed for the night. Not because I would sleep but because I could endure it, and if I endured it, it would end, and when it ended, I could have my hot chocolate with cream. That morning sip was the only happiness I knew.

(But the first sip only: with the second came fear and sickness and misery, like an inner drizzle that never lifted.)

*

"Let me be clear about this," I say. "You want to videotape me in the dramatic act of pulling down the window shade?"

He exhales audibly but otherwise manages to mask his irritation. "As I've explained, Josephine, we're going to ask you to perform a series of everyday movements — walking to the window, sitting down, turning around and such — while the camera's on, and then afterwards the three of us will watch the tape and talk about it."

"What, are you going to give me notes on my performance," I ask, "make sure it's up to Oscar quality?"

They exchange glances and I imagine the next entry in one of those files, reassembled now and tapped into alignment: "Patient hostile and uncooperative, resists Body Image Treatment; suggest we medicate."

"Josie," the nurse pipes up, in that wheedling tone I'm beginning to distrust, "none of us really sees ourselves the way we are. We all could use a little help in seeing ourselves objectively."

"Fine," I say, "videotape yourself. Also," I add, as this occurs to me, "it wouldn't be objective. I'd be comparing myself to every actress I'd ever seen on TV."

And, I don't say, This is where I bow out. Something is wrong with this picture — not the picture that the camera, neck craned, is waiting to capture, not even the outline of myself I'm supposed to crayon on the wall. Something is wrong with the picture of a twenty-five-year-old woman who has given her body over to strangers.

Instructions to patient:

Please perform the following motions slowly and deliberately but in a natural and unforced manner. The camera operator will take full-

length and close-up shots in each position, focusing on problem areas of the body (legs, hips, buttocks, stomach, face, etc.).

- Walk to the window, turn your back to the camera, reach up, and pull down the shade. (If there is no window, or no shade, please mime this motion.)
- Turn around, walk to the chair, and sit down. Cross your legs and smile.
- Turn sideways in the chair, presenting your left profile to the camera. Now do the same with the right profile.
- Face front again, rise from the chair, and walk across the room. Make one complete turn, holding your arms at a forty-five-degree angle from your sides.
- Bend over as if to pick something off the floor. Straighten up.
- Walk to the door as if you were going to open it (but don't). Look over your shoulder and wave.

I don't need a video camera. I don't need a crayon to define the edges of my being. I don't even need a mirror. I know what I am: a twenty-five-year-old female body, emaciated still in the clavicle and calves, with spindly shanks but a smooth coating of baby fat everywhere else (the back of my neck, the underside of my chin, the upper arms, the finger joints) and a large, unsightly, tirelike deposit around the middle. My skin is dry, mottled, and erupting; my hair is limp and scant. I do not look beautiful. I would not look good in a bikini. But I'm going to get out of here.

In the middle of August, he left. Watching him scurry through the boarding gate, with his briefcase clutched under his arm and an anxious tilt to his head — was he afraid the plane would dematerialize before he emerged from the tube? — a sole thought presented itself to me: now I can go home and eat anything I want because there's no one to look at me.

So I did, for several days — perhaps it was weeks. I'm not sure anymore.

I left the house only to do the rounds, by car. Sometimes I would consume everything I'd bought before I got home again and would have to keep driving, making what began to feel like an endless loop. Money was running low: my next scholarship check wasn't due until school started in a month's time, but I kept going, anxiety about each vanishing dollar spiking the stew of dread and lust in which I drove and spent and consumed and drove and spent and consumed.

I wore the same clothes every day (drawstring-waist sweat-pants and an oversized man's shirt) because nothing else would fit. I didn't wash my hair or even comb it because I couldn't look at myself in the mirror. I stopped showering because I refused to bare my flesh. If I never looked directly at myself, I had no way of recognizing this being who gnawed away, pupal in some dark, thick dream.

I ate until I slept and then, waking with a blurred cry on a cushion damp with drool, ate again. Then I slept again — at eleven in the morning or through the afternoon heat — cramped and sweaty, awakening rank with the sofa's rough weave imprinted on my cheek.

One evening the telephone rang, shocking me out of a shallow doze. A baby crocodile had been nibbling at my hand, which, when I tried to push myself off the couch, I realized was paralyzed with pins and needles. At first I thought the smoke detector had gone off, but, as the terrifying trills continued, I saw that they came from a black device under some chip bags and an empty ice cream carton on the coffee table.

The telephone.

My heart was hammering so violently, and it had been so long since I used my voice, that my "Hello?" came out as a creak. There was silence, so I tried again, this time achieving a croak.

A hesitant voice on the other end, recovering rapidly, inquired if I might be interested in subscribing to the daily paper at a special thirteen-week introductory rate.

I looked around the small, airless room, at the shag carpeting littered with torn cellophane and cookie packages and pizza boxes and soda cans and yogurt cups and the silver foil from Hershey's kisses, with magazines open and trampled next to the couch, with weeks' worth of newspapers splayed three-deep on every surface, and I imagined the day's news arriving neatly bundled at my door every morning, and I laughed.

"Ma'am?" asked the voice.

I laughed again. "But why thirteen?" I managed to gasp. "Don't you know that's an unlucky number?" In the silence that followed, it occurred to me that anyone hearing those spasms would mistake them for sobs.

"It's not 'acting out,' " I tell her. "I'm just not going to do it, that's all."

"It's part of the therapy, Josie."

"Well, as far as I'm concerned, the therapy is over."

She looks at me.

"I'm cured!" I say, and we both laugh. I'm back in my room, as punishment for "acting out," and she's sitting with me while I address my lunch.

"Look," I say, biting into a large cheese sandwich, "yum yum yum."

"Yummee," I say, crunching a carrot stick and chewing loudly, "can't get enough of that ol' vitamin A."

"Ooh la la," I say, "what do we have here? Dessert!"

She's watching my performance with disapproving lips but

amused eyes; with a small grunt and slight shake of the head, she picks up the newspaper — "Epidemiologist Notes Rising Rates of Rare Cancer" — pretending to ignore me. But I'm having a good time, I'm on a roll, smacking my lips and bulging my eyeballs like a demented character in a TV commercial. After every mouthful, I go, "Mmmn-*mmmn!*"

Nevertheless, the lunch is disappearing.

When I finally hung up, realizing that the line had gone dead, I sat motionless for a moment and then, registering what my glassy eyes were fixed on, began to scavenge in the chip bags. I crammed my mouth with salty crumbs and washed them down with something thick and sweet — no, slightly rancid — from the ice cream carton. In one of the trodden-on boxes on the floor, I found two petrified pizza crusts and gnawed on them, the jaw effort bringing tears to my eyes.

As a satisfying sickness consolidated itself between my ribs (if I still had ribs; I hadn't checked them lately, hadn't counted them, hadn't pressed painfully between the bones), I curled up again, paws tucked under my chin.

But I couldn't black out.

The afternoon light painted the outside of my eyelids a thin bloody red. My muscles ached, especially in the lower back. I could feel the gummy sweat between my toes. I began to itch all over.

The telephone had bored a hole in my dream; it was split open now, torn, and I didn't know how to seal it again.

I itched.

I stank.

The room smelled like a sewer, with putrid overtones.

I decided to take a shower.

*

Next, draw an image of your own body (life-size) on the blank paper provided for you. The therapist will then ask a bystander to draw his or her image of you, next to yours. Finally, the therapist will stand you against the wall, arms outspread, while he traces your actual outline with a crayon. These three depictions — the patient's, the stranger's and the rapist's — will provide material for analysis and for subsequent Body Image Awareness Exercises.

I thought it would be possible, if I tried hard enough, to shower without looking at my body. If I stayed away from the mirror, if I didn't look down, if I slid the bulky bar of soap across me without ever touching flesh, surely I could stay invisible, undefined in space, for just a little longer? No one had looked at me for (I think) weeks; a body that isn't looked at doesn't exist.

But something went wrong. Out of habit, perhaps — or perhaps, as at an accident scene, out of horrified lust to witness the worst — I glanced down and, through the steam, saw an immense mound, soft and swollen as risen dough.

Something gave way in me, and if I hadn't been in the shower I think I would have crumpled to the floor.

All to do again, all to do again: the awful struggle would never end. Not even for a second could I relax my surveillance; my dark, larval feeding, my drugged defection, had been a luxury I could never afford. I would have to start over, drawing the bounds again, etching the skeletal self again from that blurred mass bleeding at the edges (bad color, cheap funnies — but no joke, no punch line, the last frame's missing, printer's mistake).

I got out of the shower, toweled myself (keeping my eyes fixed front), combed my hair, and put on a clean pair of sweatpants (but no underwear, because the elastic would bind), clean socks, and an oversized T-shirt (no bra, for the same reason). In the bathroom cabinet, I found a sheet of small red pills, only three of which had been popped out of their bubble pack. I swallowed the remaining nine with tap water; they went down easily, but the glass slipped out of my hand and shattered on the floor.

A terrible little cry escaped me. This was more, much more, than I could take.

Leaving the shards where they had sprayed, I ran out of the bathroom, dived face downward on the couch and writhed, pulling the long, fine hair on the back of my head until the roots gave way. I whimpered and groaned until, tasting salt, I realized I had gnawed the skin off my lower lip. To stop the damage, I bit deep into the back of my hand; a familiar cold tingle wormed over me, and I heard someone laugh through the wall and then laugh again and then applaud.

I stood up and took a bow and the room was very large. There was lots of cold, curved space between objects, one of which was me. I understood that I could be both *here* and *there* at the same time and wondered why I had never noticed this before. I wanted to stare at myself in the bathroom mirror to reflect on this (and also to check for insects in my hair).

Oh, broken glass. Put on, what? — winter boots, for protection.

It crunched and grated under my feet, scraping against the tile with a sound that sent spasms of sensation through my solar plexus. I became distracted by this sensation and began a little dance, first stomping like a wine presser and then shuffling like Mr. Bojangles, to recreate the sound and its awful, exquisite twinge.

But soon the glass was too finely ground to make much noise, so I lost interest in the dance but couldn't remember why I was there in the first place. Looking around, nothing occurred to me. The ants were really bad now, in my hair and on the floor — no, that was just broken glass and mud from my boots. Well — with a surge of purpose — I would clean it up.

A teaspoon, obviously, rather than a dustpan, seeing I didn't have one. It looked so beautiful, like shaved ice or sugar crystals. Perhaps it would melt in my hot, wet mouth; perhaps it would score me going down, scarring my throat so I would never have to swallow anything again.

Open wide.

There's a good girl.

18

I'M IN THE DAYROOM watching Julia Child ("Oh bother," she says, dropping the fish on the floor, as if millions of people weren't watching her do something intimate, obscene), when Suzanne puts her head in and says, "Tomorrow morning?"

"What?" I ask, still thinking about *saumon en papillote:* why would anyone eat a dead fish baked in a paper bag? (Then it comes back to me: a page from my loose-leaf binder. Just one. I had to put something in my mouth.)

"Tomorrow morning," she says. "For the shopping."

Ah yes. The shopping. Shopping *therapy.*

Art therapy. Physical therapy. Nutritional therapy. Body image therapy. Frog therapy. And now, before the inmate can re-enter the world, shopping therapy.

I thought she was kidding when she first brought it up (humor therapy?), but it turns out she isn't. Predischarge routine, according to the doc. (Discharge: ugly word, gynecological word, cottage cheesy.) The nurse will take you shopping for an appropriately sized wardrobe.

"What about all my old clothes?" — my size ones, my "petites," my precious collection from the children's department?

"You can bring them in later, if you like, and we'll go through them and bundle them up and send them to the needy."

I am the needy. I need those labels to define an occupied zone: myself. I need those garments to contain me, to keep me within bounds (yes, doctor, I know I'm not supposed to think like this anymore. Fetishism? I thought that had something to do with feet).

Shopping lessons: the idea is laughable, or would be if it didn't frighten me so much. That's right, teach me to consume. What else was I schooled in for sixteen long years? What else did my mother teach me: what else did she know? So easy, then, to believe you were entitled to anything you wanted; so difficult, now, to imagine buying even a comb. (Automatically, I touch my head and run my fingers through several times: only five hairs come out today. She's told me to stop counting, but I can't.)

Behavior mod, she calls it. (Behavior Mod and the Rockers. Behavior Mod and the Off-Their-Rockers.) But over the years I managed to modify my own behavior, instituting a system of punishment and reward. First there was a rule that I had to rearrange the closet or the bathroom cabinet before I bought anything, even a tube of toothpaste; then there was the rule that I had to throw something out before I could buy anything new; then the rule that I should have nothing in the house that I didn't use every day; then, finally, the taboo on buying anything at all. Discipline for the spirit: to make things last, to do without. To use sparingly — as it says on the tube of skin medication the doctor has prescribed for me (it also says "apply to affected areas": I wouldn't know where to start).

"Why," a fellow grad student once asked — as if it were any of her business, the plump, overpainted parakeet — "do you wear the same clothes every day?"

"I don't," I pointed out, icily. "I have three pairs of jeans and the sweatshirts are different colors." (Black and gray.)

"Nor do I see any reason," I added, looking her up and down, hoping she would never talk to me again, "to become a slave to consumerism." As if it were a moral position. As if it were a choice.

"I can't," I bleat, "I just can't."

"I'll be there to help you," she says, folding towels and flattening the edges efficiently with her freckly hand.

"But you don't understand — "

"Jo, I do."

How can she?

She's so sensible, she probably just thinks, Oh, I need some socks, and goes right out that same day and picks a few and pays for them and takes them home and puts them on. How could she understand my weeks of anxious procrastination, my shame when I bring the sordid little purchase home, chewing through the tags and hiding it away, sometimes for months, before I can wear it? Does she, in the department store's desert air, look down at her body and not know whether to head for the size twos or the size twelves? Does she stand paralyzed before a rack of skirts, unable to answer the question, Am I the kind of person who would wear that?

How do you dress someone who's not there? What would a missing person wear?

I never planned to disappear.

My goal was a modest one: to be perfect.

But something went wrong, and I did without so much that I almost undid myself (so I'm told, by the doctor, who I don't believe, and the nurse, who I do).

I even remember the moment I became conscious of this —

this mission, you could call it, this vocation. Spring semester, sophomore year (eighty-eight pounds): walking home from classes one dazzling blue day, I was overwhelmed by the brightness, which, inhaled, expanded like helium in the head. My brain became a radiant blur, my limbs very long and light, and as I tried with slow-motion steps to negotiate the oddly slanting sidewalk, I knew I would never make it. (This happens, when you eat only every eighteen hours. I fainted in the drugstore once, hitting my chin on the counter's metal edge. I slid down the wall to the floor at the registrar's office, waiting to pay a bill. I learned, over time, how to stand up: very carefully.)

But that day I found a way to keep myself going. Concentrate, I said. Focus on this sensation, because the worse you feel, the better you are. The worse you feel, the better you are — the emptier, the freer, the purer. Know how it feels to be human, when all insulation (money, for instance, and fat) has been stripped away. Think of all the bodies on this planet which have no choice.

"The worse you feel, the better you are," I repeated, chanting it inside my head, timing my steps to its insistent tetrameter.

That kept me going for quite a few years.

And by the end I didn't need it anymore. I had reached such a pitch of discipline that my own abstention was beyond my control. Hunger had become abstract, food a foreign body, inert as stone (unless it had a strong smell — bread, meat, dark chocolate — in which case a valve in my throat would revolt). Most of the time, I couldn't imagine forcing masticated matter down my esophagus; it fascinated and disgusted me to catch someone in the act. In the campus cafeteria one day, sipping a Tab and trying to concentrate on a crossword puzzle, I found myself staring, appalled, at a fat woman cramming hamburger into her mouth. And then chewing, *con brio*. It was the lewdest sight I could imagine (except, perhaps, a pregnant woman, every kind of appetite inscribed on her flesh). How could anyone do something so indecent in public, especially someone who had no right to eat at all? I stared and stared, deafened by a loud, loose rattling in my ears.

A while later, I realized that I was still staring, forgetting to blink, though she had long since left. That happened, too: missing a reel of the movie, or seeing, for a spell, only the black space between frames.

"Frankly," the nurse says, "I don't understand how you were even functioning in that condition."

"I was functioning perfectly well, thank you very much. I didn't waste time eating and sleeping and chasing after sex like everyone else. I just studied all the time, I was a kind of a, kind of a 'star' in the Econ Department."

This seems plausible enough. I'm not going to tell her that I remember almost nothing from those long, mute, vitreous days, the six months or so before I came here. I remember only how slowly they unspiraled and what an effort it was to breathe.

And I remember Jane's face when she saw me in the shower. She walked in by accident once, soon after I moved in. She'd never seen me without layers of baggy clothes, and I made sure she never did again (unless, of course, she spied on me through the door, which, come to think of it, she probably did). This was precisely why I hadn't wanted a roommate in the first place, but after my trip to the emergency room I decided, perhaps too hastily, that I shouldn't live alone. Something had rattled me — claustrophobia, I think, or some other kind of craziness — so I gave up the studio (that smell of scouring powder) and moved my books, my suitcase, and my typewriter to Jane's place, which was orderly and rent-controlled. She was a grad student in

Biology ("Quiet, considerate person looking for similar to share"), a solid, dog-faced girl who lived on beer and peanut butter sandwiches. Our only real fight occurred when I asked her please to keep her jumbo economy-sized extra-crunchy peanut butter at the lab rather than at home. "Just who do you think you are?" she asked me — a good question.

Otherwise, she stayed out of my way, while I tried to be quiet and considerate and not too neat. (But those hairs in the drain, that unrinsed spoon in the sink . . .)

I think she believed me when I said I bought all my meals at school. I think she believed me when I said I was allergic to the glue on postage stamps (so would she please lick one for me). I think she believed that I had Crohn's disease.

"Come off it, Josie," says Suzanne. "You know she saw right through you all along."

Did she? How would I know? How are you supposed to know what someone else sees, looking at you? I was approaching transparency, my blue hands blood-red against the light: perhaps she could see right through me. Perhaps everyone could.

"It's time," she says softly, "to start telling the truth."

But I never have told the truth. How could I start now?

"I'm cured," I tell the doctor, "large as life, ready to go back into the world as a mature, productive individual." He doesn't think this is funny and keeps repeating, in an earnest croak, that the hardest part is about to begin. "I've had it up to *here* with the hardest part," I pun, gesturing, but he doesn't seem to get it. Then, as if announcing that I've won the lottery, he tells me we'll be seeing each other three times a week for "outpatient therapy."

"Can't wait," I reply.

I'll be seeing the dietician, too, for "nutritional counseling."

I've agreed to live in the graduate dorm (but in a single room: no more roommates, no other bodies in the same space), and I've "contracted" with the "treatment team" to eat three meals a day in public. (I imagine the dining hall, the banging plastic trays, the clatter, the yelling, the masticating crowds, the stale, mealy smell of the steam, the fogged Plexiglas shield, and the food itself, buckets and buckets of it, heaps, piles, vats. A buzz of terror goes through me, as if from a cattle prod; that's where the "biofeedback" and "relaxation training" are supposed to help. And the "menu selection" lessons from Miss Sausage-Calves.)

I don't know if any of this is going to work. But what choice do I have? (A rhetorical question: I know what choice I have. And it's comforting to know it's always there.)

"I beg your pardon?"

Group therapy, he says. Assertiveness training.

"Not on your fucking life," I respond, demonstrating, I hope, that I don't need the latter.

Target weight, he insists.

"But I thought I was there. I weigh a hundred and seven, don't I, *don't* I" — staring down at my gross belly, panicking at the thought of ever reading those numbers on the scale.

"One-oh-seven?" he asks. "What on earth gave you that idea?"

"I thought — "

"Josephine," he says, "it's only been eight weeks. You're still a long way from that. But we think you're at a weight now where normal physiological functioning is possible."

Normal physiological functioning. Growth and bleeding and hunger and decay. A long, slow rotting; meat going bad. Thanks a lot, doc.

"Doctor," I say, in a sudden panic, "I don't know if I can do this."

"You'll have a lot of support," he says, reaching over to pat me, molding the air above my right deltoid in a manner meant to reassure.

I don't need "support." I need . . .

I need . . .

It occurs to me that I have no idea how that sentence might end.

"And Suzanne?" I ask. "Where does she fit into this?"

"Well, the nurse isn't generally part of the follow-up team, but," he adds, noticing something, "in this case we plan to involve her fully in the outpatient phase."

I shrug, surprising in myself a flash of longing to find her and cling to her body, so solid and substantial, to hold on so that I never have to leave, never have to feel the chill of empty space around me.

"Oh, well," I say, "whatever you experts decide."

I watch the Frugal Gourmet, who doesn't seem very frugal, ladling on butter and cream, talking about how much he loves to eat this and that. I watch a documentary on colon cancer, then part of a slasher movie, then an aerobics program, lots of Lycra. If I weren't afraid someone would come into the dayroom, I would stand up and start flinging myself around, grinning fixedly like the women on the screen. But watching them bores me — what exactly do they suppose they're doing? — so I channel-hop, black lace and leather, must be MTV, lipstick, pizza, talk show on impotence (there's an inflatable implant now, a handy rubber bulb you keep in your pocket), more pizza, a new wasting disease: bodies that have no choice, men cachectic and bruised like rotting bananas — like me, when I used to bruise so easily — except these aren't bruises. I stare at the screen, at their dark bewildered eyes.

Some kind of sadness comes over me, so I turn off the TV and go back to my room. I lie down on the bed, where I've spent so much time — where so much time has been eaten away — and I close my eyes, covering my face with my arm. The usual images start to arrive (white noise, mouthful of blood), but — behavior mod — I try to think about something else. I think about something lost, something sun-kissed, then, I can't help it, I think of the wasting; I think of the waste.

Wasted bodies. Wasted lives.

For reassurance, I grasp my thighs and run my hands upward, probing for hipbones, but all I feel is flesh. Sitting up anxiously, I look down at my thighs, huge now, spread out to double their dimensions, with a Y-shaped fold where my belly meets them — or, more accurately, rests on them. Folding my arms across squishy breasts, I pinch a thick wad under each triceps, formerly tight fiber. I bend my neck forward, tucking in my chin till I feel the pad of fat that lives there now.

This is the body I must learn to inhabit. (To cohabit, rather: it feels like an alien fastened to me, reprogramming my DNA to produce itself instead of me.) I don't know if I can: that spare, vacant frame gave me so much space to hide.

Can I learn to be so present?

Can I learn to be so full?

"Suzanne," I say, interrupting her (she's going on about "follow-up" and "monitoring" and did she say "relapse"?).

"Yup?"

I can't think what it is I want to say. We're getting ready for the shopping trip, and she's coaxing me into my shoes, which I haven't worn since I got here.

"I . . . oh, I don't know."

I gesture vaguely and then for some reason use that hand,

while it's in the air, to touch my knuckles to her cheek, just to know what it feels like, that downy, slightly dry, dappled skin of hers. It feels surprisingly firm and resilient, someone else's face.

"Suzanne?" I say, this time more urgently.

"Yes?" she says.

"Suzanne, what am I going to do when I get out of here?"

"But, Josie," she says, "we've been through all that lots of times. You'll see me, you'll see the nutritionist, you'll see the doctor three times a — "

"No, I mean, what am I going to *do?*"

"You mean, what's the first thing you're going to do when you get to the dorm?"

No: that's simple. Only two options: eat or not eat.

Then it strikes me that perhaps the larger question is equally simple. After a while, I try out this idea. "Well, maybe I only have two options."

"Oh yeah? What are those?"

"Well, the same as anyone else. Live or die."

"Oh, for heaven's sake — "

"And even if it's, you know, I still have a choice: quickly or slowly."

She stops what she's doing (putting clothes, mine I suppose, into a garbage bag) and looks at me gravely, uncertain, trying to read my face. I watch the lines around her eyes relax as she decides I'm not serious.

She may even be right, for once.

"Oh well," she says, shrugging, "if I were you, I'd go for slowly, same as everyone else."

"But what's the difference? The result is the same."

"Yes," she says, "but you get to live in the meanwhile."

"Live?" I say. "Let's not get carried away here."

She snorts softly and returns her attention to the trash bag, but I keep going, something swelling inside me, some wave of hilarity beginning to surge.

"Live?" I repeat.

"Live?" I say. "What a novel idea!"

And we both laugh, shaking our heads, she because she thinks I'm joking, I because I think I'm not.

I thought I had it all figured out.

The less I swallowed, the more I declined, the more I hoped to pare things down to essentials. Why shouldn't all problems have a single, bare-bones solution? I needed to discover what was left when excess was stripped away, when nothing survived but the self in its minimal form.

I thought the body could be redesigned as a perfect, self-sufficient machine. But the more I denied it, the louder it cried. The more I reduced it, the less I found. The more I wasted it, the more space it claimed, until my whole mind was under occupation.

Don't say "I have a body," Suzanne tells me: say "I am a body." I can't do that yet.

But if it were true, if I were a body, what would I be?

ACKNOWLEDGMENTS

I would like to acknowledge my great debt to other writers and theorists who have explored the phenomenon of anorexia nervosa, especially Hilde Bruch, Kim Chernin, David Garner, Susie Orbach, and L. M. Vincent. I am also deeply indebted to the following first-person accounts, insights from which are woven throughout Josie's story: *Portrait of an Anorexic* by Maureen Ardell and Corry-Ann Ardell, *Am I Still Visible?* by Sandra Heater, *Solitaire* by Aimee Liu; *The Art of Starvation* by Sheila MacLeod, and *Starving for Attention* by Cherry Boone O'Neill. Finally, I would like to thank Pamela Painter, Kim Witherspoon, and Betsy Lerner for their blind faith and expert assistance, without which *Life-Size* might never have grown to just that.